The Spiritual Adventures of Russell the Dog

A Blend of Truth, Fiction, and Inspiration from the Other Side

TRISHA WATSON

Stone & Light Publishing, LLC

The Spiritual Adventures of Russell the Dog
A Blend of Truth, Fiction, and Inspiration from the Other Side
by Trisha Watson

Copyright © 2020 Trisha Watson

All rights reserved.

This book or parts thereof may not be reproduced in any form, stored in a retrieval system, or transmitted in any form by any means—electronic, mechanical, photocopy, recording, or otherwise—without prior written permission of the publisher, except for the inclusion of a brief quotation in a review.

This is a work of fiction except where noted by the author in the introduction. The characters, organizations, and events portrayed in this novel are either products of the author's imagination or are used fictitiously.

Published by
Stone & Light Publishing, LLC
TheSpiritualAdventuresOfRussellTheDog.com

Photos © by Mark Watson
Cover and Interior Design by Nick Zelinger

Lyrics for "Run Like The River Runs", "The Way We're Going", and "Beating of My Heart" by Michael Tomlinson used by permission of the artist.
Copyright © MichaelTomlinson.com

ISBN: 978-1-7333374-0-3 (print)
ISBN: 978-1-7333374-1-0 (eBook)
LCCN: 2019919962

Publisher's Cataloging-in-Publication data

Names: Watson, Trisha, author.
Title: The spiritual adventures of Russell the dog : a blend of truth, fiction, and inspiration from the other side / by Trisha Watson.
Description: First trade paperback original edition. | Evergreen [Colorado] : Stone & Light Publishing, LLC, 2020. | Also published as an ebook. | Appendices included.
Identifiers: ISBN 978-1-7333374-0-3
Subjects: LCSH: Dogs—Fiction. | Reincarnation—Fiction. | Karma—Fiction. | Forgiveness—Fiction.
BISAC: FICTION / Visionary & Metaphysical.
Classification: LCC PN3427 | DDC 813.6–dc22

First Edition
Printed in the United States of America

This book is dedicated to those with a reverence for life who compassionately rescue animals so they may have a better life.

And it's dedicated to these souls who have transitioned into the peaceful loving world of spirit:
Colleen Donovan
Elliot Cook
Kristen Michelle Vannoy
Neil Sipes

Even in the face of our most trying hardships, we are all still far more fortunate than we will ever know. It is our responsibility to not only rise to the occasion to find the beauty in the dissonance within our own lives, but to also show compassion and do what we can for others whenever possible. We all have a place and a purpose. We are all connected. We cannot forget that.

—Kristen Michelle Vannoy

Contents

Introduction		1
Chapter 1	The Pit	3
Chapter 2	Soul Families	9
Chapter 3	Rescuing Angels	17
Chapter 4	A New Life Begins	27
Chapter 5	The House of Stone and Light	32
Chapter 6	Josephine and Francis	40
Chapter 7	Shape-Shifting	48
Chapter 8	Another Day in Paradise	60
Chapter 9	Tales of Dogs Before	67
Chapter 10	Pete Comes Forth	81
Chapter 11	Waldo's Story	93
Chapter 12	Memories of Before	113
Chapter 13	Living In A Shell	126
Chapter 14	Octavia	133
Chapter 15	The Monk	139
Chapter 16	Maggie's Story	149
Chapter 17	Realizations	162
Chapter 18	The Snake in Paradise Is a Cat	170
Chapter 19	Surprise Love Encounters	176
Chapter 20	Everything Is Constantly Changing—Best to Pay Attention	179

Chapter 21	Edmond	184
Chapter 22	Tenacious Traits	198
Chapter 23	Pie Has Issues	210
Chapter 24	Life in the Physical Is a Temporary Status	213
Chapter 25	Shared Soul Memories	230
Chapter 26	We Chose Our Parents	243
Chapter 27	Weddings, Snowflakes, and Beaches	252
Chapter 28	Package Deals	256
Chapter 29	My Reason for Being Here Has Come	260
Chapter 30	Completion Brings Beginnings	273
Epilogue		279
Acknowledgments		281
About the Author		283

Introduction

Thank you for holding this story in your hands. You are about to take a remarkable journey through the eyes of Russell the dog. At times you will find reading this story takes courage, an open mind, and a willingness to laugh and cry.

The second part of the title—A Blend of Truth, Fiction, and Inspiration from the Other Side—explains the breadth of the story.

The way each of my dogs entered my life is true. Very often we take for granted the miraculous events that bless our lives. Or as time moves on, we may forget or negate those gifts. I love to share stories, mine or anyone else's, of how rescuing a dog really means rescuing oneself.

Most everything else is fiction, with a few exceptions. For instance, there is at least one organization—and perhaps others—whose members drive a four-state region around the state of Colorado to rescue dogs. Unfortunately, they have found dogs and puppies discarded into pits. Thankfully, this is not an ongoing problem, but it has occurred. I don't know if this was the case with Russell. However, from the start he was terrified and never tolerated little boys or men. His reactions to boys, especially, were quite extreme, becoming more animated as he grew.

The "inspiration from the other side" references how the story wouldn't leave me alone. It wasn't my intention to write a book. I guess you could say I was a reluctant author. When I finally began writing this story, I took a break, going back a few weeks later to reread what I had written. To my surprise,

I didn't remember writing nearly half of what the Spirit Guide characters express in the story. Even though I'm familiar with what channeling information is, it felt a bit spooky when it happened to me personally.

The characters are composites of people I've known. Some of the stories of hardship were shared by my grandmother and grandfather. For some reason, from a young age I liked to hear about the details of their lives. Although most of their stories were heartbreaking, the hardships never dulled their spirit or tenacity to continue on. Their mastery of making the best of what they were given was skillfully honed by living during World War I, the 1918 influenza epidemic, the Great Depression, and World War II. All other characters are fictional.

In my opinion, all animals, domestic or wild, are worthy of being treated with kindness, dignity, and respect. If you have space in your home and a place in your heart, consider rescuing a pet today. Other actions you can take include signing petitions to stop animal cruelty: Care2.com is one I visit regularly. Another is giving your time or sharing your prosperity with wild and domestic animal organizations. By purchasing this book, you have made a donation to an animal rescue organization. The funds raised from the sales of this book are rotated between different shelters and animal protection associations.

May you love as unconditionally as a dog. And let happiness wag your tail often.

I wish you the Light of love with all the delight you can create in your spiritual adventure!

In joy,
Trisha

1
The Pit

You never know how strong you are until being strong is your only choice.
—Bob Marley

I was sniffing the ground when I picked up the smell of something dead. I was starving and hoped it would be a morsel to eat, but it was only a small, dried up bug, which I ate. I looked around, noticing I was far away from our home spot, something my mother wouldn't like. My hunger pangs grew louder, so I didn't hear him spring from out of nowhere. The beast viciously barked as he came on me in a blaze of dust. It was Savage, a name that struck terror in the hearts of all who knew him. The surprise of his loud growling barks caused me to jump. My legs collapsed. Our eyes locked. I wet myself.

Anger twisted his face. His mouth foamed. He crouched, snarling with his ears back, ready to attack. I was frozen with terror when something suddenly pushed me into a small opening, where I was shielded by a leaning piece of metal stuck in the dirt. I was barely small enough to fit through. I trembled inside the shallow cavity just beyond his reach.

Luckily, Savage's head was too big to fit into my hiding place, though he continued trying to get me with a brutality I never knew existed.

Then I heard it, a voice desperately begging me to dig. Savage quickly gained a small bit of ground. I felt his teeth bite, then slip, pulling hair from my tail. I yelped from the pain and from the fear of being ripped to shreds!

Insane with rage, Savage spewed snot and saliva. Frustration warped his face when he couldn't quite get me, causing him to redouble his efforts. The terror took my breath away. I squeezed back against the dirt and metal to be as small as possible. I cried out for my mother, knowing I was moments away from being torn to pieces. My heart pounded. I couldn't breathe. I couldn't stop whimpering and shaking. I didn't want to be eaten by stinky-breath Savage, who smelled like he had rotting dead mice between his teeth. The crazed monster was getting closer, with almost half his head crammed into my hiding place. He managed a short lunge and bit at my back paw, narrowly missing it. I yelped. I was about to die a terrifying, painful death.

Then something astonishing happened. My mother and Wise Rex had always been terrified of Savage and had rolled on their backs in submission when he had glanced their way. But at that moment I heard them attack him with a fierceness that matched his own. Forced to abandon his attempts to get me, Savage turned on them. The brutal battle began, and I was terrified it would end in the death of my mother and Wise Rex. Their cries of pain sickened me. I wished I were bigger so I could fight Savage myself. Moving ever so slightly to see through a crack, I caught a glimpse of my mother as she hit the ground. Savage ruthlessly attacked her as Wise Rex bravely tried to stop him from killing her. All I could smell was blood and fear.

Suddenly I heard that same voice. It was the voice Mother often spoke to, and it called to me inside my mind. The voice told me where to dig and how to squeeze out; then I was to run as fast as I could to our home spot. I frantically began to dig while my mother and Wise Rex continued the fight to save my life. I also heard my mother desperately cry for me to run.

The next sound I heard was Brute snarling. He was Savage's equal. Leaping from the roof of an old truck, he landed on Savage, tearing at the back of his neck. A ferocious battle between the two warlords of The Pit let loose. They fought almost daily, but this was different. Everyone knew this was a fight to the death.

"Hurry, little one—dig fast!" the voice pleaded. I dug as fast as I could and quickly was able to squeeze out. My back scraped on the big piece of metal, but I was free!

"Run, little one, run!" the voice begged. I was shaking but ran as fast as I could. My heart was pounding so hard I thought my chest would burst.

I made it to our home spot exhausted, my tongue dry as dust, panting, watching, hoping to see my mother coming back.

Still hearing the fight in the distance, I noticed my brother and sister were hiding nearby, shaking as they came out. All at once, the barking stopped; everything went quiet. I knew it was a bad sign—I breathed a few breaths then I heard loud howling, barking, whining, and crying. I took off running back to the fight, my brother and sister following close behind.

The closer we got, the stronger the smell of blood became. Then through the dust we could see all the dog beings of The Pit in a large, tight pack, barking and anxiously whining. It was a horrible, chaotic scene. Savage wasn't moving. He lay on his side, torn up, bloody, his tongue hanging in the dirt. He was dead, and no one wished he wasn't. Not one dog would ever miss Savage, not even his mother, whom he also had attacked for no reason.

Blood was everywhere, but not just his. Mother and Wise Rex were both bleeding. Worse yet, Mother was on her side not moving, her eyes shut. We desperately began licking her face, begging her to wake up. We thought she was dead, then heard her whine as she struggled to move. Her matted red hair was caked with blood, saliva, and dirt. One of her ears was partially torn, and she had gashes on her head, nose, neck, and chest. But she was alive, and so was Wise Rex, who was also hardly moving as a few dogs licked his wounds. Brute was getting the same attention for his injuries. We were all frightened, confused, and reacting from pure instinct.

The whimpering sound my mother made from the pain deeply hurt me. She had trouble opening her blood-soaked eyes. Slowly she tried to move to her stomach, immediately falling back on her side. She was completely spent from the fight to save my life. I whimpered as we continued to lick her wounds and other dogs came forward to help.

Savage's body was now fair game for food. Brute attempted to protect his kill, but he was hurt too badly to guard it. Normally, dog beings don't eat one another, but Wise Rex said starvation brings extremes, and everything in The Pit was extreme.

My brother decided the whole thing was my fault. He said I was always causing trouble by wandering off, and because of me our mother might die. I watched my mother struggle in pain, feeling it was my fault because I had wandered too far. So, I told my brother that if she died, I'd go with her. I didn't know what that meant, but it worked—he didn't know what to say and stopped blaming me.

The fear began to lessen some after a while. We cuddled next to Mother, and my mind went back to one of my first memories. From the moment I was born, or maybe before, I felt something heavy hanging over me. I couldn't understand it, but I remember a small part of me wondering what I had done—coming here to this place. I wouldn't know why I thought that or what it meant until later, when every disturbing detail would be revealed.

Everything around us smelled of decay. Most of the smell was from old rusty cars, ripped up furniture, and trash. We were also considered worthless, left with everything else to rot in a deep depression of dry earth known as The Pit—this is where I was born. From the start, I knew the only hope I had was my mother and maybe the angels she often spoke about.

In The Pit, everything had to be fought for—rodents, food scraps, water, territory, every single thing. As pups we got very little, but early on we had no teeth to chew anyway.

Though fighting was common, most of the dogs usually got along, except for two huge males who considered themselves rulers of The Pit. They were constantly fighting for dominance, which only frightened us more, making everything worse.

The biggest dog in The Pit was Savage. Wise Rex said he was a mix of Doberman, Great Dane, and other gigantic dog breeds. Savage was mostly tan and brown with a round black mark on the right side of his square head. His other markings were a blend of scars and fresh battle wounds. Every dog was afraid of him except Brute, who was a bit smaller but stockier, especially in the chest. Wise Rex, who was older than any dog in The Pit, said Brute was German Shepherd and Rottweiler, with some other big dog breeds thrown in. Brute was mostly black, with some tan and a white patch on his chest, all mixed in with his various old and new battle scars.

Savage and Brute set an anxious tone in The Pit. They fought almost daily or attacked other dogs for no reason other than the frustration and hunger that warped us all.

From the start, our mother, Wise Rex, and other dogs warned us pups that Savage and Brute had been known to kill puppies and eat them. I wasn't sure I quite believed them—or, rather, I had hoped it wasn't true—until this day, when Savage did try to tear me to shreds and eat me!

2
Soul Families

Love forever connects us.
—Tess

The days that followed Savage's death were better in some ways. But I was scared because my mother and Wise Rex could barely get around. Some of their wounds started to heal, some not. For the moment, we were saved from starvation since everyone had eaten a portion of Savage. Nothing went to waste in The Pit—nothing except us dog beings, who scarcely continued to survive.

A few days later, the mean boys who threw rocks attacked us. They always came together—three on bikes, two on foot—making sounds that filled us with terror. Their appearance would set all the dog beings in The Pit to frantically barking and howling. A crippling fear consumed us because we knew what was about to happen.

Wise Rex was a large and at times aggressive Airedale mix who my mother thought was most likely our father. Rex said the boys were no more than pups themselves, and their pent-up fury probably came from the frustration of nowhere to go and nothing to do. He said, "They only want to escape, to stop being treated as disposable." And that's what all the dog beings of The Pit wanted too.

Our mother, whose name was Tess, was a medium-sized red chow mix with deep brown eyes. She had endured these attacks from the mean boys for years, always doing her best to protect her pups. She trembled as she limped, moving us to a small hiding place under an old rusty car roof. As they closed in, she begged us to stay close to her.

The yelling hurt our ears as every sound echoed in The Pit. Then the rocks started flying. All the dogs were hiding under old cars or the skeletons of things tossed away. The boys were aiming at us but mostly hitting what we were trying to hide under. When they did hit one of us, our yelping brought cheers mixed with laughter. Each of us had been hit many times before, causing pain that sometimes lasted for days or weeks, but some dogs were changed forever.

We huddled close to our mother, hoping not to be hit. We begged her to make it stop, but it was no use; she was only a helpless dog, shaking with an anxious whining sound in her throat.

Eventually, the boys left, laughing and pleased with themselves. They yelled out how many times they hit us, making us cry, and they congratulated one another on their cruelty. The smell of fear was thick from the time they came until they left. But our fear never completely went away—it only lessened until the next time.

After they left, I asked my mother, "Why do they want to hurt us?"

She gently licked my head. Then, with a deep sadness, she answered, "They're expressing harmful energy they'll come to regret someday. Nothing goes unseen. They don't understand yet that what they do to others, they do to themselves. This, my sweet ones, is how actions weave our future destinies."

As pups, we didn't understand. How could we? Exhausted from our ordeal, we quickly fell asleep.

The boys were another reason Mother didn't like us straying from our home spot. "Stay close to me, my pups," she'd often say to us. "It's not safe to be out in the open during the day. They could come back, and if you wander too far away, you could be hurt." Sometimes she'd deliver a little nip to my bottom to remind me of her warning when I'd stray too far.

My mind wandered to a recent hot day before the fight with Savage, when Mother warned us again, but I didn't listen. "A few dogs have died in The Pit since you pups were born, but you're all too young to remember, and you didn't know about the many that died before. Some pups were eaten by Savage or Brute, some died from being hit by rocks, some from fighting, and some died from starvation or sickness. The only way to stay safe is to remain close to me and our home spot." She tried once to explain *died*, which was confusing. Plus, my empty belly hurt too much at the time to care.

What she didn't understand was that what mattered most to me, besides milk, was playing. If we had the energy to play, it helped distract us from the pain of our empty bellies. Besides our hunger, we were always thirsty, having very little water or milk. Occasional rainstorms would leave small puddles, but they quickly dried up and then turned to dust. Sometimes, a young girl would bring a jug of water and pour it down into the rusty car parts for us to drink. All the dogs fought for it, including our mother, but we were too small, so we didn't get any. Later we'd scrounge for missed drops, usually finding none, but it gave us something to do to keep our minds off the misery of our hunger and thirst.

There were also two women who would sometimes come just before dark and toss food scraps down to us. The competition for food caused more fights, but Mother thought the two women were merciful angels who came to help us. Sometimes she'd tell us other angels might come someday to take us away from this place. I was always confused by what she meant, for I didn't understand that there were other places besides The Pit. *Where else would we go?* I wondered to myself.

The next day was cloudy when Mother began our daily baths. I was happy to be first, loving how she tenderly licked my ears and face. Some of the wounds on her neck and chest smelled bad with what Wise Rex called infection, which was the same smell he also had. It was a helpless feeling to see our sweet mother in pain, so we did our best to give her comfort by licking her wounds until she fell asleep.

It was surprising she could give me a bath because the pain made her whimper with certain movements, but she was intent on continuing. With a calm, peaceful tone, she started to explain why I was different. "My sweet one, there are things you must know that you probably won't understand now, but please promise me you'll try to remember."

I'm glad we don't talk with our mouths the way people do, or she wouldn't be able to give me a bath and talk to me at the same time.

"But why do I have to remember?" I asked, feeling lazy under the spell of her soft tongue. "If I forget, won't you tell me again later?"

With a deep sigh she continued, "I won't always be with

you. One day everything will change; then we'll no longer be together in the physical."

Whimpering, I snuggled closer. "No! What day? I don't want that day to come. Why won't we always be together?"

Trying to soothe me, she said, "We'll be together again in spirit, as we are forever connected by love."

Gently nuzzling my neck with her teeth to remove a bug, she continued my bath while my brother and sister, uninterested in what Mother was saying, fell asleep waiting for their turns.

She softly uttered, "There are beautiful things in this world, such as grace, compassion, tenderness, and love. There are people who express these things with the intention of helping others. I call them angels."

I was relaxed and getting drowsy, loving the bath. I didn't want to hear any more, but I listened anyway as I fought off a nap.

"You have a greater knowingness with a larger purpose than most dog beings," she told me in her gentle voice. "Have you noticed I don't talk to your brother or sister the way I talk to you?"

"Yes, I wondered about that," I muttered, preoccupied as she cleaned the inside of my ears, which was definitely my favorite part.

"It's because they're simply experiencing their current lifetimes *only* as dog beings. You have chosen a different learning path with a dual purpose. Your life will have a twofold objective, along with many obstacles. Please listen carefully, my sweet. This is very important: There will be one who wishes you harm, bearing a mark on the right side of the face or head. Remember the black mark Savage had on his face?"

Panic gripped me on hearing his name. "Yes, I remember." I dropped my head, sniffing my paw, pretending not to be scared. Something else returned from the day Savage came so close to eating me; it was the dark shadow of my guilt. I looked into her eyes and said, "I'll never forget how you and Wise Rex were nearly killed trying to save me," Speaking louder, I added, "But it's Savage who's dead, so we don't have to worry about him anymore!" I hoped that put an end to any more talk about Savage.

She stopped licking me and gently placed her calloused front paw on my paw. "Please understand, my precious one, that darkness takes many forms, with a purpose all its own, making no sense to those in the vibration of Light. The one who wishes you harm will come again and again with the purpose of trying to end your life. So, you must be aware at all times of possible danger. Again, you must watch for the mark on the right side of the face or head. Promise me you'll remember."

Now I was really confused. "Okay. But what darkness, Mother? I don't know what you mean. You said when something is dead, it's gone, never to come back. If Savage comes back, I'll run away or bite him." Anxiety built in my chest with the thought of Savage coming after me again, knowing I wouldn't survive another attack.

With a thoughtful sigh she moved her paw and continued. "Energy—all types of energy—can easily change form. And this is very important, my sweet. The soul that came in the form of Savage can come back in a different body."

Fear gripped me, taking my breath away. "What? How can that be? I don't understand."

"You don't have to understand to be aware; just believe what I say is true. Do you believe me?"

I hesitated. "Yes, Mother, but . . . I still don't know how this could happen."

As I look back now, I can see that her patient love was endless. She had tried to warn me, but I was really only concerned with eating.

"It will all come to light later, when you remember this moment. For now, let's talk about something else that's also very important. Do you remember feeling that something pushed you into the safe place right before Savage attacked you? Did you hear a voice inside your head that told you where to dig so you could get out and run?"

I was instantly confused. *How did she know that?* "I . . . I do, Mother, but how did you—"

"That was your spirit guide, Josephine. She played a big part in saving you from Savage, and we owe her a great deal for her help."

"Her name is Josephine?" I asked, my curiosity heightened. "Who is she, and why can't I see her?"

"Because she is a spirit and doesn't have a body like our own. She is what's called a kindred spirit, which means she's part of our soul family. She'll watch over you, but you must still be very careful. Do not let your stubbornness cause you to be reckless. You will learn a great deal as you grow while having many adventures. Josephine and other guides will be there to help you, but you must find the courage to do most of the work yourself."

"Do what myself?" I was fighting to stay awake.

"That's enough for now," she replied, finishing my bath. "Please remember what I've told you about the spiritual adventure you have chosen. Also, be aware there is much more I haven't told you. The time will come for more to be revealed to you. Please try to be accepting." She tenderly licked me. "I love you, sweet one."

It was strange, but a distant part of me sort of understood what she had said. I licked her mouth, saying, "I love you too, Mother. I will try to remember."

A sinking feeling came over me that night as I fell asleep. I dreamed our lives would soon be ending. And that is what came to be.

3
Rescuing Angels

*Saving an animal expands the frequency of love, forever
changing the lives of all who are involved.*
—Josephine

It was a cold, sunny morning when the world we knew ended.

We woke in the usual way, with our bellies aching, too sluggish to move much. As the air warmed, we smelled different people. Suddenly we saw them. They were women, but not the ones who brought us food scraps. These women climbed down into The Pit! The wire boxes they carried made odd noises. Wise Rex said they were cages. He knew this from when the women had come in the past.

The sound that echoed from all the dogs in The Pit barking, howling, and whining was deafening. Because we were weak from starvation, it was easy for the women to catch us using bits of food. After they put some of us in a scary cage, I started to bite the wire sides, desperate to escape. I couldn't. My brother and sister had been added to the cage I was in. We frantically tried get out.

Wise Rex stood on a pile of junk in The Pit, where he could barely see what was happening. I heard him tell the other dogs he could see trucks.

The women lifted each cage from The Pit with ropes and quickly loaded us in the back of the trucks. But they left our mothers and the older dogs behind. It was heartbreaking to hear their desperate barking. They begged the women to also take them away from The Pit.

I heard my mother shouting to us that it would be OK. Still, I distinctly remember the overpowering smell of fear that came from the other dogs. It was greater than when the boys came.

All of us pups hysterically barked and cried in an effort to stop what was happening. But in the end, it didn't matter. We were trapped. I realized that if the mean boys came back now, we couldn't hide, and they could kill us all! That thought terrified me even more, which made me wee.

I couldn't understand why they were leaving all the grown dogs and why they only took us pups. The terror intensified, making everything worse. I couldn't breathe. I felt dizzy. My head hurt so much that I threw up the bits of food they'd used to trap us.

With a jolt, the trucks started to move. I somehow knew we'd never see The Pit again. The thought of being away from there felt right, but it also terrified me. I felt I'd never see my mother or Wise Rex again.

These trucks smelled different from the ones in The Pit. These moved, and smoke came from the pipes below our cages, which added to my dizziness. Above the noise of the trucks, I could hear the other pups whining and yelping, scared of what would happen next. I was shaking so much I thought I might never stop.

My brother, sister, and I, in the same cage, whimpered for our mother, while the other pups did the same. And what about our mother and the other dogs? What would happen to them? Giving in to exhaustion, our whines and cries became weaker, until sleep mercifully took us to a more peaceful place.

Suddenly, I looked, and there she was, chasing our truck. I had never seen my mother run so fast! Her hair pushed back from running in the wind, and her tongue hung out the side of her mouth. She looked like a younger, determined version of herself. Then, from a passing field, the boys came from the tall grass and chased her, throwing rocks at her as she ran. They hit her, and she yelped. I cried and barked. A loud noise startled me awake. The bad dream ended.

I was panting from my nightmare. I recalled my mother explaining how I knew more than other dogs. But I didn't know why all this was happening. I missed her so much it made me feel sick.

The trucks quickly moved along the dry, dusty dirt roads. Finally, we stopped under big things I heard the ladies call trees. The trees cast shadows over the trucks, making it cooler, and gave us some relief from the sun. We'd never seen trees before, but I had a distant memory of what they were. They looked like giants with huge arms that reached over us, but they didn't scare me. I liked them.

The ladies got out of the trucks along with one man, who I didn't like. The tallest of the ladies announced, "Well, we're out of New Mexico and in Colorado now."

Another, a shorter one, said, "I know we only have permission to take the puppies, but I hated to leave the adult dogs behind." She sounded sad.

They all agreed; that was the hardest part.

Every single smell was strange. Not bad, but like nothing we'd ever smelled before. Each of the women had a different scent. One smelled sweet, another smelled like sweat, but all smelled like the mouthwatering food they were about to feed us. In the cool shade, the nice ladies fed us soft, delicious food and cool fresh water. I had never smelled or tasted anything so wonderful! The flavors burst in my mouth while my nose reveled in the smells. The water wasn't muddy; it was clear and quenched my thirst, making my tongue feel as satisfied as my belly.

Everyone ate, including the ladies and the man I didn't like because I thought he was a giant boy. They had different food that smelled even better than ours, but I didn't care. My belly was full, and I wasn't thirsty. I felt good even though I was still scared.

After eating, we drove away, leaving the big trees behind. The rocking motion of the truck and our full bellies soon put us to sleep again. Right before I fell asleep, I saw my mother's face appear, and I heard Josephine tell her we were safe. I whimpered, hoping she could hear me and knew how much I missed her. I was terrified. Would I ever see her sweet face again?

―――᭜―――

When I awoke, the trucks were driving through a gate into a big fenced place they called a farm. It had even more giant trees. We were taken out of the cages and put into larger pens with water bowls. Each pen had different families of pups—the ladies called them litters. When all the arranging was done, we were fed again. My brother, little sister, and I had our own pen. We could see the other pups from The Pit, which made us feel better.

We were confused but happy that we had food and water. And we had the nice ladies who kissed and cuddled us. They talked to us, and I wondered if they were angels—maybe the angels my mother had spoken about. But I remained on the lookout for the mean boys. I wondered if they came to this place too.

The ladies talked to one another almost all the time. That's how we learned we were in a place called Brighton, near a city known as Denver. That didn't mean anything to us, but I didn't care where we were as long as we never had to go back to The Pit. We all missed our mothers and some of the other dogs too. We couldn't understand why they weren't with us. I tried asking the ladies many times, but none of them could hear me. I wondered about this because animals could hear me if I spoke to them.

Josephine talked to me in my mind, as she usually did, and explained, "Communication among animal beings takes place on a finer wavelength not involving sound. This is also true for human beings, who are also a type of animal, but for them it requires listening beyond the self-centeredness of the ego."

The way she explained it was complex, but somehow, I sort of understood. "Do you mean all beings can send one another thought messages? And some listen to the message, and others don't?"

"Exactly. You are very smart," she said, complimenting me.

Suddenly, my brother jumped on me and my sister soon joined in. We had fun wrestling and biting one another's heads, ears, or whatever ended up in our mouths. Afterward, we were tired from playing. Then we were happily fed again. Later, we all snuggled up together and went to sleep not feeling hungry, thirsty, or quite as scared.

When I woke the next morning, my belly wasn't growling. I was hungry, but it wasn't the same gnawing emptiness I had awakened with each day in The Pit. All we knew in The Pit was our starving bellies, thirst, and being afraid almost all the time. The only exception was when I was nursing, playing, or getting a bath from my mother. At those times I didn't notice it as much, but the fear was always in the background.

Later in the morning, each pup was taken to see a tall man with dark hair. At first, I thought he was a giant boy, so I barked at him with my most ferocious bark, which made him laugh. His name was Dr. Burt.

The new smells along with new things to see were endless. Dr. Burt and the ladies smelled like lots of puppies, plus many other scents I hadn't smelled before. He looked into my mouth and ears, squeezed my sides, turned me on my back, lifted my tail, and put something sharp in my neck. But I didn't mind because when he finished, he patted my head and gave me a piece of food he called a treat. It made my tail wag. While he was petting me, he told the lady I was feisty, pointing to my black tongue, and said I might have some stubborn traits. He thought I was an Airedale and chow mix. Then he put me down on the floor to see how I walked. That's when I caught a glimpse of a puppy who was also in the room but hid when I tried to follow it. They laughed when I realized it was me, in what they called a mirror. It was the first time I'd seen myself. I was red, like my mother, but my hair was short except for a long fuzzy tuft on the top of my head just like Wise Rex had. It was strange to see myself. At first I liked it, but then I didn't and started to bark.

Dr. Burt lifted me onto the table again and gave me another treat, which sent my tail wagging again. He lifted me with one arm, cuddled me next to his chest, and said, "This one's smart and feisty, but whoever adopts him will need to have lots of patience." He handed me to the nice lady, who said, "He's so cute that I'd adopt him myself, but my husband gave me strict orders not to bring another one home."

Dr. Burt chuckled. "My wife gave me the same orders." Ruffling the fluffy hair on my head, he said, "See you around, Mr. Fuzzy Wig." He opened the door for us, and we left Dr. Burt, the odd smells, and his treats behind.

The nice lady brought me back to the pen, kissed me on the head, and gently put me down. She immediately picked up my whimpering little sister, said she must be the runt, and then carried her off to see Dr. Burt. I tried to tell my sister it was OK, that she was going to get a treat, but she was whining too loudly to listen. Then my brother jumped on me, and we started a fun wrestling match that lasted the whole time my sister was gone. When she came back, we sniffed her, searching for new telltale smells.

After all the pups had gone to see Dr. Burt, the ladies gave us what they called baths. I didn't like the water pouring on me and tried to bite it, even though it made me feel better. Then they gave us all another treat. I loved this place because

I loved treats and eating yummy food and drinking fresh water! I loved the pats and kisses too! I loved everything but the bath, and I never wanted to leave.

Afterward, they led us to a big grassy area near our pens and let us out to play. It was so much fun sniffing one another with our new clean smells and then biting, wrestling, barking, and tugging on fun things called toys.

At that moment I realized I wasn't afraid anymore. But we had no way of knowing it was all going to end. A grumpy old bulldog who lived there and didn't like us pups said they were going to take us down to the railroad tracks and kill us! I didn't believe him, but I did wonder—and he frightened my sister and some of the other pups.

"You'll all be gone by Sunday," he said with a snort as he limped his old body back inside the farmhouse he came from. I decided right then and there I didn't like bulldogs.

The ladies enjoyed watching us play and laughed at our antics. I felt they were full of love and would never hurt us. I tried to tell them what the bulldog said about the railroad tracks and killing us, but again they didn't hear me. I didn't think it was true, but I worried. What if it was true?

I heard one of the ladies say it was Thursday, with lots to do before Saturday, but I didn't really understand what Thursday and Saturday were.

I was almost positive the ladies were angels, but it was my mother who'd know for sure. I remembered, the day before we left as my mother licked my ears, she had said she'd been waiting for me. And now that I had been born into the physical, she would soon be able to leave The Pit. I wondered then how she would do that. I hoped that maybe one of the angel ladies would go back for her, Wise Rex, and the other dogs too. I missed her so much my belly hurt, and it made me whimper whenever I thought about her. I began to drift off to sleep, wondering if Josephine could hear me and whether she knew why we were here without the other dogs. I called to her, "Josephine, I'm here. Are you here too?" But there was only silence.

I woke just as the sun was coming up. There was something strange in the air. I was sniffing around on my way to the other side of the pen to wee when I heard a whooshing sound above me coming closer. I looked up in time to see a huge owl swooping down with its claws spread, ready to snatch me up. Just then another large bird flew between me and the owl, knocking me down. The two birds fought, screeching at each other; then both were gone as quickly as they had appeared! I ran back to my brother and sister. My heart pounded, but they barely stirred. Moments later I noticed the other bird, who had saved me from the owl, was in a nearby tree watching us, looking directly at me. It was then I realized it was Josephine!

She said, "I'm sharing this red-tailed hawk's body to watch over you. The owl was hungry and set on making you his next meal." Josephine looked around. "Be aware and alert to danger." Those were her parting words as she spread her wings and took flight.

"Thank you, Josephine!" I shouted after her. "How's my mother?" But she was already gone and didn't hear me. I must have been the only one she was protecting because when I asked my brother and sister about Josephine, they didn't understand the question. "What's a Josephine?" asked my sweet little sister.

That morning, we were fed as usual and then let out of our pens to play in the big grassy area again with all the other pups from The Pit. We played all day, napped now and then, and had some treats thrown in. We all agreed: the farm was a great place and none of us ever wanted to leave.

With each passing day, I was certain the nice ladies were angels, or if they weren't angels, they were better than angels. I felt a distant knowing of what an angel was, but I couldn't remember. I somehow knew angels were kind and protective, just like the nice ladies were to us.

The only problem was the old bulldog. Whenever he came outside, he'd look directly at me and say, "The railroad tracks are just over the hill, and you're going to be first."

I tried to ignore him, but then I noticed a black mark on the side of his head and remembered Mother's warning. As I recalled the black mark on Savage's face, I started to panic and began to wonder if the bulldog's warning was true and they really were going to kill us. But I couldn't imagine the nice ladies—or even Dr. Burt—letting any harm come to us. Just then an angel lady picked me up and rubbed my belly, making me forget about the bulldog.

Unfortunately, our happiness at the farm wasn't meant to last. None of us had any idea everything was about to change, and these changes would shift each of our lives, separating us forever.

4
A New Life Begins

With every ending there is a new beginning.
—Josephine

The next day was the Saturday the ladies had talked about. They were up early, feeding us and letting us go in the big play area for a while, then returning us back to our pens. It was right after that when it happened: The ladies opened the big gate, and lots of people came into the farm. Most of the people were laughing, pointing, and saying nice things. They brought a variety of smells, but some of the people had little boys with them. I started my most ferocious barking to warn the other pups that little boys were there. My brother and sister were also barking the alarm when the other pups joined in. But no one seemed to care. The people just kept having fun, calling us puppies, and one little girl with blond hair and big green eyes said, "This must be one of the happiest places on earth—there's puppies everywhere!" The people around her agreed with laughter.

Soon after, one of the angel ladies opened the pen and took my sister to a man and woman with a little girl who had sad brown eyes. I thought little girls were OK because they didn't smell or act mean the way little boys did, so they didn't scare me or the other pups. We watched as the man and woman had fun playing with my sister. Their little girl seemed shy and maybe even afraid at first because my sister was jumping on her. Then I could see the little girl's energy become similar to my sister's. Her brown eyes began to brighten. Her parents seemed pleased and gave a nod to the lady, who took my sister inside a building I hadn't been to. That, sadly, was the last time I ever saw my sister. Shortly after, the same happened to my brother, whom I would also never see again.

Josephine quietly said in my ear, "Your brother and sister will have good lives full of love. Be happy for them."

"Thank you, Josephine, for letting me know, but I already miss them. Can't I go with them?"

Josephine answered, "You have a different destiny. Be patient. Love will also come to you."

I noticed most of the pups were more at ease about the little boys because they were different from the ones who tormented us in The Pit. I remained suspicious and felt uncertain. While I was playing with a toy, people would come up to the pen and call me over to visit. All the commotion made me tired, so after a while I lay down and fell asleep. In my sleep, Josephine, soft as a whisper, said, "Something wonderful is about to happen."

I woke from my nap to the sound of talking, and a warm feeling filled my chest and belly. I sat up, yawned, and felt my heart connect to a nice lady with brown hair and blue eyes. In that moment, I immediately knew she had come for me. And I had a vague sense that I had somehow been waiting for her. But how could that be?

Kneeling, she put her fingers through the wire and I almost fell over my paws running to lick them. I could feel her expand with love, but there was more: I somehow felt I knew her, and she knew me. Josephine gave me a clue I wouldn't understand until later, "Such a feeling is known as déjà vu—coming from something predetermined." This was another thing I didn't understand or really care about at the time.

One of the angel ladies who smelled the most like treats picked me up, taking me to another pen. She left me alone to play with a ball when I heard her say, "Deardra, over here!" And there she was, the same blue-eyed lady coming toward the pen, only this time with a dog she called Waldo. I heard her say to him, "Be nice to the sweet puppy, Waldo. We want to take him home." As they came in the pen, I heard a low, throaty growl come from Waldo. He didn't want to share her, but I could feel his loneliness mixed with a deep sadness.

Immediately he ran up to me, sniffed, and asked, "Who are you?" I rolled on my back and let him get a good smell of my belly, my mouth, and other parts. Then he stuck his nose in the air, walked toward something he pretended to be interested in, and lifted his leg. I continued playing with the ball. My eyes fixed on Deardra while she stroked my back. She asked me, "Do you want to come home with me and Waldo?" She picked me up, fluffed the fuzzy part of the hair on my head, and then placed a kiss on my face. Nothing, so far, felt as right as being with her, but I wasn't sure about Waldo. He snorted as he watched Deardra hold me.

She turned to the angel lady and nodded. "He's the one."

They took me to a room in the building where my sister and brother had gone earlier, putting me in a cage with two other pups from The Pit. We were waiting for something, and none of us knew what. I sniffed the air, still searching for my sister or brother, only managing to catch a faint whiff of them. I was afraid again, so I began to bark and whine. No one seemed to care. When a tall lady put a treat in front of my nose, I stopped, learning that I couldn't bark while chewing a treat.

Eventually the angel ladies took me out of the cage, passed me back and forth, and kissed me and said goodbye. They brought me outside, placed me in Deardra's arms, and as soon as they did, Waldo let out a bark. He wasn't happy. We walked to Deardra's car and got in. Waldo continued to protest by barking even louder when Deardra put me in the back seat next to him. At first, she ignored Waldo's barking, and then she firmly told him to stop, which he reluctantly did.

As we began moving, I grew excited and wanted to play. I started to jump on Waldo. He didn't like it, growling and then snapping at me. "Stop hanging on Waldo's face, silly pup," Deardra said. I didn't listen because I was having too much fun.

The car stopped, and she turned around and looked at me thoughtfully. Then, with a big smile followed by a chuckle, she said my new name was Russell.

I liked it. Somehow, it felt right. I remembered that back in The Pit I was sometimes called Rusty, which was close to Russell. But my mother almost always called me "sweet one."

As we drove, I found Deardra liked to call Waldo a circus bear. Later I'd learn it was because she thought he looked like a medium-sized fuzzy red bear. He was chow and collie. She thought we had the chow part in common.

Deardra said to Waldo, "Try to have a good attitude, my little circus bear. Russell is your new friend." He found that ridiculous, and I could hear him thinking, *If he were hanging on your face, you'd feel differently—and I didn't ask for a new friend, especially a barbarian puppy! I miss The Newf.*

I was thinking, *What's a Newf?*

Josephine said, "He was the dog who came before you."

I tried to ask Deardra what happened to The Newf, but nothing—only silence. I recalled my mother saying, "All animal beings can hear one another's thoughts as clearly as sounds, smells, and body signals. Human beings can hear thoughts too, but most have too much inner chatter to listen or don't believe what they're hearing." This was similar to what Josephine had told me, so I thought it must be the truth.

Thinking about my mother brought a hollow feeling that filled me with grief. The motion of the car started to make me sleepy, so I lay down and fell asleep.

5
The House of Stone and Light

Home is where love resides.
—Deardra

I awoke with a start, aware of feeling a strong pull of energy as we drove a short way on a dirt road up to a house. I could feel Deardra's excitement as we got out of the car. She carried me up the randomly shaped stone stairs. Waldo was weeing on some bushes, still in a snit, growling as we went inside. Deardra told him it was going to be OK, but I knew he didn't believe her.

Immediately lots of smells hit my nose, including those of two dogs—one was Waldo, and the other must have been The Newf. His smell mostly faded. I sensed how deeply Deardra and Waldo missed The Newf. Josephine told me Waldo and The Newf were more than best friends. They had been brother and sister in another life. The love they shared followed into this one, leaving Waldo heartbroken after The Newf died.

I didn't understand where he went after he died, but I was in his former house and felt happy for it.

I briefly flashed on the old bulldog at the farm and sent

him a thought message. *Railroad tracks, huh? Guess chasing trees messed up more than your face!*

I hoped he heard me. Scaring us pups was not funny!

Waldo was upset with my sniffing everywhere and followed me, growling as we went. I ignored him. I was too busy taking in all the new smells, sights, and sounds. Besides, I somehow knew Deardra would protect me if he decided to attack. We went through the house together, with Waldo on my haunches and Deardra smiling as she watched us.

I quickly learned the front part of the house was called the sunroom. It was surrounded on three sides by big windows that filled the house with light, creating a warmth I found soothing.

Unexpectedly, I felt I was exactly where I was supposed to be. It was a comfortable feeling; I felt safe, something I'd never known before. The short time at the farm had brought some happiness, but mostly relief from no longer living in The Pit. This feeling of contentment was different somehow. I knew things would never be the same for any of us, especially me and Deardra.

I wondered about my mother, brother, and sister. Where were they? Were they safe? I could feel myself dropping down into sorrow, but that quickly turned to excitement when I smelled food and heard Deardra call us to eat.

It took a while before Waldo got used to me. He started to enjoy our playing together, which helped take his mind off The Newf. We had rousing games of tug-of-war with old socks. And we played with the ball and wrestled, which Waldo always won because he was bigger. But my favorite game was playing with the green bone! Deardra originally bought it for Waldo. He never liked it much, but I sure did! She laughed at the green bone being bigger than my head, but that didn't stop me from wanting to carry it almost everywhere. There was something I really liked about it. I especially enjoyed sticking it in Waldo's face. I'd hit him in the head with it until he'd bite it, play tug-of-war, or chase after me to get it.

Deardra was pleased Waldo seemed happier after being so sad about the loss of The Newf. She seemed happy too. I could tell she enjoyed me being part of our new family pack. She'd often play with us, giving us lots of love and affection.

But there were problems. I didn't like the word no! No ruined everything. It was when I was having the most fun that Deardra said it a lot. I wanted to please her and not be a bad dog, but there were limits on how much I was willing to give up of what I wanted to do.

Much to my dismay, and the entertainment of Waldo, she didn't like my habit of taking a mouthful of food from my bowl, running into the sunroom, spitting it on the carpet, then carefully examining it to make sure it looked right. Next was the important part: rolling on it with my head and neck. Then, and only then, would I eat it. I'd run back into the kitchen for another mouthful, starting the whole important process over again. For some reason, Deardra didn't like it, saying no each time I did it. Clearly, she didn't understand how satisfying it was for me to eat in this carefully planned way.

After a week or so, we came to a temporary understanding. I agreed to eat at my bowl without leaving the kitchen if she didn't say no all the time. This mostly worked—except for those times when she left the kitchen. I'd sneak a mouthful of food and spit it out on the sunroom carpet, doing the whole, wonderful rolling thing again before eating it. Somehow, she always seemed to know when I did this. As soon as she entered the sunroom, she'd scold me and even call me a "bad dog." A few times she'd laugh while scolding me. This was confusing because I thought she only laughed when she was happy. Waldo watched each time, thinking it was funny. He said sooner or later she would win, and I'd have to eat in the kitchen at my bowl like a good dog. I didn't want to be a good dog if it meant I had to completely give up this satisfying way of eating. It wasn't what I wanted, bad dog or not.

One night while I was hitting Waldo with my green bone, trying to get him to play, Deardra was watching and laughed. She said I was "Puppa-fied." She shortened it to "Puppa," and this became one of my many nicknames describing my behavior or looks.

As time went on, Waldo and I spent the days having fun, playing, being pals, and doing important dog things. Waldo taught me about protecting Deardra, the house, and each other.

The hair all over my body grew to match the fuzzy tuft on my head. This led to Deardra calling me a red teddy bear dog. She liked to brush my curly hair. However, I hated the pulling and tried to bite the brush when she tried to use it on me. She said I was stubborn as a mule, sometimes just calling me a mule.

Deardra called our home the House of Stone and Light. I loved it here! It was more than a refuge from the madness of

The Pit; it was a home, a real home, my home, our home. It was here I understood what it was to love and be loved by others besides my mother, brother, sister, and Josephine.

I was content, and I liked to roll onto my back, wag my tail, and gaze at Deardra with love. I wondered why she seemed familiar; I was sure she had never come to The Pit.

That night, I dreamed about Josephine. In my dream, she had the ghostly outline of a woman who was distantly familiar. In a reassuring tone, Josephine told me I was loved and watched over. And I shouldn't be afraid no matter what happened. No matter how bad things seemed to get. As she parted, she gently said, "Everything is going to change when you're one year old."

I woke from the dream feeling anxious. What did she mean? Was something bad going to happen? Living in The Pit was bad enough! Would Deardra send me back to The Pit because I was a bad dog sometimes? My belly ached from worry. I missed my mother. Then the sound of dog food filling my bowl shifted my mind to eating.

The days flowed into weeks, then into months. Waldo continued training me on how to attend to all the important things we had to do while on a walk. We lived in the mountains. Our walks were in the woods surrounding the house, where wild beings lived. It was very important to sniff, then wee on the right spots. This was critical to let other dogs and wild animal beings know we were on the job and not about to tolerate any threats or misbehaving. This included bears, foxes, cats, or coyotes, which we sometimes saw and often smelled.

When at home, it was a never-ending job keeping all the pesky animal and bird beings who lived outside the sunroom in line with our rules. Worse, they were everywhere right outside the house—in the trees, on the ground, among the rocks, in the bushes, in holes—wherever a home could be made. We tried to keep them off the deck and away from the house by chasing and barking at them. There were so many of them that it was a never-ending task. Deardra made it harder because she liked all the animal and bird beings and told us to leave them alone. She didn't understand. Keeping animals and birds away was in our nature as dogs, but she didn't want us to hurt the pests. That didn't stop us, though. Since I was getting bigger, quicker, and smarter, I was able to help Waldo with this huge job.

One morning I wanted to go out early. Deardra opened the bedroom door, and she and Waldo went back to sleep. I was on the deck sniffing where a raccoon trespasser had been during the night when I heard "Hey, Fuzzy Wig!" I looked over the edge to see a fat chipmunk sitting on his hind legs making clicking noises as he spoke.

"That's right, Fuzzy Wig. It's me talking to you."

"What do you want?" I asked with irritation.

"Could you dogs take it easy on us chipmunks? Our lives are hard enough without you making it worse with your barking and chasing us all the time. We're just trying to have a life. Eat, not be eaten, and have some fun in the process. You need to lighten up and stop giving us grief."

I couldn't believe the nerve of this chipmunk. "Sorry, Chubby," I said, filling my voice with authority to sound more like Waldo. "That's not going to happen. You need to quit coming on the deck or in the yard. Then we won't chase you. It's that easy. Now leave me alone! I have more important things to do than talk to you." I went back to tracing the scent of where the raccoon had been.

He made more clicking sounds. "But we need to come on the deck; that's where all the easy seeds from the bird feeders fall. And who are you calling chubby? My mother says I'm pleasingly plump."

"Pleasingly plump . . . really? If it wasn't for me and Waldo chasing you, you'd be *really* fat—and bored too, I bet."

A red squirrel dashed up, running the mouthy chipmunk off. At that point, the exchange ended.

I heard Deardra singing the "Morning Song." She sang it to us every day when she got up. I ran through the open door into the bedroom in time to hear.

"Time to get up, get out of bed, live, love, laugh, and be happy."

Compared to the music she played, she didn't have a good singing voice, but we didn't care. We could feel all the love and joy she put into the song, signaling our day was officially beginning. Waldo told me she'd always sung the "Morning Song" since he'd come to be here. And The Newf told Waldo she'd sung it to him since the day she found him.

As the months passed, Waldo and I grew closer. We basked in the gentle, affectionate love Deardra showered on us each day. We especially enjoyed the delicious food, fun walks in the woods, playing, and doing our job of protecting everything in our domain. Our lives were wonderful. I felt great.

Then, when I was a year old, it all fell apart. I'd never again be the same.

<u>6</u>
Josephine and Francis

We are your Guides. We will see you through.
We never stop watching over you.
—Francis

Josephine had many concerns about the next guidance she and her old friend Francis had voluntarily accepted. The soul to be guided was soon to be born into the third dimension of the Earth plane. This was referred to as the physical.

Her thoughts quickly moved to meeting Francis in the sixteenth dimension. This was one of the most magnificent areas of the etheric field. The etheric, or spiritual, realm consisted of an unlimited color spectrum where matter was effortlessly created with a thought. Each color had a sound frequency, creating music so beautiful that many souls would come to listen. Then, resonating with the sound, the souls would become the music. The sixteenth dimension magnified this experience, adding emotion that was usually only felt while in a physical body.

Francis arrived in the sixteenth dimension as Josephine reveled in the ecstasy of being in spirit again. Josephine had recently returned from her last incarnation. Playfully, she sent energy sparks toward Francis, who was one of her oldest and dearest soul companions. Thrilled to see Josephine, Francis observed that with each incarnation she was a more illuminated and delightful soul. Unfortunately, this wasn't true of all souls. Now and then, a few got bogged down, choosing not to move forward.

"The etheric field is magnificent!" Josephine declared. "I especially love the bliss of weightlessness. And the sixteenth dimension is presently my favorite. Thank you for meeting me here, my treasured friend."

A flash from Josephine's most recent incarnation consumed her for a moment. She had been the mother of Pete, whose life had ended tragically. Because of the tragedy, she glimpsed the difficulty of the soul guidance to come.

Francis was slightly distracted, deciding what he wanted to do next. "Yes, I also revel in the peaceful joy of being in spirit," he said. "After all, it is our natural state, something we easily forgot when in the physical." He decided on spinning before exploding into a rainbow of colors that reverberated in sound ripples, creating a blissful sensation.

Josephine laughed. "What a display, Francis! I didn't know you were so showy!"

"It's something I brought forward from one of my favorite lifetimes, when I was a circus acrobat. But that life ended quickly when I attempted to put my head in a tiger's mouth." He paused and thoughtfully added, "The lion was OK with it, but the tiger chomped down on my head, killing me instantly."

Josephine chuckled. "And your lesson?"

"To remember my soul is immortal. And a physical body is mortal, no matter how invincible one may think one is at seventeen."

"It is amazing how many young souls leave incarnations early to learn that one basic lesson."

Josephine jumped closer to Francis and engulfed him in a pulsing energy field, filling him with a burst of love. "When I was a young soul, I recall three of my previous lifetimes ending abruptly at an early age for the purpose of that one lesson," she said. "Experience is a great teacher. However, sometimes the student continues to push the boundaries of the physical, and zap, a lifetime ends!"

Josephine's thoughts drifted as she considered how souls have no gender or physical bodies in spirit. Then she lightheartedly said, "I'm in joy with our decision to temporarily keep the genders, first names, and physical outlines from our most recent incarnations. It helps us stay in character, so to speak, at least through the end of our next Guidance. And the variety is fun!"

Francis reflected on how that worked. He recalled that when a soul chooses to keep its physical outline from a previous life, it's only an astral form that can be shown at will and that contains no physical mass. It's what might be referred to as a ghost image.

"I agree," he declared. "Especially since our next soul Guidance has the potential to present many complexities."

Josephine manifested a brilliant ball that burst into a thousand shades of blue and purple and surrounded their astral forms. The music that accompanied the activity was the sound and breath of heaven. She paused to consider her answer. "Let us refer to the gender that has been chosen by the reluctant soul we are to guide, which is male. He's been very resistant, and to a small degree, still is. He now believes he's ready to move forward and is doing so."

"It is a rare occurrence indeed for a soul not to allow the life review process to begin at the end of a lifetime," Francis said. "Even knowing what a soul can choose is unlimited, it is still an oddity."

"Agreed," Josephine replied with some concern. "It is an unusual soul path."

"What has shifted for him that he wants to move forward now?" Francis asked.

Josephine twinkled. "Many Guides have worked to help him overcome the denial of truth he deeply held. That denial, driven by fear, had frozen his soul in a paralyzed state of not wanting to move forward. His refusal to review his last life, but then to finally decide to have that review take place in a new incarnation as a dog is extraordinary! This choice emphasizes how essential our Guidance is for the success and completion of his upcoming lifetime."

Francis hesitated, then spoke: "I sense he wills to enter the physical very soon to begin his soul's journey. He now seems to understand that reviewing his past life is the only way to accomplish his growth forward. However, to review his past life as a man while experiencing his present lifetime as a dog is quite bold. Even for souls who have reached higher frequencies, a dual experience on the Earth plane is an enormous undertaking. It will be a complex challenge for us all, and we may not succeed."

"Yes, it is an attempt to move ahead," Josephine said lovingly. "He has stifled his growth by refusing his life review, thereby willing his soul into a state of limbo. Now that he has chosen to move forward, all we can do is give inspiration, guidance, love, and what protection we can."

Francis nodded. "We should not underestimate the level of complexity with this soul. The Guidance Counsel has advised us of the many challenges we are likely to encounter with him."

"He will be our greatest guidance challenge thus far," Josephine said quietly. "It is helpful that I was his mother in his last lifetime, as Pete, and that you have been his sister and father in previous incarnations. Our souls have expanded in the love we all have shared. Plus, we have a sense of his soul essence, just as he does of ours, making us well suited for the challenge. Therefore, I am at peace with our decision to volunteer for this enormous test."

Francis considered the Counsel's advice again. "The shadow soul will also find a physical presence in this incarnation as part of his karmic pattern," he said. "It will ruthlessly hunt him with a fanatical intention to destroy him."

"Yes," Josephine sadly acknowledged, "this is a truth. A test that has been repeated over many lifetimes with these two souls locked in bitter hatred for each other. This time he desires to ultimately overcome the evil of the shadow soul."

"And we must not underestimate the role of free will, as a soul can take opposite directions without thought or warning," Francis said. "We know this well from our lifetimes on the three-dimensional Earth plane. The ego has many appetites in the physical. The choices he makes could cause him to increase or inhibit his soul's progress."

"Yes, my dear Francis, you are correct. It will be complicated. It is his soul's chosen journey, his spiritual adventure. As we know, his choices reveal what he needs to learn and what he has learned. This will be one of his most defining lifetimes.

Let us visualize our success so it may align with the energy of our intention."

Joining together, Josephine and Francis projected their intentions into the field of unlimited possibilities. Holding the vision of their success in accomplishing this huge task, they stated as one, "And so it is. And so it shall be."

"His name was Pete in his last lifetime. What name has he chosen for this lifetime as a dog?" asked Francis.

"His name, this time, will be Russell until he returns to spirit."

"A good name—" Then Francis said with excitement, "He is born! And as planned, unaware of his purpose."

"Yes, and it is a good plan that he will not become consciously aware of what he has agreed to until he reaches one year of age," said Josephine. She paused to watch his first few minutes as a newborn puppy. "That is an excellent design. If most souls knew what they signed up for in the physical, the opportunity to demonstrate one's growth would be lost. All choices would be easy, making the lifetime boring. It would be better to stay in spirit than to assume a physical body and not be tested to reveal what a soul has authentically learned."

Francis also thought how perfect the design was. He considered how most souls do know what their spiritual objectives are on a subconscious or soul level. These levels are usually only accessible to the conscious mind in states of relaxation, such as during sleep, meditation, hypnosis, or chanting. Otherwise, a lifetime would be too easy, and the soul would lack the motivation to seek specific answers.

"My concern relates to when he discovers he is experiencing his lifetime as a dog while another part of his consciousness is reviewing his past life as a man named Pete," he said.

"Fear not, my precious Francis. For his life will be guided by Infinite Source, plus you and me. Other Guides are available, depending on what assistance his soul consciousness needs. And so it is, and so we shall do our best to guide him to accomplish his extraordinary soul aspirations."

"A powerful truth, Josephine. Russell does have many souls dedicated to assisting him. This includes Tess. She agreed to be his mother, bringing him into his physical incarnation as Russell the dog."

"As you know, Francis, Tess is an advanced soul—a perfect choice for guiding him early in his life. One of his most useful blessings is that he'll be able to hear others' thoughts when appropriate to his path. And they won't be only from other animal beings, which primarily communicate that way anyway. Sometimes he'll hear people. Especially the one who is in the physical and will provide some assistance to him in his life review as Pete."

"I understand that the one you speak of to assist him will not consciously be fully aware of this agreement," said Francis.

Josephine was absorbed in the music of the color green as she answered. "That is correct. Therefore, not disturbing her primary spiritual path."

Together they peacefully contemplated as they bathed in the illuminating vibrations of color, music, and love always present in spirit.

Francis spoke first: "To hold past fear and refuse a life review does bring a most difficult lesson plan. But he would not have chosen to do so had he not needed it as a learning tool. Ultimately, the decision of how to move forward was between his soul and Infinite Source."

Josephine smiled, exuberant in her faith—knowing she and Francis loved this soul, who had been Pete and was now known as Russell. "He is brave to have agreed to a dual design, especially considering the other added complications that will plague him."

Francis agreed. "Yes, and he may still choose to resist the process. We can only attempt to help him rise above the obstacles of the egoic fearful mind. It is he who must make the hard choices followed by appropriate actions. It is promising he *wants* to move forward in his soul's evolution."

"Yes, that is promising," Josephine said. "However, we both know there is much at stake. If he doesn't succeed in reviewing his previous life, he will likely choose to return to a suspended state, leaving his soul's growth stifled, affecting the Collective of Souls."

"The Grand Design is so intricate that even the smallest part contributes to the whole of—" Francis stopped, hearing the panic in Josephine's voice.

"Oh no! He's already in trouble with the shadow one, this time known as Savage!" With that, Josephine vanished.

Francis understood he wouldn't show up in Russell's life until it was time for the details of Russell's spiritual path to be revealed at the age of one year. Even with the danger and many obstacles, Francis felt ready to take on his biggest challenge yet. With the knowledge they had, he and Josephine would do their best to successfully guide the spiritual adventure of Russell the dog.

7
Shape-Shifting

Shape-shifting is a transformational state that is possible with unlimited thinking.
—Josephine

Deardra liked to read something inspirational in the morning, often out loud so that we were included. On this day it was from *Illusions* by Richard Bach: "Learning is finding out what you already know. Doing is demonstrating that you know it." Smiling, she said it was a good thought to start the day. Petting us, she picked up her coffee cup and headed for the kitchen.

We often heard her say, "Everything is subject to change without notice." What was about to happen gave this statement new meaning. I had no way of knowing *everything* was about to shift, changing in ways no one could have ever predicted or prepared for, especially me.

It was early on a late summer morning; I was dreaming about my mother. In my dream she was dead, dying from her wounds soon after we had been taken away by the angel ladies. They were the same wounds she had received while trying to save me from Savage. I was ashamed, overcome with the guilt of believing it was my fault she was dead. In my dream I said to her, "I'm sorry, Mother. I love you. Please forgive me."

I awoke absolutely sure it wasn't a dream. I was so miserable from the grief that gripped my heart that I could hardly move. Then something extraordinary happened that completely changed everything as I knew it.

I was lying on my side seeing a red-tailed hawk I often watched as it flew high in the sky. I sensed her joy as she sailed on the wind. Then suddenly, in midair, she came to a dead stop! I could see her looking into my eyes as if she were right next to my face. Startled, I sat up, finding she was right next to me.

Then I realized the red-tailed hawk was Josephine. I was thrilled. "Josephine! I'm so happy to see you!" I said, recalling how she'd saved me from Savage and the huge owl when I was at the angel ladies' farm. "How's my mother?"

Gently she said with love, "Your dream showed you the fate of your mother, Tess. Her mission to guide you was complete, so she was able to move beyond the physical. She is in spirit now and pleased you are doing well, with your path unfolding as planned."

My happiness from seeing Josephine turned to sorrow when she confirmed my dream was true. My sweet mother was dead. "Where is she?" I cried out.

Josephine always spoke in soft, peaceful tones. "She deeply loves you and may be one of your Guides. We will see how your river of learning flows. Her life purpose as your mother was to be the conduit for you entering the physical and to prepare you for the difficulty of your chosen incarnation."

Somehow, I mostly understood what she said, and learning that my mother fulfilled her purpose oddly brought me some peace, but I still felt responsible for her death.

I whimpered. "It's my fault she died. I should have stayed close to her. If I had, she might still be alive."

"Everything happens as it should," Josephine said with ease. "Tess was happy to leave The Pit knowing her purpose to bring you into the physical and guide you was fulfilled."

"If that's supposed to make my pain go away, it doesn't. I laid my head back down on the deck, still feeling a deep, guilt-ridden anguish.

Josephine gracefully flew to the bird feeder. Landing on it, she began preening her feathers while she watched me. The sunlight shining behind her made it difficult to look directly at her.

She was right to the point. "We have much to cover, with a great deal for you to learn in your present incarnation as Russell the dog. You have chosen a challenging lifetime, but one that contains great rewards if you see it through to the end."

"See what through to the end?" I asked, confused.

"The dual path you have chosen for this incarnation," she casually replied. "You will learn as we go. Shall we start with shape-shifting to assist you with unlimited thinking?"

"What's 'shape-shifting'?" I sullenly asked.

"The ability to experience different forms." Then, with enthusiasm, she said, "Come fly with me, and you will feel what it's like to be in this hawk's body. You will be able to see what I see and experience what it's like to have wings."

I couldn't believe my ears. "Really, Josephine? I'm a dog, not a bird."

"Trust in me," she said. "You will see; then you will understand."

Somehow, I knew I could trust her completely, as if I'd always known her. "All right," I reluctantly replied. "I don't understand any of this, but I suppose I can give it a try. What do you want me to do?"

"Embrace unlimited thinking. It brings unexpected gifts." She said it as if reminding me of something I already knew.

"Just like that? But I'm a dog. How do I think unlimitedly?"

"Oh, my dear one, you are not just a dog. Again, it is called shape-shifting." There was a pleasant energy radiating from her as she continued on. "You have the ability to shift your consciousness by imagining what it is like to be in this hawk's body. Imagine what having wings covered with feathers feels like. Imagine looking out of my eyes as I fly, seeing the ground below, feeling the air currents rise under my—your—wings. You can shift your current shape any time you want—if you think beyond limits."

"What did you mean—I'm not just a dog?" I asked with interest.

"We will discuss more about that later. Let us do this exercise first," she patiently said. "To begin with, watch me fly, but wait until I'm at a point where I level out; then imagine you are in my body. Feel the breath moving in an out of my nostrils. Feel the fine bones of my fragile body, with my wings extended, sailing on the wind. See from my eyes as I view the earth below and the sky above. Imagine. Feel. Experience. In that order."

With a sudden launch, she took off for the sky. I watched her until she leveled out; then I closed my eyes and tried to imagine myself being inside her feathered, delicate body. After a moment, I felt the beating of her heart and imagined looking out of her eyes, with the sensation of breathing as I was flying. I could see treetops and the ground far below, and I could feel the wind giving my wings lift as the cool air rushed against my face. I could smell unique scents. I could see other birds in flight and watch earth-bound animal beings moving below. I was experiencing an unparalleled freedom beyond anything I ever imagined possible! It was an exhilaration that can't be explained, but only experienced. I joyfully laughed inside as I glided and then swooped gracefully through the air, when abruptly I remembered that I was a dog—not a bird! I had a brief sensation of falling; then instantly I was Russell the dog again.

Josephine quickly but gracefully landed on a nearby tree branch. "You were doing an excellent job of shape-shifting until your mind limited you. The mind is a wonderful tool when it serves, but it's stifling when it limits you with fear. It is a lesson worth noting."

I was disappointed my shape-shifting experience was over. Then my doubtful thoughts started. "I should have done better—"

"It was your first time, and you did very well," Josephine said.

Her words helped, and she was right; it was my first time.

As I started to recall the excitement of flying, I said, "Being an earth-bound dog is good, but flying—now, *that's* exciting!"

A cloud of doubt drifted in. I started questioning if what I felt was real. "Was I just dreaming, or did it really happen?" I asked.

"Did you just experience what it was like to fly as a red-tailed hawk?" She stated the question with an air of patient love.

"Well—yes, I suppose I did. But was it real?" I probed, not knowing which to believe—my limited mind or my experience.

"Anything you can imagine is possible, but you are the one who decides what's possible for you. Was it real for you? Did you have physical sensations created from shifting your consciousness into another shape, bringing forth an expansive experience?"

I sighed. "I did have an experience of flying, of shape-shifting, as you call it. I guess I can't deny that, but can I do it again?" Part of me wanted more, but part of me didn't. Too much was happening too fast for my mind to handle.

"Being in the physical can produce many limitations, specifically concerning what is believed to be achievable," said Josephine.

She looked at the seeds Deardra put out each day for the birds and other animal beings to eat. She asked with a smile in her voice, "Anything else to eat around here besides seeds?"

I couldn't resist some humor. "Yeah. There's a fat, sassy chipmunk you could have for a snack."

I sensed Josephine's amusement. "That little one? Oh, he's a sweet soul with a different destiny, one that doesn't include ending up as a snack. Perhaps you should consider shape-shifting as a chipmunk. It may expand your empathy for other beings of that type."

Now she was the witty one.

"No, I'll pass on that. Perhaps something else, but what?" I asked, not completely sure I wanted to try it again anyway.

Josephine, as usual, was helpful. "You can shape-shift anytime you see a being into which you want to shift your consciousness. Once you have had an experience, you can do so again. But it will be necessary to train your mind to think in a less limited way, which can be helpful in accepting your reason for being here."

"My reason for being here? What reason is that?" I asked. Then I immediately remembered Josephine's prior warning about things changing when I was one year old.

"We will address that reason soon enough, but first, what would you like to shape-shift into next? Perhaps a tree? A butterfly? A squirrel? Maybe a rock? However, a rock is quite boring. Anyway, the point is to understand that you're not trapped in a body. Your mind is free and unrestrained, and it can take you anywhere. Embracing the power of your consciousness enables you to experience just about anything you can imagine, but always imagine what is helpful, not harmful, to yourself or others."

I still struggled with some doubt. Not as much, because of what I had experienced, but it was still there.

Josephine, knowing my thoughts, gently said, "Doubt should not prevail over what is obvious. Doubt is a tool used by the ego to limit you with fear. Does your intuition doubt you experienced shape-shifting?"

"How do I tell the difference?"

"When you learn to feel intuitively, without your ego involved, emotion tells you what is right and what is not. Hold the question or thought; then notice how it *feels* in your body."

I held the question. After a moment, I realized I felt peaceful. That was the assurance I needed to believe it was real.

Another small part of my ego was still trying to create doubt, but I ignored it, focusing on what I felt to be true. "Thank you, Josephine. I can see how doubt can be used to trick someone into rejecting the truth."

Questions started firing through my mind. First, I had to ask, "So what is the reason I'm here? And you're familiar to me, but I think even before I was a puppy. I can't explain it, but have we known each other before?"

The aura of love that filled the air with her presence increased with her answer. "I was known to you as your mother in your last incarnation as a man."

"I was human?" I asked with amazement.

"The time has arrived for you to know why you are here, which may be hard to hear at first. Yes. You were a human man named Pete. The primary purpose for you being here is to review your last lifetime as Pete." Josephine radiated a sentimental love. "I dearly love your soul and loved you as Pete, partly because you were my son, but there are even greater connections between us. My purpose, along with that of others yet to come, is to guide you to successfully embrace the truth of the pain you could not face as Pete. Your spiritual plan is designed so that you may finally be free of past encumbrances you could not and would not accept, stifling your life review. If you accept the review of your life as Pete and experience your current life as Russell the dog, the expansion of your soul may once again take place."

I was stunned—not knowing what to say, I didn't reply, trying to sort out what she had just said. I had no memory of a Pete or of Josephine as my mother from when I was Pete. Overcome with frustration and extremely confused by what

I had heard, I decided to change the subject. I asked with some annoyance, "Where is my mother? It broke my heart seeing her dead body in The Pit covered with flies. You said she's fine, but how can she be fine if she's dead?"

"Your mother, Tess, is not dead. She returned to spirit. She is right here with me."

I clearly heard my mother say, "It's me, my sweet special one. I'm not dead. Only my physical beingness is no more. I incarnated as your mother in The Pit to clear some past karma and to wait for you. My primary purpose was to help prepare you for the extraordinary spiritual adventure you had chosen. Align with Josephine and the other Guides coming to assist you on your journey. Always remember that you are loved and watched over by Infinite Source, me, and countless others."

I was delighted to hear my mother lovingly reassure me as she had done so many times when I was a little pup. I felt her presence as if she were right next to me, so I jumped up, looking around, expecting to see her, but she was nowhere to be seen.

"Mother? Where are you? I want to see you!" I desperately wanted to look in her eyes one more time.

Josephine softly said, "What you are recognizing is the essence of her soul."

It was true then; she was no longer in the physical.

It was soothing to feel her peacefulness even if it was on a different plane of existence. Knowing she was alive lifted a weight from my heart, but I was still sad and scared, and frustration was welling up from deep inside me. "Thank you, Mother, for letting me know you still exist. But it's very confusing that I feel sad and scared, but also happy. And what's this about a Pete? How am I supposed to sort this out or even believe it? I'm a dog but not a dog? How can I be reviewing a life as a guy named Pete while I'm in a dog's body? Whose idea was this?" I hoped the elk poop I ate earlier was causing this crazy dream, but deep inside I knew this was the truth of why I was here, in this body.

My mind briefly wondered about what Waldo, who was so wise, would think about all this.

"Josephine and other Guides will help you now." Mother's voice was soft. "Try to rise above resistance and replace it with acceptance. If you don't, resistance will cause you more pain. I will always love you and watch over you. We will be together again, my sweet one." Her voice faded as I felt her spirit leave.

Josephine gently answered my earlier question. "It was your idea to incarnate as a dog, and there is much more, which will be revealed to you in Divine timing. You will still experience your life as a dog, but with an expanded purpose of reviewing your last lifetime as Pete and perhaps other lifetimes that are relevant."

"I must have been in a hurry when I agreed to this past-life-review thing, and I don't want to do this now. Can't I do this in my next life, leaving me to just enjoy my life now as Russell the dog?" I felt panicked, angry, confused, aggravated, relieved, happy, and ecstatic—all at the same time.

"No, you weren't in a hurry," Josephine responded. There was no judgment in her tone as she fluffed her feathers. "Everything happening in your realm of being is for your highest and greatest growth forward. Resist not, as resistance to an unchangeable reality causes pain. Accept that ultimately you chose to have your previous life reviewed while experiencing life as a dog. Your soul is not simply having an experience of what it's like to be a dog. You are a soul who has chosen to experience being a dog with the complexities of reviewing previous incarnations, one in particular."

"What if I've changed my mind and don't want to do this? What if I just run away?"

"Where would you run?" she asked, slightly amused.

I felt silly. I'd spoken without thinking. Of course, there was nowhere for me to run. I whimpered with the anxiety that panic brings.

"Relax, breathe, take a nap; you'll find more clarity when you wake," Josephine quietly said. "I will watch over you as you sleep. Please remember, in all ways, in all time and space, in all dimensions, you are watched over and loved."

Suddenly I was relaxed, feeling the warmth of the sun, hearing a slight breeze encouraging the aspen leaves to bring forth the sweet melody they make when caressing one another. I easily fell into a deep sleep from exhaustion, prompted by fear of the speed with which all this strangeness was happening. I was hoping that when I woke, the emptiness of not knowing would be gone, and I could just continue being myself, Russell the dog.

Once I was asleep, Josephine was there, waiting in my dream world.

The more she explained, the more I heard, but a big part of me remained resistant. I felt I'd been knocked down by a wave of confusion.

"I know this is overwhelming to you right now," she said sympathetically. "Many Guides are here to help you; you are not alone in the reflection of your life as Pete. Be *in* peace.

Trust the progression. The clarity of spiritual evolution awaits you."

As I started to wake in the sunroom, the message began resonating deep inside of me. It was like a loud gong that vibrated to my core, but with so many emotions that I couldn't sort them out. My thoughts immediately went to shape-shifting. I watched a blue jay that sat on a branch outside the window looking in at us. Deardra loved listening to music, having it on whenever she was home. The song, "Run Like The River Runs" was playing by Michael Tomlinson. Certain parts of the song rang loud in my ears:

"Feathered friend I wish that you could say
Why you sit on that wooden post and watch me play
The sky is yours and the ground is mine.
Do you want to trade some time?
And let me soar above these trees
See the earth through golden leaves
Breathe the air and watch the rivers from above
There are many things to love
But it's these that call to me
If I run like the river runs
If I fall like water falls
Oh if I breathe like the wind
Will I ever learn it all?"

The soft swaying melody soothed me back to sleep. I immediately began to dream of shape-shifting. Once again, I was flying as a red-tailed hawk, sailing on the wind with Josephine by my side. The music played in the distant physical world with my troubles, for that moment, left behind.

8

Another Day in Paradise

Life is constant transition.
—Josephine

Deardra told me I'd be a puppy until I was two. Then I'd be a dog and wouldn't be "puppafied" anymore. I'm not sure what that meant because I'm just me, and I love being a puppy!

I wake up in the morning, jump off the bed, rub my face on the carpet, roll on my back, and kick my legs for a full body carpet rub while I'm snorting and snarfing. Then I sit up, with my hair sticking up in all directions, and sneeze twice. Deardra watches my morning ritual and laughs while scratching Waldo's belly.

Next, she sings the morning song, and we head for the kitchen, where all the delicious food smells live. We eat twice a day, but I'm always hungry, happy for the treats we get between meals.

After breakfast we play one of Deardra's favorite games. She shines a flashlight on the carpet, making spots for me to pounce on and run after as they move. Her laughter adds to the fun, and she really seems to enjoy the display of expertise I exhibit. It's a type of playing for us both, but I'm much more serious about it than she knows. For me, it's an obsession. Afterward, she switches to throwing the ball—a game Waldo likes better. He has no interest in chasing spots.

Deardra and I had a long ongoing battle that continued for months about my taking a mouth full of food, then spitting it on the carpet in the sunroom. It was so satisfying to rub my head in the food before eating it, but she didn't like it and wanted me to stop. I tried to stop; for a while I could keep from doing it, but then couldn't help starting again. The final allowable activity we agreed upon was that I could eat all my food in the kitchen, and when I was finished, I could go to the sunroom and rub my face on the carpet without spitting out any food.

What Deardra didn't understand about my face rubbing was that when you have shaggy red hair all over your body, you have to deal with what I call orts. Orts are food bits that accumulate in the hairs around my mouth and rubbing my face on the carpet is the only way I know to remove them. But, of course, Deardra doesn't understand about orts. Although she finds my ritual amusing, she asks if I can't find a different way to clean my face. I want to tell her no, I can't. I've already changed from spitting food on the carpet to just face rubbing, but that's as far as I'm willing to go. When I do it again, she tells me I'm stubborn as a mule, but I'm just being myself, taking a stand on what I want.

Sometimes I see a little boy go by on a bike. It reminds me of the boys from The Pit and how cruel they were to me.

Thinking about the misery of The Pit helps me appreciate being here with Deardra and Waldo. We all love one another, and Waldo told me I would never have to go back to The Pit.

One of our favorite games is chase, in which Waldo and I take turns chasing each other around the house. Then we end by jumping on the bed and wrestling. Waldo usually wins because he's better at pinning me down first, but it doesn't really matter if I pin Waldo or not. He's my pal, a true friend, and as Josephine once said, he's a great soul in a dog's body.

Not too long after Josephine's red-tailed hawk visit, we were resting on the bed following an especially fun wrestling match. Waldo surprised me by saying, "It's important for you to know, Russie, that someday I'll leave my body like The Newf did, but you shouldn't be sad since I'll be waiting for you in the Light."

I didn't understand what he meant; well part of me did. "What do you mean? What light?" I asked, afraid of the answer.

We heard Deardra talking to us. "What are you two fuzzy boys doing?" We jumped off the bed and ran to the sunroom, where she gave us lots of pets, and we lay down next to the couch while she read a book.

Waldo continued with what I didn't want to hear. "One day I'll leave my body, not existing here in the physical, but still existing. I'll be dead—or what animal beings call the next place."

"I don't want you to ever go, Waldo," I whimpered, with the same stabbing pain I'd felt when I found out my mother died. "I love you. What would I do without you?"

"It's OK, Russie," he said, obviously touched. "I love you

too, but leaving the physical is inevitable. I just want you to be prepared before it happens.

I liked it when he called me Russie, but I didn't like the rest of what he said.

Deardra heard me whimper. "What's wrong, Puppa? Are you OK?" She flattened down my spiky hair around my face and eyes; then she softly stroked Waldo. What she did for one she always did for the other.

The sunroom was getting too hot, so we decided to go outside. We found a comfortable spot on the deck where the sun filtered through the trees, giving us shade mixed with warm light beams. Summer was a favorite time of year for us.

Waldo continued. "Someday you'll leave your body too. It's the way things work here in the physical."

I felt melancholy. "Then when you go, I'll go with you since I have to leave here anyway." I sincerely hoped I could.

He yawned, looking at me with his golden-brown eyes surrounded by his fuzzy red hair. "That's sweet of you, Russie, but it doesn't work that way. Every soul that comes to the physical is here for a limited time. Some are here a shorter time than others, and some longer, but I've heard when your time is up, it feels like it went too fast."

He pawed his nose and sneezed. "I know this because when Deardra first brought me home, she had a black-and-white cat named Henry. He was a sweet cat, really more like a dog than a cat, and because he was so small, he resembled a large kitten. Deardra loved him and would sing him songs she made up. But Henry had a heart condition Deardra didn't know about. We knew about it because when Henry would sleep with me and The Newf, sometimes he'd stop breathing, dying for a few minutes, and then he'd come back. Henry told us about a bright Light he would see. At first it was far away in the distance, but each time it happened, he'd go further into the Light. Waiting for him were other animals he had known in this life who had passed, and there were people and animals from other lifetimes. Each time Henry came back into his body, he gave us more detail. He said he'd miss us when he went to the next place and would be waiting for us in the Light when our time came to leave."

Two magpies landed on one of the bird feeders, we jumped up and chased them off. Squawking, they loudly protested as they flew away. Magpies, blue jays, and crows weren't allowed on the bird feeders. They were loud, bossy, and always acting like they were in charge, so we constantly had to remind them who was *really* in charge of the feeders.

We settled down again, and Waldo's tone softened. "Henry was just five years old when, on a gray snowy day, he didn't come back into his body. The sadness crept in as we were sure he wasn't coming back. The anguish was mostly for us and Deardra because we knew Henry was doing fine in his new life beyond the physical. When Deardra found Henry's lifeless body, she was heartbroken, which added to our sadness. You see, we dogs are created to be empathic beings, but we don't have a verbal way to let our human companions know we feel their pain and want to help them."

I felt sad and began to lick Waldo's face.

When I was done, Waldo said, "After Dr. Les examined Henry's body, he told Deardra it was Henry's heart that caused his death. We were right there next to her as she wondered if she had given him enough love. She began softly singing his name as the tears ran down her face. She imagined blessing him and releasing his spirit to the sky."

Waldo's story made it clear how profoundly Deardra loved us. I love her, but it's with a feeling of deep regret I can't explain. Josephine told me the day would come when I would understand why I felt that way about her.

"All beings have experiences of leaving their bodies and then coming back," Waldo said. "Those experiences have always been shared in the animal world. Animals have greater knowledge of these things than most people do."

"What about people?" I felt anxious and started to chew on my green bone.

Waldo seemed far away as he continued on. "People have what they call near-death experiences and have written books about such things. Deardra had a near-death experience when she was twenty-six."

"She did?" I replied, surprised. "How do you know that?"

"I heard her tell a friend about it once. It gave her a deeper sense of how temporary life is. And how aware every being is. Have you noticed she sometimes reads us things that pertain to dogs or animals?"

"Yes, I like it when she does that."

"One night, she read a story to me and The Newf about a woman who, after a car accident, left her body. In the ambulance her heart stopped beating for eighteen minutes, after which she was declared dead. Later, after she was revived, she talked about her encounter with a loving Guide who advised her to go back into her body since it wasn't her time to leave the physical yet. She also remembered going in a tunnel of light. Her loved ones who had gone before her were waiting there.

Guess who were two of her waiting loved ones?"

"I don't know. Who?" I had an empty feeling in the pit of my stomach.

"Dogs! Dogs she'd once had in her life. One when she was a young girl, the other when she was a grown woman. Deardra told us that lots of people who leave their bodies and come back talk about seeing family, friends, and animals they loved—dogs, cats, horses, and other sorts of animals too. The form doesn't survive, only the love. It matters the most because we take all the love with us."

I liked hearing that we take the love with us. It brought a warm, reassuring feeling deep inside me.

"But, like people, animals also become attached to the experience of being in the physical, so they feel sadness and grieve when a life ends." Waldo seemed sad for a moment. I could tell he was thinking about The Newf. "One of the best parts is that all beings have a life review that shows a soul where it did well and where growth is needed."

For some reason, the last part about the life review scared me. It almost felt like someone else had spoken to me through Waldo. We looked at each other with amazement, then jumped to our feet when Deardra said, "Let's go for a walk." The spell was broken, and out the door we went to investigate the ever-changing smells, sights, and sounds of the woods.

Later, when I told Waldo everything Josephine had explained to me, he wasn't surprised and began to tell me the story of Deardra and The Newf.

9
Tales of Dogs Before

*Dogs have a way of finding those who need them,
filling an emptiness we didn't know we had*
—Deardra

After our walk, we settled in the sunroom, where Waldo rolled on his back and then scratched an itch. After finding a comfortable position, he began the story he had observed in Spirit before he was in his present body. He'd been watching over Deardra before he came into this life to be her dog.

"Deardra was convinced Nicholas The Newf was the reincarnation of a stray puppy she had brought home from a reservation in New Mexico the previous September. It all started when she went on a four-day vacation with her new friend Marcy."

"It was a hot Labor Day afternoon when Deardra and Marcy stopped at an Indian pueblo that was open to the public. As they approached the reddish-brown adobe buildings, Deardra thought it was truly an exceptional place, like no other she had visited. When entering the pueblo, she felt a mild pulsing energy in her hands, mixed with a sense of déjà vu.

"The native people and tourists formed moving clusters of activity. Bright-colored handmade wares, jewelry, and clothing were displayed outside and inside some of the adobe homes.

"The other thing that struck Deardra was the number of dogs and puppies running loose. Naturally, being an animal lover, she started to pet some of the pups. She asked Marcy to go ahead, saying she'd catch up later.

"There were many puppies at the pueblo, but there was one in particular she noticed and was especially drawn to. The pup was laying on its side in the dirt, watching her, his tail wagging, radiating what Deardra found to be an irresistible sweetness. He looked like an Australian shepherd mix—black, with some white, and his eyes crowned by distinctive light-tan eyebrows. She picked him up, noticing his nose was crusted over. Her heart connected to the sick pup, whom she'd later call Auggie. For a moment her mind wandered; I bet Les could help him, she thought to herself. Les was Deardra's boyfriend at the time. His veterinary practice was in the small mountain town where they both lived. She looked in the pup's eyes and asked, 'Do you belong to anyone?' He licked her hands and wagged his tail."

All this talk of dogs and puppies running loose caused my mind to flash on The Pit, sending a stab of fear and sadness through my belly. I shook it off, going back to hearing Waldo tell the story.

"Tired of shopping alone, Marcy made her way back to where she had left Deardra, only to find her still playing with the pups. Marcy wasn't a dog lover. She preferred cats."

"Cats?" I asked. "Over dogs?"

"I know, but that's the way she was, and cat beings do have their place in the world. Remember, Henry was a cat," Waldo said thoughtfully. "Anyway, Marcy sounded a bit annoyed as she asked, 'Are you going to explore this place with me or just hang out with the dogs all day?'

"What Marcy didn't know was that Deardra had made up her mind to take the pup she was holding home with her. She decided to keep Marcy happy, so she put the puppy down and agreed to do some shopping.

"As she shopped, Deardra remained distracted the whole time, thinking about the puppy she was determined to take home. Just as they were getting ready to leave, Deardra carried the pup around, asking if he belonged to anyone. Like most dogs at the pueblo, she found that the pup was a stray.

"Marcy was anxious to leave, so Deardra put the pup down, telling him, 'I'm coming back tomorrow to take you home, Auggie, so be ready.'"

I couldn't wait and wanted to know. "Did she go back and get Auggie?"

Waldo gave me a look and said, "You'll have to wait until the end of the story to find out."

He patiently continued. "Marcy, who had a germ phobia, heard Deardra tell the pup she was coming back to get him the next day. This really upset Marcy. Her voice was shaking when she told Deardra, 'I won't go all the way back to Denver with a stinking, dirty, sick puppy in the car. I'll walk first!'

"Deardra finished saying goodbye to Auggie, stood up, and informed Marcy, 'I don't want you to walk, but it's my car, and I'm coming back here tomorrow on our way home to get

Auggie." Then she turned and started to walk toward the parking lot.

"Marcy was shocked. 'Now you've named him. Really? He's filthy, his nose is crusted with yellow greenish gunk, and who knows what kind of diseases he has.' Her disgust was apparent by how she emphasized certain words, like filthy and gunk.

"But Deardra's mind was made up. She stopped, and so did Marcy as they faced each other. Deardra's tone was quiet but firm as she said, 'I'm fully aware of all those things, but Les will be able to help him. Would you have me leave him here to die?'"

"'Yes!' Marcy yelled, causing Deardra to jump. 'There's lots of dogs that die all the time! You can't rescue all of them.'"

"'Well, I'm going to rescue this one if he's still here tomorrow. And you don't have to yell.' Irritated, Deardra started walking toward her car.

"Marcy wasn't in a position to argue since Deardra drove, but she hoped she could sway her to reconsider this seemingly crazy idea.

"After breakfast the next day, they started toward the pueblo. Marcy was repulsed at the thought of riding in the same car as a sick puppy and tried one last attempt to change Deardra's mind. 'I've never seen you dig your heels in with such disregard for health or safety,' she said. 'I mean, if you don't care about yourself, what about me? I don't want to get sick from a dying dog!'

"Deardra's patience wore thin, and she told Marcy that Les had been a veterinarian for almost ten years. Never had he gotten sick from any of the animals he'd cared for.

Marcy said that there was a first time for everything. She asked Deardra one more time if she would reconsider.

"Deardra told Marcy that she was sorry she was scared, but that Marcy needed to understand that this was something she had to do. Then Deardra's eyes filled with tears. That's when Marcy knew she had lost the fight. If Deardra was crying, it was done—the puppy was going to Denver."

Waldo scratched his face and then continued. "When they reached the pueblo later that morning, it was crowded. The search began, with Marcy half-heartedly helping, but to her credit, she did look for the pup. It was odd, but Auggie couldn't be found, so Deardra asked some of the residents about the puppy. Some knew which puppy she was talking about, most didn't, and no one cared. The only answer she received was from an older man, maybe in his seventies. The lines of a long life accentuated his face, framing his deep-brown eyes. 'Too many dogs here. No one will care,' he said."

"After searching for nearly an hour, Deardra thought that maybe Auggie had died or that he did belong to someone. Reluctantly, she said to Marcy, 'I guess it wasn't meant to be.' So they started back to her car. Deardra's eyes filled with tears. She was deeply disappointed.

"Marcy was thrilled! Not having to ride back to Denver with a sick puppy was her ideal outcome. 'Yes, I guess it wasn't meant to be.' She tried to sound sympathetic but was relieved things had shifted her way.

"As they walked back to the car, Deardra felt depressed. For a moment they forgot where they had parked among the multitude of other cars. Then Deardra spotted her car at the same time that Marcy shouted, 'I see it!'

"They were about ten feet from Deardra's car when the miraculous happened. Auggie scurried out from underneath Deardra's convertible, stopping them both in their tracks! They were stunned as Auggie scurried up to them. 'Oh my God!' Deardra said, scarcely believing it.

"'What are the chances?' Marcy said, shocked as she looked at Deardra, who had tears running down her face. Her voice cracking, Marcy added, 'I can't believe the things that happen when I'm with you. I give up! You two are clearly meant to be together.' This new attitude relieved the tension between them. Deardra quickly hugged Marcy and then she scooped up Auggie. He was adorable, even with the yellow crust on his nose and the smell of a dog desperately in need of a bath.

"Deardra tearfully said to him, 'I was so worried about you, but you believed me when I said I'd come back for you, and I did. How did you know this was my car?' Deardra cried with joy and worry, seeing he was weaker than the day before. More reason, she thought, to get him to Les as soon as possible. He wagged his little tail and licked her hands as she thought about his tan eyebrows on his black fur and how they lit up his face.

"After Auggie ate a few morsels of puppy food and drank some water she had brought, they began the six-hour drive back to Denver.

"Deardra thought about the amazing difference a few moments can make. Now they were driving back to Denver with Marcy in the passenger seat, holding Auggie on a towel in her lap. This was something Deardra didn't think she'd ever see Marcy do; she was pleased this was a growing experience for all concerned.

"Deardra silently thanked God and all her Spirit Guides for the extraordinary gifts of love that continued to unfold in her life. She intuitively sensed the beginning of a new path, but one she didn't anticipate would contain so much sorrow.

"Auggie was sick the entire way home, causing them to stop several times. Deardra, concerned about the delays, wanted to get Auggie to Les for medical attention as soon as possible. Dr. Les, as we sometimes call him, was waiting at his animal hospital when they arrived early that evening."

Waldo stood up, yawned, stretched, and walked outside into the yard toward our favorite aspen tree. I followed close behind. Reaching the shady spot, he scratched the cool dirt, releasing an earthy scent, and lay down. I liked to do whatever Waldo did, so I also scratched the dirt and lay down next to him. Once we were both comfortable, he picked up the story again. "Auggie was Deardra's first dog, and his life purpose was precise. It was to help open Deardra's heart to feelings she'd been denying, and it was also for Auggie to fulfill another part of his soul's purpose, which was to create a path for his next incarnation as Nicholas The Newf."

"Did he do that?" I asked.

"Yes. Even though Auggie only lived eleven more days, he accomplished his mission."

"He died?" I asked, surprised.

"Yes, I'm afraid so. Auggie had parvo and distemper. Each one is very serious, but both together is a deadly combination. Dr. Les did everything he could to save the pup. Of course, once Auggie left his body, passing beyond the physical, Deardra was heartbroken."

I whimpered at how sad that was for Deardra.

Waldo continued. "With Auggie's passing in mid-September, Deardra noticed how the sweet pup had filled a lonely place deep within her heart that she had only been vaguely aware of. It was clear to Deardra that Auggie had rescued her, which accentuated her loss of him, and it caused an emptiness she tried to push away."

I felt so bad for Deardra and told Waldo, "I wish Auggie hadn't died."

Waldo looked thoughtful, then said, "It was sad, especially for Deardra, but everything has a purpose. After Auggie passed, Deardra felt a deep need to find a pup to love, so she began to search animal shelters, dog pounds, pet stores, and wherever else she thought she might find a sweet puppy with eyebrows like Auggie had. She believed the eyebrows would be a sign a pup was meant especially for her."

I was anxious. "Did she find one?"

Waldo seemed a bit amused by my eagerness. "Well, not right away. She couldn't find any puppies with eyebrows, which seemed odd to her. She mentioned this to Dr. Les, who also thought it was unusual. Eventually, though, after looking on and off for three months, she decided to wait until spring. December was a cold, snowy month in the mountains—not the best time to be house-training a puppy. Besides, she had Henry, her small black-and-white cat whom she deeply loved. A puppy would have shaken up Henry's world at the time. Waiting would give her more time to talk to Henry about a new pup joining their small family."

Waldo paused. Then he suddenly announced, "That's when it happened!"

"What happened?" I was startled.

"Deardra was staying the weekend with Les. It was a bitter cold December morning when she awoke to find herself engulfed with a sensation of love—along with a phrase that kept repeating in her mind: 'Something wonderful is about to happen.' The phrase kept repeating in her head throughout the day until midafternoon, when she had an overwhelming urge to go outside. The feeling was so strong, so compelling, that she felt it was impossible to resist. She knew she was being directed by her Spirit Guides, as had happened many times throughout her life.

Waldo stopped to lick one of his front paws.

I was on the edge of my tail, wondering what was going to happen next. "Did she go outside? What's out there?" I rolled on my back, gazing at the blue sky, mingled with big white sailing clouds that brought shade as they passed.

Waldo glanced at me but ignored my questions as he continued the story. "It was an extremely cold day, ten degrees below zero! Deardra didn't like bitter-cold weather, so she had no desire to go outside, but she couldn't resist her relentless intuition to do just that. Finally, she gave in and told Les she was going outside for some air. Then she quickly opened the sliding glass door. He didn't hear, consumed by a football game. The frigid air hit her like a cold slap in the face, but Les's two Irish wolfhounds, Thaddeus and Truman, pushed by her in a rush to get outside. Closing the door behind her, she stood on the deck as the frozen air bit at her face as she gazed at the frozen, snow-covered trees. She tried to make the most of the situation by noticing the beauty of the winter scene. After a few minutes, she began questioning her decision to be outside in such frigid weather. A few more minutes passed before she decided it was too cold. She turned toward the house when she heard something. It almost sounded like a grunt—Thaddeus and Truman heard it too, and they ran down the deck stairs to ground level to search for the strange noise. Wearing only slippers, with a light jacket over her sweats, she carefully walked down the icy, snow-covered stairs. Once in the carport she saw the two gentle giants pushing something with their noses. All she could see in the dim light was something fat and furry, grunting louder. The light was dim. At first she thought it was a raccoon, but it sounded like a pot belly pig. It wasn't either one."

"What was it? Was it The Newf?" I asked impatiently.

"Russie, you're going to have to be patient and wait until the end of the story." Waldo shifted a bit. "It was a puppy! Deardra couldn't believe her eyes as she carefully made her way to where Truman and Thaddeus had the puppy corralled. She immediately scooped up the fur ball. Walking back to where the light was better, the first thing she noticed was that the pup had eyebrows! She hugged him while tears of joy rolled down her cheeks. Silently she thanked God, and her Spirit Guides for sending this wondrous gift of love. She knew this was another profound experience, showing she was watched over, guided, and loved.

"Deardra quickly went back into the house to show Les what she had found. He didn't realize she had gone outside, and suddenly there she was holding a puppy with eyebrows! Shocked, he asked, 'Where did you find him?'

"She told him she'd found him downstairs in the carport, where Thaddeus and Truman had him pinned. She was shivering from the cold along with the amazement of what had just happened.

"Les gently took the pup from her arms and said, 'I didn't know you were outside on such a cold day. That's not like you. Did you hear him making noise?'

"'No. I was directed to go outside by my inner voice. And so I did. Look at his eyebrows! He was definitely sent to me.' She felt she was walking a faint line somewhere between a dream and reality.

"Les wasn't sure. 'He probably belongs to someone. We'll have to put up signs,' he said."

"'That's fine, but he was sent to me, and you won't find anyone who claims him,' Deardra said with confidence. She was delighted by the knowledge that something wonderful had happened, just as her intuitive inner voice had promised it would.

"The pup had the same sweet energy as Auggie. Since it was close to Christmas, she named him Nicholas Auggie. Les thought he was part Newfoundland, so later she often called him Nicholas The Newf, or The Newf for short. She had rescued Nicholas, but she knew that, as was the case with Auggie, Nicholas had been sent to rescue her. He filled the lonely place in her heart. And there was another gift; finding him brought a deeper reinforcement that she was right to have trusted her inner guiding voice."

The rest of the tale had to wait until later. More dog duty alerts brought a busy but pleasant sunny afternoon.

After Deardra fed us dinner, we settled in for the evening. Waldo continued. "One of the reasons I came here was to be The Newf's friend after Charlie moved beyond the physical—and, of course, to watch over Deardra.

"Who's Charlie?" I asked.

"Charlie was the dog Deardra had before I came to be here. He was The Newf's buddy."

"Oh," I said. "And he died too?"

"Yes, he got sick and died when The Newf was about four years old. Deardra was very sad about losing Charlie."

Waldo snapped at a fly buzzing around his nose, then continued on. "Anyway, me and The Newf were great buddies. We spent many hours dealing with neighborhood raccoons, foxes, coyotes, chipmunks, squirrels, and birds—plus lots of other animal beings. Most were fun memories, some not."

"Tell me about the run-ins you and Newf had." I loved the stories Waldo shared with me, always wanting to hear more.

"I'll tell you another time, Russie, but right now let's finish The Newf's story."

I sensed some sadness as he continued. "By this time, I was here, in the physical, to be with The Newf. In his tenth year, he started to have severe pain from the ongoing hip dysplasia he'd had since he was a pup. After Deardra tried everything to make him comfortable, the day came when he was no longer able to get up, eat, or drink. I could sense Deardra's heart was breaking, but she knew what had to be done. The tears streamed down her face as she called Dr. Les, by that time her ex-boyfriend, saying it was time. She sobbed when she hung up the phone. She said it was the worst phone call she'd ever made. Dr. Les came to the house a short time later and gave Nicholas a shot to end his suffering so that he could easily leave the physical."

"Deardra and I were with The Newf as he breathed his last breath. Then he separated from his body. Deardra was sobbing, and I was too on the inside. A piercing grief filled us that's hard to describe."

Waldo seemed far away when he said, "A vacant, empty void overtook the house, expanding the depth of our pain from losing The Newf."

I felt his sadness as he recalled The Newf leaving the physical, but then he went on to explain a most incredible thing that happened next. Waldo said, "Right after Dr. Les left with The Newf's body, a bird, with a white line above each eye that looked like eyebrows, appeared at the flat bird feeder outside the sunroom window. I instantly knew that it was Nicholas The Newf; he was sharing the bird's body. I could feel the immense love as The Newf told me that he wouldn't leave until Deardra and I were doing better. Then he told me not to be sad since he'd never felt better. He was free from pain, running through beautiful shimmering grass with Charlie and Henry. He reminded me that we'd be together again someday.

"Deardra was face down on the sunroom floor, crying. The Newf's passing was very hard for her. When I lay down next to her, she buried her face in my fur and cried her heart out. A few minutes later, she lifted her head, noticing the bird with eyebrows standing on the feeder. It was looking directly at her. She also seemed to instantly know it was The Newf since she sat up, dried her eyes, and then put her arm around me. She softly said, 'See that bird, Waldo? He has eyebrows. That's a black-headed grosbeak, which we rarely see. It's the evening grosbeaks that are here almost every day. I think it's The Newf's spirit telling us he's not quite ready to leave us.'

"We continued to watch the bird sitting on the feeder. He wasn't eating but only watched us through the window. Then I heard The Newf say, 'I loved being with you both in the physical, but know I am still with you in a different way. I'll be waiting for each of you on the other side when your time comes to leave. My dear Waldo, take care of Deardra. She is a sensitive soul with much ahead of her. Always remember, we take all the love that we give and receive with us. It is beautiful!'

"The Newf's words helped soothe my pain, and I wanted to share them with Deardra, but judging from the faraway look in her eyes, I sensed she also had heard him on some level.

"Amazingly, the bird stayed for four days, always on the feeder or on a branch just above it. Deardra began calling him The Newf bird. She'd get up during the night to see if The Newf bird was still there, and he was, every time. On the fifth day, she brought The Newf's ashes home. She had planned a service and invited one of her friends who also thought The Newf was special. Right before we went outside for the ceremony, The Newf bird was still in the tree. Afterward, when we came back in, he was gone, and not another bird like it was seen again for over a year."

Waldo closed his eyes as he continued the story. "I watched The Newf bird fly away. As he did, The Newf said to me, 'I love you Waldo. It's only a matter of time before we're together again.' I bid The Newf farewell, letting him know I loved him too.

"To this day, on the rare occasion a black-headed grosbeak visits, Deardra refers to it as The Newf bird."

Waldo let out a soft whimper when he finished the story. He said he was grateful for the unbreakable bond love forges.

I could tell at the end of the story that a new chapter began that day for Waldo and Deardra. Neither would be the same after having known and loved Nicholas The Newf, and both were better for it, as love expands and refines us all.

10
Pete Comes Forth

Each soul has a specific agenda for entering a physical body. The type of body chosen is in perfect alignment with the plan put forth to bring the greatest spiritual growth.
—Francis

I was thankful for the break from the strangeness after Josephine had revealed why I was here. While her explanation answered a lot of questions, I had many more. Needing a break, I decided to lie down for a nap. As I was falling asleep, I was aware of the trees inhaling and exhaling. I was breathing their breath. They were my witnesses along with Waldo. He didn't say much when I told him what had happened so far. He felt I should be accepting, which was one of the hardest things for me to do.

Later, when I awoke from my nap, a vision began. It was a memory with a rush of immense sadness that washed over me; there emerged the scene of a boy with curly brown hair and big brown eyes who was being laughed at by his second-grade class. During school, a well-meaning teacher had given him a bag of old clothes that were too big. I realized the boy was me—a part of me still, but no longer me at the moment.

From a deep well of confusion, my angst grew. I blurted out, "I can't deal with this! Am I a dog or a boy?"

A large presence came forth with a strong but different vibrational frequency than Josephine or my mother Tess. This spirit being, like Josephine, spoke to me in a warm, loving, nonjudgmental tone that resonated in my heart, mind, and soul. Every cell of my physical and nonphysical being was suddenly engulfed in love. My fear melted away. I not only felt safe, but I also believed I was safe.

The male voice gently answered my question. "You are both. You were a human being in your last lifetime plus many others before, but now, in this lifetime, you are a dog being. The soul has no boundaries related to the forms it can choose in different incarnations. This time, you are both these expressions of existence along with numerous others you have experienced on many levels, traversing multiple dimensions and time periods—all resulting in immense spiritual growth."

I was stunned. Not able to move. But I wasn't afraid; I was awe-struck.

The voice continued. "*Feeling* that moment as a boy, who was poor, was in direct correlation to many moments you created in another lifetime as a wealthy girl. You were known in that life as Octavia; she/you enjoyed seeing others grovel. You easily used cruelty with humiliation to create pain for those less fortunate. Because you derived the sensation of pleasure from these harmful actions, the karmic effect resonated with greater force. One of your common behaviors as Octavia was throwing rocks at stray dogs and cats. Cause and effect is an effective learning tool when coming to the three-dimensional Earth plane. What is done to others is done to oneself."

The message was conveyed with a relaxed certainty, and the meaning seemed unavoidable. I was blank as I tried to understand what I had just heard. Having it expressed without judgment made the message sound matter-of-fact yet compassionate. My mind, however, continued to resist because I didn't want any of it to be true. I just wanted to be left alone to enjoy my life as Russell.

The voice knew I was resisting and said, "Consider the knowledge previously imparted to you: resistance causes pain."

I sensed my awareness expand. I understood that I couldn't dismiss what I was hearing. Still, a big part of me wanted to run, hide, escape, cry, laugh, or scream because I couldn't wrap my mind around this disturbing information. I was conflicted. I was a dog at the moment and a human before. I couldn't make sense of it and didn't want to.

The voice continued. "You cannot dismiss your soul any more than you can deny your existence as a dog in your current lifetime. Let us examine, as a reminder, the plan you chose before coming to the physical. Everything you perceive going forward will be the experience of being in a dog's body, with the memories of previous incarnations. The most emphasis will be placed on your last lifetime, when you were known as Pete. This is how you have chosen to finally experience your life review as Pete. Other lifetimes may be woven in to bring a cause-and-effect clarity. Octavia is an example of another incarnation with overlapping karmic energy related to your lifetime as Pete and as Russell the dog. At another time we shall explore your lifetime as Octavia in more detail."

When I answered, I was angry, even resentful. "And the primary reason for all this is to review my life as a guy named Pete? I don't understand why this can't wait until I'm older or my next life. What's the hurry? I like being Russell the dog! Can't we leave it at that?" I could sense my panic was viewed as more resistance, but I didn't care. Josephine had already somewhat prepared me, but I still couldn't get beyond not wanting to do this crazy thing.

A patient love continued to resonate from the voice. "You requested to experience your life review in a physical body. It was decided by Infinite Source, your Guides, and, most importantly, your soul, that you would experience one year as a dog being before your awareness would open to your past-life review. You agreed to this design, but you don't remember due to your soul entering the slower frequency of a physical body, in which the density stifles higher levels of awareness. A dog being feels more deeply in some ways than a human being. So, for the purpose of your life review, it was agreed that enhanced *feeling* would bring the greatest clarity, creating the most powerful instruction before continuing on your soul's evolutionary journey. In the spirit state, only the highest frequency of love exists. Slower frequency emotions do not exist there; those are only felt in a physical body. This is so the great teacher of emotion can be felt, then expressed. It is for the highest growth of your soul that your life review takes place at a pace of your choosing, therefore unfolding perfectly in this matter."

"I'm still confused. So I'm a dog, but not a dog—having a dog experience to review a life I can't fully remember because I'm in a dog body. I don't like this! I already told Josephine how I felt about it."

"If that is how you wish to view it, so it is for you in this moment. Resistance will only cause you more pain. There is going to be a great deal of emotion to come. Some will be very painful and some joy-filled, but all will be for your soul's highest and greatest good. Accepting this truth will bring you a sense of peace with less self-inflicted pain."

A confused panic washed over my mind. I decide to take a calmer stance. "I'm not trying to be difficult, but this is all very hard to accept. I want to understand, yet being in a dog's body after being in a human body is a confusing experience. Tell me in more detail why I'm here as a dog reviewing a lifetime as a man."

The response was serene. "The answer has multiple levels that cannot be revealed to you now. The part of the answer for you to know now is that dogs have an innate ability to give and experience authentic love due to the absence of a human ego. Usually, this authentic love flows through a dog's consciousness like oxygen nourishes every cell in the body. In order for you to realize the important lessons from your last lifetime as a man, it was granted, and you agreed, to incarnate as a dog, not only to embrace and understand unrestricted love but to contemplate the important lessons of your last life as Pete. Dogs have a great deal of time to contemplate in an awake or sleep state. A dog's job is to love and hopefully be loved. However, there is much more that will be revealed to you later."

I still didn't like what I was hearing. I listened more closely, hoping to find a flaw in the plan so that I might use it to end this madness.

I heard Josephine, in the distant background, say, "Stubbornness will only help you to remain stuck."

The message from the voice continued. "When a soul enters a physical body, its vibrational frequency is slowed to the appropriate frequency of the body type chosen. As a dog, you possess all the instincts, challenges, observations, and ideas of a dog, but by design you have limited ways to convey those to humans. This brings forth the opportunity to love, be loved, be reflective, and acutely observe from a fresh perspective. This plan has been designed by Infinite Source for your soul, with your soul, to provide the greatest movement forward."

"Is this how it works for every soul?" My heart pounded; fear was back fogging my brain. "And if I agreed to this, why can't I accept it?"

The explanation continued to unfold from the patient voice. "Every soul chooses a different learning path for each lifetime. Many are here to learn and then grow by experiencing the repercussions of what their past actions have created. Positive or negative, each soul will know what it has brought forward so that it might recognize the opportunities of expansion beyond lower frequencies."

"I need some examples of what you're talking about." I was still scared that this was all true, but at that point I was curious.

"Some advanced souls have chosen a specific path to guide and teach. Other souls have many lessons to experience and learn. Some choose only one lesson. For some souls, a lifetime has nothing to do with past life karma and only involves cause and effect of the present lifetime. Then for others, karma is not the most effective teaching instrument because they have evolved beyond cause and effect to other levels of instruction. As you can see, there are no absolutes, only limitless possibilities. What a soul selects, with Guidance, ultimately provides the most appropriate growth path."

While in the midst of having this conversation, I noticed my knowledge, my very awareness, had grown beyond what my dog mind contained. Perhaps I was at that point plugged in to what Pete knew. "What about free will?" I asked. I hoped I could use that as a reason not to continue. After all, it was against my will. I just wanted to be Russell the dog.

"Free will is available to most all who come to the Earth plane, in varying degrees. Remember, the possibilities are unlimited. Some have a great deal of latitude with free will, and others are limited. It all depends on the identity path chosen. In the instances of limited freewill, this is usually due to a specific, finely focused purpose for entering a body again. Sometimes it involves a short lifespan to accomplish the desired specific learning or teaching objective. This assists a soul to stay with its intended plan. This is *your* self-designed specific lesson plan. Your free will in this incarnation is mostly limited to two choices."

"Which are what?" I was more discouraged with each passing moment.

The voice answered with a matter-of-fact tone. "Leave your dog body or stay until you complete your purpose for being here."

I was riding an emotional roller coaster, racing from angry resistance to acceptance and back to confusion. Suddenly, I started to calm a bit as I began to understand I had to accept my fate or leave. "You said 'most all' referring to free will. Do some come here without free will? Having fewer choices than my two?"

"Exceptions exist relative to a soul's specific learning objectives. The possibilities are endless in every dimension of consciousness."

I could see there was no point in continuing to try and get my way. I had two choices. One was to leave my body and die as Russell the dog or stay with this crazy plan that I couldn't remember agreeing to. I was tired of trying to make sense of the senseless.

Then the questions struck me: "Who are you? Are you God or an angel?"

"I am one of your many soul Guides. Josephine had been your mother in your previous life as Pete and is now choosing to be one of your Guides. I am here to guide you as well, perhaps being one of your most frequent advisers. You and I have also shared past lives as family members. The Guides that assist you will be determined as your life review unfolds. Precisely what you need will show up when appropriate."

"Do you have a name?" I meekly asked.

"Not in spirit. We in spirit are known to one another by the unique vibrational frequency each has according to that soul's current level of spiritual evolution. Usually, similar frequencies resonate together, creating soul groups. In spirit, we are not female or male. Gender is a tool used in each incarnation to aid in our learning, but only on the planes of consciousness where gender is relevant. However, it is easier in the physical to have a word to anchor with, so you may refer to me as Francis, a name I once had in a past incarnation we shared.

"Where's God?" I felt a bit more at ease with each answer Francis gave.

"We refer to God as Infinite Source. The Infinite is everywhere, all there is, all that exists, all that was, all that will ever be—the Source of everything beyond what you can imagine, reaching Infinitely beyond everything you can't. It's the ultimate limitless vibration, contained in every wave and particle, physical and nonphysical, which all spirits are part of, and evolving to, so we may be rejoined with Infinite Source. What some call heaven, we in spirit call Elation."

"You said rejoined. What does that mean?"

"In spirit, your awareness contains all this information. It is my pleasure to remind you of that since you have the amnesia of the physical due to the slower frequency of the body's density."

Francis's way of explaining the profound was exceptional, allowing me to slowly embrace the information that had begun to become distantly familiar. Something else was happening. With less resistance, I had more clarity, as if the mist of fear was lifting. But deep down I still felt uneasy.

I had the impression Francis was relaxed, comfortable in the loving act of being my Guide. I briefly wondered about our past lives together. He continued. "All souls originally come from, and continue to be part of, Infinite Source. We are always connected to that highest frequency of Light, which in essence is the frequency of Love. While in the physical, a soul may accept or reject that awareness." Francis paused and made an observation. "There is difficulty in attempting to explain what is without limits so that it makes sense within the limited comprehension of a physical brain."

"So far I think I'm following." I had definitely shifted into a different state of understanding. Yet I was still fully aware I was a dog.

Francis agreed I was doing well and picked up where he left off. "Infinite Source is ever expanding, bringing forth newer parts of itself. These are points of Light known as souls. The new souls are not yet resonating at the same frequency as the whole of Infinite Source."

I was curious. "So where were we before we became souls?"

"Always we are a part of the essence of Infinite Source. Our conscious awareness becomes greater as we become a soul." Francis spoke casually, as if he were simply explaining that dogs have four paws.

I scratched my ear. "I don't really get that, but I'll take your word for it."

I had the impression Francis smiled as he continued. "We are of a slower, ever-expanding vibrational frequency. Therefore, we are not fully resonating to be completely rejoined with the whole of Infinite Source. However, we are never separate from the Infinite—just not fully rejoined but always connected. In all ways, we are compelled to evolve our souls. The purpose is to rejoin the Infinite once our highest frequency has been achieved through demonstrating actions based in the wisdom of love, which results in our souls' evolution. At first, we seek to evolve through experience on different levels of consciousness. Each incarnation brings knowledge. Knowledge that is put into action brings forth opportunities to demonstrate growth through deeds, revealing what our soul has truly learned or has yet to fully learn. It is the growing awareness, along with the demonstration of what has been learned, that leads to growth. What is shaped by choice in the physical is what persists until the desired growth is achieved. This shows what is needed to continue, eventually completing the evolution of the soul, which is followed by rejoining with Infinite Source."

Everything Francis was saying resonated with parts of me that I didn't know existed, baffling my mind. "Whew. That's a lot to take in, but I think I sort of get it."

"Remember, this is already known to you on a different level of awareness that is not accessible to you right now. Be still, at peace, secure in the knowledge that no soul is lost or left behind. Each individual soul is of equal importance. All are a part of Infinite Source and will never cease to exist. Hold in your awareness the love that surrounds you. You may move forward at the rate you select."

My mind was stuffed. l couldn't hold another thought. "It's overwhelming to consider it all," I said. "It was easier and more fun when I was just Russell the dog. I don't think I can hear any more right now." Secretly, part of me was still resisting, hoping it was just a weird dream from something I ate. As a dog, there are all forms of things that are appealing to eat that people would never consider an option. Like elk poop.

Francis understood. "I will leave you now to reflect on what we have spoken of. A great deal will be unfolding. I shall return."

When Francis left, there was a distinct energy shift indicating our communication was over. It was somewhat of a relief having learned more. However, I was sad, and I wasn't the same. I wasn't just Russell the dog anymore. I was Russell with other past selves mixed in.

Deardra was listening to the song, "The Way We're Going," by one of her favorite artists, Michael Tomlinson. Some of the words echoed in my ears, reflecting the way I felt:

"All I know is folding in together
Colors on the run
Fade away forever
The circle's never done
I'm just barely breathing
Face up in the rain
I give in to the living.
We seldom know
The way we're going
The seeds we're holding
Let them scatter where they will."

I yawned with the soothing sound of the melody. I was exhausted, so sleep came quickly. In the background of my dream were distant echoes of other selves from other lifetimes.

I wondered what Waldo knew about such things. I was anxious to tell him about my recent visitation, hoping he might have something helpful to share.

One week later, my world as Russell the dog began to slowly shatter, with levels of pain that can't be described.

11
Waldo's Story

*My eyes filled with tears as I looked into the cages
and wondered how it would feel to be looking out.*
—Deardra

Waldo and I were lazing in the yard on a breezy summer afternoon when he told me the story of how he came to be here with Deardra. This was another part of Deardra and Newf's life he observed from the spirit realm before he came into his body to be Waldo the dog.

After scratching his nose, he softly looked my way. "It began when Charlie died. He was The Newf's pal and companion. Deardra and The Newf immediately loved Charlie, perhaps somehow knowing he wouldn't be with them long.

"Charlie was a young pup when he was found under a bridge by a kindhearted homeless man. He tenderly cuddled Charlie. 'Don't worry, Little Ink Spot. I'm homeless too. Nobody loves me either, but I'll take care of you,' he said. He affectionately cared for Charlie until one of Deardra's friends, Julia, who worked at an animal hospital in Denver, tried to convince the man to let her find the puppy a home. He resisted because Charlie was all he had and was his only source of love. After a few days, he decided the pup deserved a better life, so he tearfully surrendered Charlie to Julia. She later told Deardra, 'It was sad to hear him sob as he pushed his neatly organized shopping cart down the street.'

"Deardra adopted the sweet little black pup the next day, naming him Charlie."

Waldo sneezed and said, "Charlie and The Newf had lots of fun adventures because Charlie was a 'Houdini dog,' as Deardra liked to call him. He had a talent for finding endless ways out of the fenced yard, always making sure The Newf could get out too. She even had to go before a judge once because Charlie and The Newf escaped and were captured by animal control, which put them in dog jail! A few pooches said that dogs and cats who were there too long were 'put to sleep,' which meant *killed*! After hearing this, Charlie and The Newf were terrified that they could be killed too. It took almost a whole day before Deardra found out where they were and finally came to take them home. It was a terrifying experience they never forgot."

My stomach sunk. Then I wasn't sure I heard right. "People kill dogs?"

Waldo looked at me as if he suddenly remembered I wasn't aware of things like that. He answered with a tone of despair. "Yes, it's true. Dogs, cats, wild horses, lots of animal beings' lives are ended. Some people say there's not enough room for everyone, so they decide who isn't loved, and that's it. . . . Efforts are made to stop more unwanted animals from being born with what is called spaying and neutering. This makes it impossible to create more animal beings."

I whimpered. "It's so sad—I can't understand why anyone would hurt us animal beings." Then I thought about the mean boys who threw rocks at us in The Pit.

"It's very sad, but we as dogs have no control over what people do." Waldo stated with a heaviness. "But you don't have to worry, Russie. We're safe. Deardra would never let anything happen to us."

Still feeling a heaviness, I agreed, and Waldo continued the story. "The next day a man came to fix the fence. He smelled of smoke, unclean body odor, and fish. He made it impossible for Charlie and The Newf to have any more exciting adventures beyond the yard.

"In the fall of that year, not too long after the dog jail incident, Deardra moved to the House of Stone and Light. It was one of the saddest times of her life, and it came after she had experienced two overwhelming losses within a few months. The heartbreak brought immense pain that shook her faith, which caused her to feel abandoned by God and more alone. The little happiness that broke through the numbness came from the love of Nicholas The Newf and Charlie. The tranquil energy of her new home became an ongoing source of her healing.

"Sadly, for Deardra and The Newf, Charlie died less than two years later from a flipped stomach. The Newf was so lonely after Charlie died that all he wanted to do was mope and bark. From the time Nicholas was a puppy, he'd had aching stiff hips that affected his ability to run or move quickly like other dogs. Deardra felt it was one of the reasons The Newf was sent to her—so she could care for him. With a loving tenderness, she did her best to make him comfortable.

"Losing Charlie was a hard loss for them. It added to her pain that Nicholas was grieving and lonely without the companionship of his buddy.

"A few months before Charlie died, I was born into the physical to begin my lifetime as Waldo the dog. My Spirit Guides kept me aware of the important things I needed to know.

"Another month or so passed after Charlie died, and Deardra began looking for a new friend, mostly for The Newf, but for her too."

Suddenly, Waldo was tired. "We'll finish the story later." Then he immediately fell asleep!

I was surprised, thinking it was strange, when I heard Josephine's voice say, "Over here." I looked up to see her in a nearby tree.

"Josephine! You're a crow this time?"

"Yes, I love to fly. Crows are one of my favorite bird beings. They're very smart and playful."

Sometimes Waldo and I watched the crows play a game with a small pinecone. First, one would fly high, then drop the pinecone while the others below tried to catch it. The one who caught it would let it go until another crow would catch it. They seemed to enjoy the contest, squawking loudly as they played.

I was worried about Waldo and asked Josephine, "Is Waldo OK? He was telling me his story when he suddenly decided to take a nap."

"Yes, he is all right. Just very tired. I will finish his story from here."

I was still surprised Waldo was so tired, but I listened as Josephine continued on.

"One day while Deardra was at work, she felt sick and decided to go home. As she got into her car, her familiar inner voice urged her to go to the nearby animal shelter, emphasizing, 'He's there waiting.' The crisp clarity of the message indicated the importance.

"'Who's there waiting?' Deardra asked."

"'Your dog,' the voice responded. She sat behind the wheel sensing her nausea getting worse by the minute. She angrily shook her head.

"'I'm sick! Can't he wait until tomorrow? I just want to go home, get in bed, not throw up, and feel better.'

"Instantly the answer came. 'He won't be there tomorrow.'

"'Great!' she said with aggravation. 'OK, I'll go. . . . I hope I'm not delirious—that my dog is really waiting there.'"

Josephine stretched her wings, moving up the branch before she went on. "After Deardra drove to the shelter, she sat in the parking lot, considering whether her stomach was too nauseated to handle the strong smells inside. Taking some deep breaths and grabbing a plastic bag in case she got sick, she closed her eyes, making the decision that it was now or never. The faith she had in her inner voice made it possible for her to push through the nausea enough to go inside.

"For her, it was always the same heart-wrenching experience to walk through the shelter. She wished each dog could come home with her so she could lovingly ease the confusion each held in its eyes. The heartbreaking frustration of knowing what would happen to some of the dogs drove tears down her cheeks. She stopped to compose herself, blew her nose, and continued on to find the reason she was there.

"Suddenly, as Deardra turned the corner, she clearly heard, 'There he is.' And there he was, a fuzzy red puppy who appeared to be part chow. Instantly she felt he was the one. He was lying down, not lifting his head, but he closely watched her as she squatted down in front of the enclosure. Softly she spoke to him, noticing he didn't move much. This concerned her, so she quickly moved forward with the adoption. After finalizing all the paperwork, she left the shelter with the fuzzy red pup asleep in her arms.

"Once in the car, she felt much sicker than before, but she was grateful she'd listened to her inner voice. There was a sense of relief that something important had been accomplished. She understood that this little puppy was significant in her life. Together they started the forty-minute drive home, though she worried about whether The Newf would like this new pup. She wondered how they'd get along and hoped they'd be fast friends. She reflected on dogs being brought together and never learning to like each other. Then she decided to stop the negative thoughts and trust the direction her inner voice guided her to take."

Josephine's tone was soft. "Before they made it home, Waldo threw up in the back seat. Deardra almost got sick too, but she was more concerned about the yellow color, which she knew was a bad sign from her experience with Auggie. She took a quick detour to Dr. Les's animal hospital. On the way she decided on a name. The first name that came to her was Waldo, which was the name he had picked."

That got my attention. "Waldo picked his name? Do we all pick our names? I like my name, but I didn't think I had picked it."

"Yes, we do pick a name before we come into the physical. That name is conveyed to the ones who agree what our name shall be."

"Is that true for people too?"

"Yes, for people too." Josephine sounded amused. "This is all part of each individual soul plan."

Sweetly, she said, "Let us return to the story. Waldo was hospitalized for six days and nearly died from parvo. Because this was not his intended time to leave the physical, his life continued. Deardra intuitively knew it wasn't an accident that Waldo lived. She recalled how her inner voice had directed her to find him and how she had been told that if she waited until the next day, he wouldn't be there. That was correct; Waldo would have been put to sleep at the shelter as soon as he started vomiting. This fact was later confirmed by one of Dr. Les's classmates, the director of the shelter. For Deardra, this was more confirmation from the other side that she, The Newf, and Waldo were meant to be together."

I chimed in. "Waldo was so lucky that Deardra listened to her inner voice." My thoughts went to the moment I first saw Deardra. I thought of how I felt I'd known her from before. I wondered if her inner voice sent her to get me too.

"Yes," Josephine confirmed. "It all worked out. She could have resisted, using freewill and caused the fabric of all your futures to shift. If Waldo would have left the physical, she would have missed a point of Divine assistance in her life plan."

"When Deardra brought Waldo home from the hospital to the House of Stone and Light, he met The Newf, who watched him from a distance at first. Slowly he became more curious and sniffed Waldo's face. The Newf was big—from Waldo's perspective, really big. He was just over four years old, with stiff, painful hips that made it difficult for him to get up. Deardra told Waldo, 'The Newf came to me with severe hip dysplasia. Because I love him, I want to make his life as easy as I can, along with yours, my sweet Waldo.'

"Waldo received lots of love, tenderness, and good food, so he recovered well. Each day his love grew for Deardra, The Newf, and the House of Stone and Light."

Josephine finished the story. "Later, after The Newf moved beyond the physical, it was your time, as Russell the dog, to come to the House of Stone and Light. There are many reasons for your presence here. One was to assist Waldo and Deardra heal their sadness by filling the empty space The Newf had filled."

"I'm so glad to be here, Josephine!" I said. I let out a happy bark, which woke Waldo from his nap. Josephine spread her beautiful black shining wings, gliding from the tree branch into the distant sky.

I told Waldo that Josephine had come and finished his story. "That's good," he said. "I guess that's how it was meant to be." He scratched his ear and then sat up.

Suddenly, we were on our feet in a full run, barking as we raced to the end of the fence. We smelled the fox before we saw it, and we launched into immediate action due to the closeness of the scent. The fox emerged from behind a pine tree growing between two large rocks, looked our way, and casually said, "Relax, domestics. I'm just on the way to my den. Do you really have to bark and growl so spitefully every time when you know it's just me on my rounds?" He sounded annoyed. "You're scaring all the chipmunks and squirrels away. How am I supposed to eat?"

We kept barking. Waldo answered, "As long as you keep coming so close to us and the house, you're a threat! A trespasser! I shouldn't have to explain it!" Waldo was aggravated by the fox asking the obvious.

The pesky fox seemed relaxed, defiantly sitting a few feet from the fence that separated us. "You domestics don't have to hunt for every meal. Your bowls are filled with food twice a day. You know nothing of hunger. I don't interfere with your eating; why should you interfere with mine? Let's make a deal. . . . Leave some of your dog food for me each evening on the flat stone by the gate, and then I'll do something for you."

"Like what?" I blurted out.

Waldo turned to me and quietly said, "I'll handle this."

"See, even the puppy knows I might have a good idea." The fox sounded encouraged.

Waldo sniffed the air, only smelling the fox—he thought for a moment. Without warning, he suddenly lunged forward with a loud roaring bark that scared me and the fox so much that it caused us both to jump. "Be gone you want-to-be dog!" Waldo said with a snarl. He continued to aggressively bark as the fox disappeared in a flash. We laughed, amused by the speed of his exit, not knowing a fox could move so fast. He deserved what Waldo gave him because he liked to taunt us. Then with a serious look, Waldo said to me, "Never make a deal with a fox, Russie. They're sly and always crafting a trick. It's their gift for survival from the Creator. Do not test that gift."

I just had to ask. "But what if he had a good idea?"

Waldo's tone and expression were serious. "A fox only thinks of ideas that are good for a fox, and they enjoy making fools of us dogs. Promise me you won't ever make a deal with a fox."

"OK. I won't, Waldo, even if it's the best deal a dog could make."

Waldo gave me a look of concern. "Better yet, promise me you won't even talk to a fox."

"OK," I said. "I promise, even if a fox talks to me first." Waldo gave me another worried look. I felt good that the fox business was handled as I drifted off into a nap.

Later that day, I told Waldo I had started thinking about The Pit again. He thought it was tragic that such a place existed, but he felt there was a purpose for all things. Perhaps providing possible clues for why we were here in the physical.

One terrible day a few months later, when I was just over a year and a half old, Waldo started throwing up. Deardra put us in the car and drove to Dr. Les's animal hospital. I noticed Waldo had an increasingly bad smell, but I thought it might be from a dead chipmunk he ate.

When we arrived, Deardra rushed Waldo inside, where she stayed a long time while I waited in the car. I didn't mind because it was fun to watch the pet parents arrive with their dogs or cats. Of course, I had to bark to let them know I was the watchdog on duty. All the coming and going kept my attention while I waited, but I was worried about Waldo and hoped he'd be OK for all the playful adventures ahead of us.

I decided to lie down on the seat when Francis gave me an indication of what was to come with a message I didn't want to hear.

"Life in a physical body is temporary; only the soul is eternal. All who are together will be together."

I think it was meant to prepare me. Instead, it instantly caused a stabbing pain in my chest—the same kind of pain I felt when I found out my mother, Tess, had died in The Pit.

Finally, Deardra came out, but she was without Waldo. I moved from the driver's seat to the other front seat, noticing her eyes were red from crying. After she got in the car, she brought her hands to her face and cried for a long time. Her eyes showed her pain when she looked at me and said, "Waldo has to have an operation." She blew her nose while crying more. "He may have cancer." Tears ran down her face. Her lip quivered.

Cancer! I knew that was bad. I felt a heaviness push down on me; that must have been what I have been smelling. For a moment I was numb, and I began whining.

I pleaded for help. "Francis, please stop this." My stomach felt sick. I prayed, "Dear Infinite Source, please don't take my brother, Waldo, away from me. I'm already faced with great challenges. Please, please heal him."

There was no response from Francis. I felt alone, terrified by what might happen, knowing how empty my world would be without Waldo. It wasn't fair. I wasn't ready. But I'd never be ready to be without Waldo.

Deardra cried all the way home, and so did I, on the inside. When we got home, it didn't feel like home without Waldo. I only felt a hollow emptiness. Our melancholy mood hung in the air as dark clouds moved over the mountains, bringing heavy rain. Later it hailed so hard that I thought the windows would break. Deardra said the weather was reflecting our turmoil.

Over the next few days everything felt different because everything was different without Waldo. Deardra spent the time worrying, praying, and crying. Between going to work and visiting Waldo, she wasn't home much, which left me alone to feel even more isolated. I missed him so much, but all I could do was wait and pray. Of course, I had experience waiting since it's how a dog spends most of its life. Waiting to eat, waiting to go for a walk, waiting to be petted, waiting to be talked to, waiting for treats, waiting to poop or wee. But this was the worse waiting of all, filled with pain driven by the fear of more pain to come.

When Deardra came home from visiting Waldo, that same bad smell was on her hands and clothes mixed with other scents. We were overtaken by worry because we loved Waldo with our whole hearts. But who wouldn't?

I heard Josephine say, "Waldo is a great soul deserving of all our love and admiration." Francis agreed.

Four days after first going to the animal hospital, Deardra finally brought Waldo home, but he was moving very slowly, without his usual trot. His side had been shaved, and he had a long cut with metal stitches. I greeted him with my green bone, but he didn't want to play, eat, or drink. He told me he was glad to see me, but he only wanted to lie down and sleep. I didn't bother him even though I wanted to play. My excitement waned as dread took hold with the reality of how sick he was. It was frightening to see him so weak. I continued to send pleading prayers to anyone who would listen. I begged for Waldo's healing. I cried out to Francis, Josephine, and Infinite Source. "Please save Waldo. I love him, I can't be here without him. I promise to do anything you ask if you will please let Waldo live." I was in so much pain I felt raw inside.

A gentleness came through as Francis lovingly answered, "It is not possible for you to presently know the agreement

Waldo's soul has made with the Infinite. There is no death of the soul. Only the physical embodiment dies. It is used as a vehicle for the soul's purpose to evolve."

I sobbed as the answer resonated on a deep level, where I felt I wasn't alone. But it didn't help the pain, and what I heard wasn't what I was praying for. I lashed out. "That's not what I want to hear! I only want to hear that Waldo can stay here with me."

A few minutes later I heard Deardra crying as she talked on the phone to a friend. She said, "Les told me it was an aggressive form of cancer with no hope of recovery." Hearing that caused a wave of despair that knocked me down. Waldo was going to die. I was hanging by a thread, dangling somewhere beyond agony and disbelief.

I felt sick and pleaded with Francis. "Please let me die with Waldo." Then I corrected myself. "No, I *want* to die with Waldo." Watching him sleep, I fully realized how much I loved and needed him. The thought of being here without him was unbearable on every level of beingness.

That night, when we were sleeping on the bed with Deardra, I told Waldo more about my visits from Francis and Josephine. He gazed into my eyes and said, "Yes, it's part of your learning path, as is my passing beyond the physical. Please try to accept it, or the resistance will cause you more pain." In that moment I understood. He was also guiding me. He was truly a great soul! I was thankful for the honor of being his companion. But I refused to give up.

I whimpered and said out loud, "No, I don't want you to go! If you *must* go, I'll go with you!"

"Not this time, Russie. Don't diminish the importance of your life. You didn't show up here by some strange cosmic accident. It's time for you to embrace your reason for *being* in this lifetime."

"But I love you, Waldo, and I don't want to be here without you." I was whimpering and whining as I pleaded with him. Deardra stirred but didn't wake up.

I could see he was ready to fall asleep again. "I love you too, Russie. Remember, all will be well. I will be with you always."

I felt defeated. Waldo slipped into a dream world where I couldn't follow. Eventually I put my head down next to Waldo, falling into a deep sleep where Francis waited.

Francis again attempted to comfort me. "Surrender to what is beyond your control. Waldo is watched over, safe, and deeply loved. He is fulfilling his chosen purpose for this incarnation. Be compassionate by releasing him to his path."

I tried to accept the message Francis gave, but somehow, I just couldn't. Each day I continued my begging prayers, trying every angle, which included more bargaining for him to stay here with me as Waldo the dog. Then I finally realized Waldo was at peace with his coming transition. It was only me who was suffering because I didn't want to let him go.

The next two months slowly passed as Deardra and I watched Waldo's body deteriorate. He improved a bit and was able to slowly walk, eat, and drink small amounts, but he was no longer able to play. He loved having me sleep next to him so that we were touching, which gave us both some comfort. Deardra would often lay on the floor, petting us, singing songs she made up about Waldo the circus bear and my being puppafied. She'd kiss us both, telling us stories of how we came to be with her. She spoke of how God, all the angels, and the Spirit Guides sent us to her, to bring healing love into her life. She didn't know how much her love expanded in our hearts, how it managed to reach beyond the pain. The moments we so tenderly shared, filled with the sweetness of true undying love, slightly eased our suffering, but they also deepened the dread of what was yet to come.

The day came when Waldo was vomiting again, unable to eat or drink. He was barely able to move. Deardra called Dr. Les's office, saying it was time. She hung up the phone and fell to her knees weeping. She begged to wake up from this nightmare, pleading for it not to be true. But it was true. She lifted Waldo onto the bed. Then I jumped up, and we all cuddled and waited together. Softly she cried as she caressed his head while telling him about the treasured memories she had of him. First, she talked about when he was a puppy, laughing through her tears over the funny puppy things he did. She recalled the time he was harassing a raccoon, and it bit his bottom, causing him to get five stitches. How he loved to wander the neighborhood where everyone knew him. She talked about attending a party down the street where she only knew a few people, but everyone knew Waldo and had a Waldo story to tell. He was touched by her memories and felt sad to leave her, but he said he knew the love they felt for each other would continue.

Francis softly reminded me: "We take all the love with us."

Then we heard the doorbell. I jumped off the bed and ran down the hall whining. Deardra sobbed as she carried Waldo's thin body from the bedroom, placing him on a soft bed she had made from sheets and blankets. I could smell and feel her sorrow mingled with mine.

When Dr. Les came in the house, his energy reflected his somber mood. He had saved Waldo's life when he was just a pup. Eleven years later, he was going to end Waldo's life. For him it was the most heart-wrenching part of veterinary medicine.

I spoke to Francis. "Everybody liked or loved Waldo. He will be missed." The weight of my heart was so great I could hardly move.

"Yes, Waldo has accomplished immense growth in this incarnation. He has also done well Guiding you."

One last time I pleaded with him. "Francis, please stop this. I know you could if you wanted to."

"No, I cannot interfere with what a soul has designed—especially involving the end of a lifetime. This is between Waldo and Infinite Source."

Deardra cried while petting Waldo's head as he lay on the makeshift bed in the sunroom. Dr. Les spoke to Waldo about running through fields of green grass as he put the needle in. Waldo looked deeply into my eyes for the last time and said, "You're the best, Russie. We had great fun! I'll see you on the other side. Remember, love is forever, and I love you and Deardra." Waldo's golden-brown eyes were soft as he gazed at us for the last time, breathing his last breath. My heart felt as if it shattered—and I sensed Deardra's did too. Not wanting to let go, she clutched Waldo's now-empty body, quietly sobbing.

"Waldo is in spirit now," Francis softly said. "Free of the physical, he is in the etheric field leaping, running, jumping, and doing somersaults—a common response to the lightness of returning to spirit."

For the first time I heard one of Deardra's Spirit Guides speak to her. To my surprise, it was Josephine! She comforted Deardra with basically the same information about Waldo that I was receiving from Francis.

Suddenly the reality of Waldo being gone set in. It made everything else in my awareness insignificant. Now, on every level, in every way, all I could feel was the pain of loss.

"Waldo is fine. Only his body has died," Josephine said. "This you know but cannot embrace because you are still in a physical body. He is present—only a thought away."

Dogs can't scream or sob out loud. We have fewer ways to release and express our emotions, so what we feel is contained. Every part of me felt broken. The pain I felt at that moment attached itself to the pain I felt when I was taken from my mother, and later when I found out she was dead. That much agony combined together was unbearable. My devastation took my breath away even though I could feel him as he looked down at us from above his body.

I know Deardra felt him too, but it wasn't the same to have him with us only in spirit. Her tears flowed when Dr. Les wrapped Waldo's body in a blanket to take him away for cremation. I sniffed the bundle one more time, pushing it with my nose in case he wasn't really dead. Dr. Les picked up Waldo's body to leave. Deardra hugged him and the bundle. It was her last hug for her sweet fuzzy red bear she knew as Waldo, who would always live in her heart.

The door closed with Dr. Les and Waldo on the other side. It was the beginning of a dark reality without Waldo. A huge wave of grief overtook us. We returned to the sunroom, where Deardra sat on the couch. She patted the cushion as a signal for me to come sit next to her. We were only allowed on the couch at special times by invitation only. This was one of those special times. She cried and cried and tried to soothe me with her words of love. "It's just you and me now, Puppa. We'll have to help each other through this, and together we'll make it to the other side. Waldo is with us, aware of how much we love him." She smiled at me through her tears, moving the hair from around my eyes. "I love you, puppafied Russell." With my most gentle licks, I slowly caressed her hand with my tongue to let her know, in the only way I could, that I loved her too.

Later that night, Waldo was still close by. He told me with delight that he loved the weightlessness of being without his physical body. His joy increased the closer he traveled into the Light of Infinite Source. The Newf and Henry were waiting for him, along with others from this life and other lifetimes. He said it was blissful to reunite with his soul group, which I was also a part of.

I felt some relief that he was happy. He said his life review went well. Next time he could come back in the form of his choice. It was a significant graduation. He was content with the progress his soul had made as Waldo the dog. He assured me he would be there to greet me someday when I left the physical. He was off to a state of beingness he couldn't explain, reminding me once again he was only a thought away. "Not in the same place, but always together" was his parting promise.

His message gave me some comfort, but I was still here in the physical, devastated with grief and feeling lonely, heart-broken, and with a hollow emptiness amplified by Deardra's grief. I sensed she also heard his message. She cried herself to sleep on the couch, but I felt a slight easing in the heaviness of her energy. Waldo's message was assuring, though it didn't take away our pain. Francis said that the passing of time plus the acceptance of our loss would help lessen our sorrow.

A few days later, the light beams in the sunroom soothed me as I slept. I dreamed about Waldo. Wrestling, rolling around, play biting, we carried on with the feeling of pure love filling us—lots of love. He was my soul brother in the dog-being world, as I was his.

Francis showed me we had been brothers three lifetimes ago in human bodies. At odds with each other, we didn't get along. This time was different. Together as dogs, we healed the past, spending joyful fun-filled days due to the lack of human ego concerns. I woke from the dream deeply missing him. I knew he was doing well, still very much alive, but I missed him being in his fuzzy body since I was still here in the physical world trying to adjust without him.

Francis shared a thought: "Sorrow hones us deeper so we can contain more joy."

I heard what he said but just stared at the trees in the distance. I could sense them breathing. I had no energy and said, "I'm dog-tired down to my soul, Francis. Is suffering supposed to be a big part of my lifetime plan? If it is, I don't think I can take anymore."

"All is set in motion with a purpose. It is an opportunity for you to rise above an unchangeable reality. Remember, resisting an unchangeable reality causes pain, and acceptance brings healing. Losing Waldo didn't just happen to you alone. Deardra is also suffering. Your love can bring her the support she presently needs. Keep moving forward. A new phase of growth awaits you both." His words were hollow to me in that moment.

The next few grief-filled months passed with a dullness that's impossible to explain. I wasn't my usual "puppafied" self. I wasn't interested in food, walks, or playing with my green bone. Everything reminded me of Waldo. I carried a deep, lonely ache from missing him so much. Deardra wasn't her usual happy self either. Overcome with her own grief, she also worried about my suffering. She said pain was distracting when she forgot to sing me the morning song a few times, though when she did, her usual enthusiasm was missing. No matter what happens, I know Deardra loves me. In my limited ways as a dog, I let her know I love her too.

After a time, we came to accept Waldo's absence as we slowly began to heal. A few months later, a noticeable shift happened. It was time to move forward. A new pup was in our future. For me, this was another waiting disaster.

12
Memories of Before

I remember him as something left behind upon the road of life—as something I have passed, rather than have actually been—and almost think of him as of someone else.
—Charles Dickens

It wasn't too long after Waldo moved into spirit, and I was on the deck relaxing while I chewed on my green bone. I began thinking how nice it was to have a break from the stress of my past life review. With that thought, what was waiting in the background let loose.

"Daddy, let's build a snowman!" The memory began as I looked to my left, seeing two beautiful little girls in their snowsuits laughing. I/Pete was gently throwing snowballs at my young daughters, ages three and seven, who were doing their best to throw snow my way. Each had big, beautiful eyes framed by long eyelashes and shiny brown hair. I was enjoying the time with my girls, happy to see them having fun.

"Daddy, where's Mommy? Can she come out and play too?" asked my younger daughter, Annette. My older daughter, DeDe, seemed to know Mommy wasn't well.

The question brought a deep sorrow. My fear was that my girls might never know what it was to have a loving mother. A mother like I had.

I heard their sweet little girl voices as if they were a few inches away from my ears. Seeing them again brought delight mixed with the stinging pain of regret that I hadn't been a better dad.

I was a young man nearing the end of my twenty-ninth year as I attempted to navigate my overwhelming life. I worked part-time and was going to school full-time at one of the toughest schools in the country. There was little time left for me to spend with my girls.

I knew it was better that my wife, Gretchen, wasn't part of this sweet memory. She was profoundly depressed and she spit a venomous, resentful attitude that often caused the girls to cry. She'd yell at them or me for no reason. My marriage to her was beyond miserable, with no workable way out. Divorce was not an option in the Catholic Church or acceptable to my family at the time. The family's biggest fear was this: "What will the neighbors think?" I guess it was better to live for the opinion of others and suffer rather than live authentically. So, I did my best to keep moving forward, constantly trying to keep everyone happy. It was a constant effort not to allow my own depression to rise to the surface.

My mother, father, two brothers, and sister lived next door to us in a run-down fourplex. I was very close to my mother, Josephine. She fully understood what I was living with because she had also been abused throughout her life.

As Russell, my heart seized in my throat, remembering what Josephine had revealed to me as the red-tailed hawk on the day of my shape-shifting lesson: "I was known to you as your mother in your last incarnation as a man." Now I could clearly see her, in her body, as Josephine, my mother. This brought a sense of familiarity although my mind found it overwhelming. I noticed she was the same kind, loving soul in the physical as she was in spirit. She lovingly protected me in both worlds. My heart overflowed with love for her. I wept with a strange mixture of grief and happiness from witnessing the undying, far-reaching power of love.

Francis informed me of what was to come. "Initially, you will see certain parts of your life as Pete. There will also be parts of Josephine's life before and after she was your mother. Your father, Samuel, and other family members may also be included. The purpose is to give you a larger view of what each experienced that shaped that person's *personal reality*.

As Pete, I was my parents' second child. My brother and I were born in New York City during the Great Depression. Poverty consumed our family as it did millions of others whose daily fight revolved around one thing: survival.

I watched as the view became more expansive in observing my earliest memories as Pete. My family constantly experienced the hunger and humiliation of poverty. We were consumed with a never-ending anxiety from the constant fear of not knowing what would happen next. It was my mother who stood in the breadlines to feed us—my father was too proud. He'd been beaten down by his past and took to drinking in an attempt to drown his pain. He was a good man in many ways, but the times were brutal, with little hope of a better future.

During that time, many men left their families in an attempt to cover their pain with alcohol made from stills.

They often ended up in hobo camps, usually called Hooverville's, after President Herbert Hoover, who believed the government should stay out of people's lives and not interfere with individual rights. This philosophy allowed the acting out of the dark, greedy side of human nature, which brought about the collapse of the American stock market. The "crash" brought destitution to the masses as many of the rich continued living their lavish lifestyles.

As Pete, I observed my father become one of the men who took refuge in a hobo camp. After three months, he returned with stories of "riding the rails," carefully explaining how he and others would jump on railroad cars as the trains left the station, most not knowing where they were headed. It was very dangerous because most of the men were drunk as they tried to catch a railcar. A few were killed or lost limbs, forcing the railroads to try and stop the practice. The camp he stayed at was raided by the police, which prompted his return home.

He described the hobo camps as a sea of men in an ocean of chaos. They'd been stripped of their dignity. He said they all felt trapped like drowning rats on a sinking ship with no way out. Many were driven to steal, causing fights, which fed more violence. He said we were all victims of the greedy parasites who'd never be held accountable for their thievery.

On his first night home, we couldn't help noticing my father's black eye, split lip, and protective mannerisms toward his ribs. He didn't want to say what caused his injuries, but we knew it was most likely a fight. A short time later he wept until he fell asleep, clutching the corner of the mattress on the floor as if it were a lifeline.

Everything I observed, I also felt. This made the experience captivating, but also painfully unnerving.

Next, I was in a room in the White House. From the corner, I watched President Franklin Roosevelt in the midst of his first hundred days. I could see he truly cared about people, especially the working class. He understood it was the real backbone of the country. Its members were the ones whose sweat built the railroads, grew food, and labored in foundries and factories. They were the ones who fought the wars created by the rich for the benefit of the wealthy. The most recent war was World War I, which claimed over 17 million lives, mostly from the working class. It was the powerless who spilled their blood and gave their lives for their country. And sadly, no matter what happened, or how bad it was for the majority, it didn't stop the greedy from continuing to exploit capitalism without conscience or concern for the misery they caused others. They did it because they could. Most of the wealthy referred to the working masses as "the herd." Francis said that the elitist reference hadn't changed. President Roosevelt, who came from a wealthy family, was aware of this mentality and was determined not to let the opposition of a few stand in the way of saving millions from starvation.

"From a spiritual perspective Franklin Roosevelt was a powerful, compassionate soul with numerous difficult tests," Josephine said. "His determination was fixed on saving as many as he could from the devastation of sociopathic narcissism."

I was reliving history, observing with amazement as the New Deal was crafted and then started in 1933, the year I came into the world as Pete. With the New Deal, President Roosevelt and the Democratic Party created jobs plus emergency relief programs. These programs kept millions from starvation and death. The breath of hope started to replace the apathy of defeat. It took a year before the programs benefited my family, but it was a lifesaver for us and millions of others. It gave my father a job, put food on our table, and got him some of his dignity back.

Next, Francis moved us to observe banking reform. This was also passed in the first hundred days to avoid another devastating exploitation of the American working class. Later, Social Security was added, with programs to aid tenant farmers and migrant workers. The Republicans viciously fought using every tactic, especially fear, to obstruct the lifesaving programs by calling them "socialist."

"This dimension is not intended to be only positive and loving," Francis pointed out. "If it were, only one reality would exist, with no choice between darkness and Light. Therefore, as an example, there would be no free will to choose between cruelty versus care. It is actions that reveal intentions." He paused, perhaps waiting for me to digest what he had said so far. Then he added, "Many levels of pure love exist, but each soul is tested to prove it has evolved to that point."

"So is there accountability for those who express the brutality of greed, or are they just being tested?" My mind felt crisp when I was in this state of reexperiencing Pete's life. I had expanded far beyond my consciousness as Russell the dog.

Josephine was precise in her answer. "Souls who come to the physical are not just taking a test without accountability; that's a different dimension. The purpose for those souls who choose this test is whether they have truly overcome the ego sickness of greed and its companion, cruelty. Consider the brief look you had of your incarnation as Octavia. Many opportunities are given in a lifetime to choose and express actions of love, compassion, empathy, and mercy. The insight a soul needs for direction comes from Infinite Source, the soul's own past experience, Spirit Guides, and other teachers. However, the Guidance is often ignored. If not ignored, the vibrational frequency of kind actions increases. This expands the *constructive* energy of Light, thus diminishing destructive frequencies. The result increases the harmonic vibrations of the souls involved, benefiting all. Each advances with a loss of desire for cruelty, eventually elevating the collective consciousness of the third-dimensional earth plane."

I was amazed. "Wow! That's a lot to take in, but it *feels* right. I'm encouraged to say I kind of understand it." Feeling worn out, I took a nap.

When I awoke on the deck, I stretched, hoping for some time to chase squirrels. They needed a reminder of who was in charge. However, Francis had other ideas. "You are doing well. Let us continue," he said. Next, I watched parts of my father's childhood. Both of Samuel's parents were abusive. Love was especially foreign to his mother, who was tall with a cold stern face framing empty brown eyes. His dad ruled with an iron fist, mirroring the way he'd been raised as a boy. "Spare the rod, spoil the child" was what people believed at the time.

As a new scene unfolded, I watched my father at age fourteen be heartlessly blamed for his younger brother's death. His mother hysterically shrieked, "You're to blame for your little brother dying."

His dad yelled, "You should have been watching Matthew, not letting him climb a tree." Then I observed his little brother falling from a tree, hitting his head.

My father, Samuel, yelled back. "It's your fault! Because you don't believe in doctors and wouldn't get him any help! That's why Matthew is dead!" After hearing the truth, he punched my dad in the face, knocking out some of his teeth. Then as he fell on the floor, he was repeatedly kicked in the stomach.

His dad screamed, "The blame is yours. I hope you rot in hell and your back breaks from carrying the burden of your brother's death. Never blame us again for not calling a doctor. You're useless, and you'll always be useless."

His mother yelled, "Get up and get out of my sight! You have killed your brother."

I felt the depth of his pain. Barely able to get to his feet, he hobbled outside. Gagging, he threw up blood mixed with vomit. He slept in the yard that night, crying himself to sleep from the beating, but it was the brutality he'd endured that did the most damage.

I had a hard time with what I had witnessed. The intensity of all the emotions I felt was frightening. Shaken, I asked Josephine and Francis, "Why am I seeing all this? Is it really necessary for me to relive the suffering of others? I have enough of my own agony."

Francis was clear. "All is for the benefit of your greater understanding. Do you wish to postpone this overview for later?"

I thought about it. "I guess not, but this is very difficult. I need a moment." After a short time, I reluctantly said, "OK, go ahead."

Francis and Josephine moved ahead one year in my father's life to what was significant for my benefit. Sadly, nothing had improved for my father. The punishment of blame continued, making him the family scapegoat. The verbal abuse, beatings, and relentless stain of guilt drove him to leave home at fifteen. The shame he carried reached the boundaries of his soul. Broken, he had no one to turn to and nowhere to go. After a few weeks of starving on the streets of Chicago, he decided to lie about his age and join the Army. He was stationed in Panama as a cook.

My mother, Josephine, met my father, Samuel, in 1927. After a short courtship, they married that same year. He was twenty, she was nineteen.

Unexpectedly the scene shifted to the last day of my father's life. It was a day I remembered as Pete, only this time I witnessed it from a higher perspective. That morning my father dreamed of his little brother, Matthew. In the dream Matthew told my father he loved him and was waiting for him. My mother, Josephine, said my father got up at the usual time. After his shower, her husband of over sixty years surprised her by putting on brand-new clothes he'd been saving for a special occasion. He sat in his favorite chair, staring out the window. With tears in his eyes, he said to her, "I just don't know how it happened. Matthew fell. Then a short time later he was gone. I hope he knew how much I loved him and still do." Five hours later my father died of a massive heart attack. It was his time to leave the physical. I watched his spirit embrace Matthew, along with many others who lovingly greeted him. I was surprised to see the souls of his parents, who had been so cruel, also embrace him with love.

As we moved on, I felt a profound empathy for his pain. I had a better insight into the many times he had treated us so harshly. By *feeling* his pain, I was able to have compassion for him, finally being able to forgive him. The strength of forgiveness freed me from the prison of resentment where I had kept my heart. I thanked Francis and Josephine for the peace the power of healing brought.

Next, Francis began to show me parts of the life of my mother, Josephine. Her parents had also immigrated from what they called the "old country." Her father had been a violent alcoholic, who was lost in his own personal hell, unleashing his seething anger on his wife and thirteen children. Three of the children didn't survive. Everyone in the family was beaten by him when he was drunk, which was most of the time. Or they were crushed by the ongoing hunger his alcoholism caused. He spent all his pay on alcohol, gambling, and some food for himself, though he typically liked to drink rather than eat.

Then we watched my mother, Josephine, as a small child of five, when she was also accused of her younger brother's death. I could clearly see this was a trauma bond my parents shared. On the day Francis showed me, she was excited to find a frog and ran in the house, slamming the screen door. Within an hour her eight-month-old baby brother Harry had died. When her father found out, he felt nothing; for him it was one less mouth to feed. But it was devastating for her mother and some of the other children. Due to the misery and anger that filled her family's lives, family members wanted and needed someone to blame. So it was decided that Josephine had scared him to death when she slammed the door. The truth was, Harry was sickly from the day he was born. Their father spent every penny on alcohol, with nothing left for a doctor. Even so, blame can distract, making the pain of loss a little more tolerable for those deeply wounded. On that day, Josephine became her family's scapegoat.

Next, we observed another tragedy, of which there were many in Josephine's lifetime. This one also happened when she was five, a few months after Harry's death. She was playing in a field with a few friends when she climbed on a fence, losing her balance. She fell on a broken bottle, severely cutting her left cheek. A woman passing by who heard Josephine screaming walked her to the hospital. It took thirty-six stiches, with nothing to kill the pain, to pull the left side of her face back together. No one from her family came. Alone, she cried from the pain of her injury and the agony of abandonment. The nurse, who lacked compassion, yelled at her to stop crying. When she continued crying, the nurse suddenly slapped her on the other side of her face with such force that Josephine passed out from the pain. When she came to, the nurse was still screaming at her. "Now you shut up and stop crying, or I'll hit you again!"

Francis explained its significance. "This was a new action, or first karma, the nurse had created. Later, as her life unfolded, her brutal, merciless actions were reflected back to her in many forms. When her lifetime ended, her life review held all the pain her words and actions had caused others, including the agonizing, painful sorrow she had caused Josephine. Be aware. A soul is responsible for the energy it creates and the repercussions it later receives."

As Pete, I was familiar with the scar on my mother's face. It reached from just below the bottom of her left eye to her chin but extended much deeper. For the rest of her life, every time she caught her reflection, it was a reminder of that day and the nurse's brutality.

As the scenes quickly moved on, I witnessed how the physical, emotional, and mental abuse continued for Josephine at home and in school. Kids are cruel, perhaps because their parents don't consistently teach the value of kindness. So there was name-calling, endless bullying, and never-ending stares, pointing, and whispers about her scar. After a period of time, a numbness covered her emotional pain. She tried to pretend it didn't matter, but the accumulated abuse took its toll. Even so, she was never abusive or violent with anyone.

At age nine, Josephine's father put her to work in a factory, ending her education and what was left of her childhood. Some of her older brothers and sisters had worked in the hat factory for years. He kept all the money his children earned to feed his alcohol sickness. Her mother was a shell, broken from the regular beatings, hunger, and birthing a child every year. Josephine had no one who loved her and no one she could depend on. Yet she made it through. As a young woman she considered herself lucky to have found a man who wanted to marry her, even if that man harbored many of his own scars. He was also somewhat violent and a drinker, as she learned later. However, her marriage contained much less abuse than she had become accustomed to. And it was less than what many women had to endure from their husbands at the time.

I watched as the severe harshness of Josephine's life continued into her later years, but through it all, she always looked for reasons to laugh. The depth of what she endured would have broken most to their very core. It was sad to see she never achieved lasting happiness, though her heart continued to be compassionate. Somehow, she remained a gentle soul who wouldn't harm anyone. The triumph of her spirit over the pain of darkness is the example she lived. This was her legacy—the legacy of resilience she gave her children, grandchildren, and all who knew her.

"She endured, finding enough joy to laugh, even when there was no hope of anything better," Francis pointed out.

Feeling discouraged, I asked, "So what does a lifetime mean? Is it just to suffer and die?"

Francis was precise. "Perhaps the question you're asking is this: what is lifetime *for*?"

I tried to answer the question myself. "Is it to learn and demonstrate what has been learned?"

Josephine enthusiastically answered. "Yes, very good. That is a big part of it. Keep in mind, this is your transformational time on the earth plane. This is your story, in addition to the stories of other souls who share and have shared an incarnation with you. Each lifetime is a different spiritual adventure that compels the chosen transformation for each path."

Now that I knew some of Josephine's pain, it enormously deepened my loving respect for her. I realized that when I was Pete, she was my rock, my only stability. I fell asleep basking in the warmth of my love for Josephine.

13

Living In a Shell

Look, but only if you will not deny what you see.
—Francis

It was a new day, and after Deardra went to work, I was back to observing Pete's memories. Francis advised me to watch for patterns of denial.

My mother, Josephine, was the only one I could trust. I depended on her to take care of the girls while Gretchen worked, and I went to school. Even so, Gretchen consistently complained about my mother because she wanted to stay home with the girls.

The memory focused on the toxic emotions I had for Gretchen when I was Pete. I knew why she really wanted to stay home. It was to completely indulge her laziness, which she had no shame about. She'd never admit we would have been worse off if it wasn't for my mother taking care of the girls.

The scene with Gretchen continued, containing all the bitterness I held so deeply. I was experiencing it again as if a scab had been ripped from a painful wound.

Gretchen didn't put any effort into getting herself off the couch. Her favorite expression was "Don't push yourself." Her refusal to take care of herself or our two young daughters was an added stressful burden on all of us. I believed her self-indulgence was unfair, breeding more resentment that festered inside of me like an infection. So I was cruel, lashing out, trying to hurt her for constantly hurting us. I told her many times that if she didn't work, she'd be "totally worthless." Once, DeDe heard me say that and started to cry.

I wondered at the time what was happening to me. I could feel the damage accumulating, hardening my heart as my spirit withered. What was left formed a hard cocoon around my emotions. I had no regard for the pain I intentionally caused Gretchen. The truth was I wanted to hurt her for continuously injuring me and the girls. However, I was also aware that expressing my pain passively and aggressively was hurtful, even harmful, to my daughters. Because I was trapped in my rage, I couldn't seem to help myself.

I tried everything I could think of to reason with her to change. It was a hard lesson for me, but I learned that trying to change someone into something they aren't is impossible. I wanted her to be, or even pretend to be, something she wasn't—maternal, caring, and kind. So I was less caring, which I could clearly see was the wrong way to be, especially for DeDe and Annette.

Our marriage wasn't based on love or even liking each other. It was a trap, a sham, a lie we couldn't escape. We stayed together for the girls, the Catholic Church, and our families— all mixed in with what the neighbors would think. All our negative feelings for each other morphed into a marriage of bickering, with a mean vindictiveness that resulted in a never-ending game of tit for tat.

Gretchen was especially cruel; it seemed nothing was beneath her. She lied, made horrible accusations, hit and screamed at the girls, and called us all names or whatever else she could think of. She never drank alcohol, so there was no reason for her behavior other than her own misery and desire for everyone else to be miserable as well.

I should have divorced her but didn't. I was afraid. Afraid I'd become more overwhelmed, particularly since I thought I had no real skills in being a good dad. My immediate concern at the time was to stay focused on graduating so that I could provide a better future for my family. The only parenting I knew was how I was raised. While my mother had been loving, she was also flawed, sometimes adding her own emotional frustrations to the drama of the everyday chaos. A constant undercurrent of antagonism was ever-present, driving the whole family to claw at one another by fighting, bickering, attacking, or criticizing one another. Each day presented varying degrees of a war zone with short reprieves.

It was all there as I watched—crystal clear in the memory of spent moments that played out before my eyes. Included were all the sights, sounds, smells, and highly charged emotions, swirling with an intensity I could hardly bear. All were memories I longed to forget.

In the next scene I watched big tears running down DeDe's face as she begged through her sobs. "Promise me, Daddy, you won't hit mommy again, even when she's mean." My heart broke as I witnessed the pain of my actions in my daughter's eyes. I also realized DeDe knew her mother had purposefully pushed me to the brink to provoke my punishing response, which was no excuse. It was wrong to react violently by slapping Gretchen. By doing so, I gave her what she wanted, a reason to justify her misery by making me at fault because I was at fault. I hated myself even more for hitting Gretchen, partly for allowing her to push me into losing control of my temper. My father had also lashed out with abuse at times, demonstrating that the use of violence as a solution can create more abuse.

Instantly, a strange feeling hit me. I looked around, acutely aware I was not remembering this alone. It was part of my life review as Pete, but someone else carried the memory, and that someone was remembering at the same time I was. Who could it be? Thinking of the possibilities, I thought, could it be her?

Francis had no judgment of what had transpired in my recent review. "All will be revealed concerning your shared memory," he softly said. "Presently, let us examine how you chose fear over love by staying with a troubled woman who was twisted by the force of her own thoughts. She believed her own imagined fiction, willfully feeding the darkness that poisoned her mind. She consistently chose to put herself above everyone, including you and your daughters. Aware of this, you continued hiding in the shell of denial, knowing she was causing harm to your girls. Your fear of what others would say overwhelmed your desire to bring about change; the fear of that change kept you paralyzed."

I felt defensive. With bitterness I said, "I was paralyzed with fear. And she was pregnant! I had to marry her. I don't remember you or anyone else helping me navigate that impossible situation!"

"These observations are not condemning, only instructive, to help you see from a different perspective," Francis gently said.

I tried to relax in an effort to release my defensiveness. "Go ahead. Continue. I'll try not to be so touchy."

"It's important to remember that you're reviewing the personal reality, or *personality*, you created as Pete. This includes your thoughts, beliefs, perceptions, emotions, memories, and ego."

"OK. What other observations do you have?" I was still smarting, but I wanted to hear.

"Did you notice how you fed denial with misplaced optimism? You hoped all would be fine without any indications of how that might occur. You effectively created a voluntary state of blindness, as an ostrich does with its head in the sand. As you continued to deny your unhappiness, your frustrated anger festered, growing to greater levels each day. The effect was internalized violence that pushed outward. That's another example of how limited thinking produces a limited reality."

Again, I felt criticized. I had the need to defend myself as Pete surfaced, but my argument was half-hearted. I was aware of the real truth, not the defensiveness my ego as Pete blurted out. "Yes, it's true. It's all true. I was a failure! Is that what you want me to realize? And yes, I tried to have faith with the hope that things would change. What's wrong with faith and hope?"

I felt a loving warmth emanating from Francis as the answer came. "Faith and hope can be gifts. Each soul has the opportunity to awaken in the power of love and then to express love in any or all of its forms. Intuitively you knew, and were guided to be aware, that your overly optimistic faith was misplaced, leading to a deeper level of denial. This denial caused you to continue to expose yourself and your daughters to the damage of one so damaged."

Josephine tenderly spoke: "Again, our observations are not to function as a judgment or criticism, but for you to observe, with the wisdom of guided accountability. The idea is not to just see, but to emotionally *feel* a larger picture of choices, including thoughts leading to actions where a different choice might have brought happier outcomes. This knowledge of other options is not to create regret. The purpose is for the expansion of awareness to enable you to see the entire picture of choices related to forming probable futures. With the completion of your entire life review as Pete, you will decide what you have learned. Then you will declare your earned wisdom. This will also determine what lessons you need to bring forward into your next incarnation. It is the opportunity to demonstrate through your actions what you have risen above—highlighting what you have not."

Honestly, I hadn't sensed any judgment from Josephine or Francis, only loving support. It was my ego that chose to be wounded by the truth.

I listened intently, trying to understand what I required in order to shift into what I most needed to learn. I felt soothed by the essence of love resonating from Francis and Josephine's guidance. I asked, "If I bring something forward into my next life, is that my karma?"

Francis said, "A tenacious trait is a self-defeating behavior that shows up until it is overcome. If that trait inspires actions, which is usually the case, then karma becomes involved. Each soul designs the learning situations required for that soul's desired growth forward. The right people, situations, circumstances—everything is designed before entering the physical. However, free will is a factor that can enhance or stifle the strategic design."

"OK. I guess I understand that part. So why would a soul choose poverty?"

"To answer that question, let us revisit two of your past incarnations," Josephine answered.

"Wait." I felt desperate wanting to know. "Who was I sharing some of those memories with?"

"In time, you shall understand," Josephine gently said. "All your questions will be answered. For now, behold—"

14
Octavia

*Wealth reveals the richness of one's soul or
the poverty of one's ego.*
—Josephine

Instantly I was in a different body—that of a girl. The body felt familiar, but I had no connection to it, as if it were a skin suit that I'd outgrown. The memories of this previous life came flooding back, and I knew exactly who everyone was.

I sat in a silk dress with undergarments that confined my torso, especially my ribs. I was terribly uncomfortable as I sat in a velvet parlor chair reading the latest book, *The Man of Feeling*, by Henry Mackenzie. According to the date on the newspaper my father read, it was September 2, 1771. The room was filled with beautiful furniture, paintings, and expensive keepsakes collected from around the world.

My parents were sitting across from me on an overstuffed couch, warming up with their brandy for the evening lecture. On this particular night they would preach about the responsibilities of aristocracy—specifically, the importance of understanding my superiority over others of a lesser station.

My father was a lord by birth, and my mother was a lady by marriage. We were wealthy, with disdain for anyone who wasn't. My father believed everyone below our station was a commoner. And the poor he referred to as beggars or rabble.

I was nineteen, poisoned with the resentment and anger of someone many years older. Most of my bitterness began at age three upon the birth of my brother, Augustus. They called him Gus, and he became the center of my parents' world. He was to be the sole heir, with a small stipend for my support, which Gus would control, as a motivator to encourage me to marry. If I didn't marry, I would be dependent on Gus for my survival. His resentment for me had built over the years, and rightly so. I'd bullied and antagonized him as far back as he could remember. He liked to say that I was meaner than a cobra, just as ugly, and no man in his right mind would ever have me. Perhaps he was right, but he was a milksop! He was always nice and agreeable with everyone, even to those of inferior class, including servants. Everyone loved him. In contrast, no one liked me. We were opposites, with no love or tolerance for each other.

It was a strange experience to peer out of the eyes that were once mine and at the same time observe myself from a few feet away. I put my book down and walked across the parlor to a mirror. I was startled when I gazed at my reflection. My hair was a dull blond. My hazel eyes were small, close together, and deeply set in my oblong face. I was perhaps five foot four. I wasn't ugly—plain was more accurate. Even so, the bitter anger I contained showed through, giving me the appearance of sucking a lemon. It was no wonder no one liked me.

My parents were taking turns lecturing me about the responsibilities of our class. My father was first. He took a gulp of his brandy, then puffed on his stinking pipe. "Yes, Octavia, it's incumbent upon you to always remember your station in life as a lady. Those you encounter of an inferior class should be treated as such in order to help them remember their place, which is always beneath you."

My mother sipped her brandy. "A young lady who is kind makes herself a target for beggars who prey on the sympathies of others, using trickery to extort money from the wealthy." She had the annoying habit of clutching her throat when a subject made her anxious. Neither of my parents believed in generosity or mercy, clearly stating those things were better left to the church.

A few months later my parents went abroad for one of their long holidays. My brother was away at school. In their absence, I was in charge. Shortly after their departure, I was approached by one of the coach drivers of our estate. He asked for an advance on his pay so that he might summon a doctor for his young son, who was ill.

I never liked the look of him. He was borderline dirty, with a sly, untrustworthy demeanor. On his right temple he had hairs growing out of a dark birthmark, which I found revolting.

I gritted my teeth, addressing him with distain. "How dare you speak to me without asking permission. I will not give you an advance since every servant would then expect it. Let this be a lesson in how to better manage your money."

"But your ladyship, my son is very ill and may die without a doctor," he implored. Everything in his face was pleading for my help. Ringing his hands, he bowed his head, this time begging. "Please have mercy, my lady. I will work double to make up for the few shillings you would grant me in advance. Please, my lady, my son is very sick."

At that point I was seething with anger. I yelled, startling him. "Mercy is for God and the church, and I am neither." Turning on my heel, I went back in the house proud of myself, even taking pleasure in my control over this inferior.

The following week, I heard his son had died, and he blamed me. This was a despicable insult that sent me into a rage. I felt nothing when he pleaded for the advance, and I felt nothing hearing his son had died. I would not tolerate the impertinence of this—this—driver. So, I personally fired him and took great satisfaction in doing so.

I couldn't wait to tell my parents of how I had successfully handled an intolerable situation. Upon their return, they were pleased with my steadfast decision in handling the coach driver's request.

Two years later, while shopping in London, I noticed a well-dressed man watching me as I gazed in a store window. My heart jumped. I felt my face flush as our eyes fixed on each other. The connection between us was captivating. I nervously smoothed my dress and smiled as he approached. He wasn't handsome, but he was attractive enough to suit my taste. Bowing with the manners of a gentleman, he introduced himself with a strong Scottish accent as Gavin Dunbar. Gazing at each other for what seemed an endless moment, I nervously released a small cough, breaking the silence. I couldn't understand it then, in that moment, as Octavia, but I felt loved—truly loved. And I sensed that he felt the same, as if we were twin souls united again. The hardness that surrounded my heart became softer.

We decided to have tea. He didn't want to tarnish my reputation, so for a few shillings he quickly found a willing bystander to act as a chaperone.

At first, we talked with a nervous tension, but after a few minutes, it seemed the most natural thing to be in each other's company. There was magic in our meeting. I knew in every cell of my body he was the one who would redeem my heart and soul. And perhaps I would do the same for him.

As I observed, I was permitted to see a larger view. We had loved each other in three different incarnations. Unfortunately, each time we were unable to fully realize our love for various reasons.

We left each other that afternoon, flirtatiously agreeing to meet the next day for a walk. I was ecstatic; my mind reeled with images of marriage. Now I wouldn't have to depend on Gus for my maintenance when our parents died.

About ten minutes later, I was crossing the street in front the hotel where I was staying when I was purposely run down by a coach. In the last seconds of my life, I recognized the coach driver. It was the man my cruel actions had ruined because I had allowed his son to die and then had terminated his position.

My life review as Octavia began. Every harmful thought, word, and deed from my life was before me. But at that point I deeply felt the suffering of the ones I had injured, along with my own pain in fully comprehending the anguish my actions had caused. The few good things I managed were also in my review, but that part was very short. I was very sad to have missed being with Gavin again. From my review as Octavia, I clearly understood that love, in all its expressions, is the salvation for the darkness of the ego.

    Francis moved me forward into my next life, in which I was running from a murderer.

15
The Monk

Only God can save me now.
—Brother Gabriel

In my lifetime following Octavia, I was a monk in the year of our Lord 1808. I lived in an old stone monastery located just outside a small town in southern Scotland.

As this past life memory progressed, I observed myself coming from a very poor family that had survived mostly from the generosity of the church. Then I recognized them—they were the same parents I'd had when I was Octavia. We were together again, only this time we were the beggars groveling for scraps. Reaping what we had sowed from our previous arrogant superiority, we had determined our future destiny. The law of cause and effect was a platform upon which we built our own karmic hell. And we had no one to blame except ourselves.

In the distance I heard Francis say, "Very good. You are beginning to understand why a soul would choose to be born into poverty."

"Does it mean all who are born poor were once rich and selfish?"

Francis replied. "It does not. Each soul chooses its own perfect learning path to evolve further."

"If poverty is chosen, why should we have compassion for those who are poor?" I thought this was a fair question.

"As Pete, you were born into a poor family," Francis said. "Did you think you and your family were not worthy of compassion? From compassion comes grace, which enriches the soul. Lack of compassion exposes the need for humbling lessons. The expression of mercy, benevolence, empathy, and generosity for those less fortunate reveals much about a soul's progress. Material wealth can infect the ego to crave more self-importance and to be easily consumed by greed. Greed is an insidious narcissistic trait that can be difficult to overcome."

"When I was Octavia, I was raised to be cheap, greedy, cruel, and selfish," I said. "I felt satisfaction when I caused others pain, which went far beyond my upbringing. Why was I so mean-spirited?"

"In spirit," Josephine answered, "your soul considered its next incarnation. It was your belief that you had evolved beyond greed, cruelty, and narcissism. So, with the aid of your Guides, you designed your lifetime as Octavia. You did so intentionally, with many challenging tests, in the hope of graduating to the next level of consciousness. The difficulty you planned was to be born into material wealth with an upbringing that reinforced arrogance and greed. With wealth comes great responsibility, and it is one of the ultimate tests of the ego versus the soul. Often the ego wins until the soul has finally progressed beyond greed. The challenge overtook you when you *allowed* your egoic self to consume the kindness in your heart. That was the kindness you rediscovered through your love for Gavin."

"How can I ever forgive myself or be forgiven?"

"Know that nothing is unforgivable, as reparation is made for all actions when the soul's objectives are met," Josephine said with compassion.

"But I failed the test miserably and probably created more bad karma," I said with shame.

Francis pointed out. "You did not fail but only revealed what you had not yet mastered. The opportunities to master each level of consciousness are endless. Each soul moves at its own pace of demonstrated wisdom. Accept what you have learned and move forward."

"Damaging karma," Josephine noted, "is created when thoughts generated by unkind beliefs become actions. If harm is the *intention* of the action, the resulting reaction resonates with greater force. This brings a similar experience in order to balance the polarity of past or present action. Good karma is also thought-and-action-based, but with the intention of helping, not harming. When the soul, without anticipation of reward, genuinely comes from heart-felt love, kindness, generosity, compassion, or anything in the spirit of love, then that soul expands and evolves. Release your fear. You are exactly where you need to be."

Francis added, "There is also first action or first karma, which we previously spoke of. This is when new actions create a new lineage of positive or negative cause and effect."

Now I was afraid I was destined to suffer. "This sounds like revenge for things I thought were right at the time. Well, maybe some things I knew weren't right and did anyway. But why should I be punished now for actions from another life? I'm in a new lifetime now. Can't I just start fresh?"

I could feel Josephine send me waves of loving reassurance as Francis continued. "Accountability is not vengeance; it is simply cause and effect," he said. "What you put into another's life comes back into your own. When in the physical, accountability is a basic, yet effective learning tool. Souls come to the earth plane to create and demonstrate what they have learned and what needs to be learned. The wheel of karma continues turning for the souls at that learning stage. As your soul expands, you will evolve beyond karma to the next phase of knowledge."

"OK. But since I'm not there yet, it's very uncomfortable watching myself fail over and over."

Josephine corrected me. "You cannot fail; you can only postpone your progress. Let us continue to examine your lifetime as a monk."

I began observing myself again as a monk. Even though my family was made up of beggars the church had fed, my deep compassion to help others was observed. And I was allowed to join the brotherhood of monks. I was called Brother Gabriel. My daily life consisted of prayer, eating, reading, helping the poor, and sleeping. I didn't want for more. The outside world was a brutal, cruel place in which I had a chance to spread God's word of love. I was secure with the protection of the church and believed I was on the perfect path to saving my soul.

As we continued, I noticed that I was becoming more accustomed to observing and experiencing myself as other personalities. It was eerie, but distantly familiar. Somehow, I was mostly OK with it since I had no choice.

All was well in my life as Brother Gabriel until one day a new monk appeared. He was short and heavyset. Oddly, I was immediately afraid of him. His presence was so threatening that it cast an aura of darkness around him. It was something I couldn't quite define, but when he looked my way, I could literally feel his hatred. Then I noticed a black mark on his right cheek. I instantly knew what the black mark meant, but Brother Gabriel didn't.

Guided by Josephine and Francis, I knew he was the coach driver who had begged me, as Octavia, to save his son's life. I sensed his taste for revenge had grown to an insatiable hunger. I was also aware that his son, who I had let die as Octavia, was a young girl in the village I often helped during my visits.

An overwhelming sensation of being hunted consumed me. I wanted to run, hide, escape—anything to stop the terror. The evil monk sneered at me as he was led to his quarters. The peace I had known was shattered.

Suddenly, the scene moved to a year later, with the evil monk chasing me through the woods by the main road to the village. Over the past year he had tormented me in numerous ways. One was by telling me over and over how he had easily killed others. And at that point, as he had promised, he was going to kill me.

I was terrified and running for my life. The morning rain caused the hillside to be muddy. I slipped and fell flat on my back. He slowed his run to a walk and laughed as I tried to get up and kept slipping.

He was seething with anger, declaring with a sick tone of amusement, "I will take great pleasure in slowly slitting your throat. I'm not sure why, but I will." His hatred for me oozed from him like pus from a wound.

I was able to sit up, and he punched me in the face and knocked me on my back again. He sat on my chest, pinning my arms under his knees. The weight of his body and his strength were far greater than I had imagined. He punched me in the face again as he laughed. I could smell that his breath was heavy with drink. He was drooling with pleasure as he hit me over and over. Then he pulled a knife from the pocket of his robe. "Now I will cut your throat, starting right here."

He placed the knife below my left ear, slowly starting to cut toward my throat. I continued to struggle, attempting to break his hold, but he was too strong. I screamed with pain. I felt the warmth of my blood as it ran down my neck and shoulder. I cried out, hoping to be heard, while praying to be saved from this monster. Unexpectedly, a surge of adrenaline doubled my strength. I pushed my pelvis up, knocking him off me. He fell to my left side. I was frantically kicking him away from me as I struggled to stand. Grabbing a rock, I hit him in the face with all the force I could gather. He fell, and when he did, he fell on the knife. He shrieked as he unintentionally stabbed himself in the chest.

Rolling on his back he lifted his head defiantly, spitting blood at me, and said, "I will get you; I promise you." Those were his dying words as his head dropped back to the ground.

For a few moments, I was beyond thoughts or words, reliving this long-ago trauma. I felt defeated, not wanting to continue this pain-filled excursion into layers of the past I wanted to forget.

My thoughts raced while I tried to make sense of it all. I could see the parallels—the threads of deeds woven together that produced a karmic tapestry of regretful experiences.

When I was finally able to speak to Josephine and Francis, my emotions were overflowing. I had hit my breaking point. I whispered, almost to myself, "This is all too much! I'm afraid—so afraid that I don't think I can face what might be coming next." I could feel my dog body shaking.

Josephine lovingly said, "All is working on your behalf for your highest and greatest movement forward. The complicated choice to review your past life or lives while experiencing an incarnation as a dog was recognized by all involved to contain an extremely high level of difficulty. This fact did not dissuade you."

"This is hard for me!" I yelled. "And why wasn't I protected from this evil monster who's hunted me life after life and probably still does to this day?"

Francis said, "That will be revealed to you later. For now, let us remain focused on your obstacles to growth."

"I realize I'm stubborn and hide in denial, but I had hoped I was making progress. What was it you said? Stubborn means stuck? I want to be unstuck, but the pain is too much for me to bear!"

Francis' tone was soft with compassion. "Your life review as Pete will happen now or at another time—but happen it will. We are reviewing the full range of polarities you created in your lifetime as Pete, along with persistent traits from other incarnations. This is so you may see a larger view. The purpose is for you to finally face the fear-encased anguish you denied as Pete by numbing yourself with addictions. By using gambling, alcohol, and other devices of denial, your choices constructed a trap of your own making. These decisions played a part in slowing your growth. The effect brought forth a violent end to your life as Pete."

"What violent end? I can't take anymore. Your tone is nonjudgmental as you neatly outline my faults, but your words are condemning." A tidal wave of shame, fear, and frustration overwhelmed every part of me. Trembling, I continued, but with a panicked yell, "I don't want to go on with this! I'm tired of it. I don't feel I can win. The terror, disgrace, guilt, and sadness I'm suffering is unbearable. I just want to be Russell the dog—that's it—nothing instructive or complicated!"

Francis was unphased. "As you know, this was not one of the options."

With those words I instantly popped out of my dog body! I was looking at my physical form from my etheric body, which was next to my physical form. It was a strange, unnerving experience to be staring at the vehicle for my soul next to me—I wasn't sure I liked it—no, I didn't like it!

Lovingly, Francis said, "You have free will. You can decide to leave this incarnation, or you can continue on with your life review as Pete while experiencing your life as Russell the dog. I momentarily removed you from the slower frequency of the physical so you could decide without the interference of emotion what is best for your soul's growth."

Being out of my body, my clarity was razor sharp. "What are my options?"

"If you stay, to continue this predesigned path forward, your soul's development will be immense. If you decide to return to spirit, very little will have been accomplished. This will create the need to revisit a different path forward with the same intended result. You would only be postponing the inevitable."

"Are there other options?" I asked, hoping something had changed. "An option that's easier, like just being Russell the dog with a few memories here and there? It might be wise to take this enormous task in bites instead of the whole thing compressed into a dog's short life." I found the out-of-body weightlessness was heavenly, but the pull was strong to reenter my body to be Russell the dog again.

Josephine tenderly replied, "Your option would accomplish very little. Each incarnation has a purpose. The time will come when you have reached a level of expansion entitling you to request a lifetime experiencing only the joy of being in the physical. However, this is not the stage your soul has achieved. As Russell, you are working on persistent traits brought forward from other lifetimes. As an example, stubbornness is rooted deeply in the ego. It can often cause poor choices, resulting in undesirable outcomes."

In my etheric body, I was flat—emotionless—as I considered my lack of alternatives. Just as before, I still had only two options: stay or go. Since I was destined to do the process no matter what, the answer stood out as obvious.

"OK. I'll stay and continue with my intended plan. I'll try to be more courageous, less fearful, negative, judgmental, and stubborn. Can I go back into my body now?"

Instantly, I was back in my body as Russell the dog. The heaviness of the physical density was noticeable. This time I had a newfound peace that came with acceptance, which was comforting.

"Pain can be transformed into purpose," Josephine said. "It is an available choice you can select. This is one of the gifts of free will. There is the choice to reach beyond the suffering with the purpose of rising above it."

"I would like to do that, Josephine, but don't know if I can. I'm wondering, did I have a high level of free will as Pete?"

Francis seemed pleased with the question I asked and my decision to stay. He answered. "The amount of free will you had as Pete was a fairly high degree. However, denial inhibits free will by blinding you to the choices and truths that are needed for your soul's growth. Dogs have far less free will, which is partly why you requested to experience your life review in this form. However, there are finer details involved. But enough for now. Time to wake."

I woke somewhat apprehensive, not knowing what to expect next.

16
Maggie's Story

*When we are no longer able to change a situation,
we are challenged to change ourselves.*
—Viktor Frankl

A few days later Deardra woke early, sang the morning song, ate breakfast, and said we were going to meet my new sister. *What?* I grunted. I wanted a brother, a buddy who could wrestle and play for a long time like Waldo.

Josephine gave me some background on this new puppy as we drove away.

"Maggie was about two months old when she was found eating trash in a downtown Denver alley. Since she didn't have a collar, the nice people who found her brought her to a no-kill shelter close to where she was discovered. She was a honey-blonde pup who was thought to be Great Pyrenees and golden retriever. This was the best guess from the shelter staff, and they were right."

Deardra first noticed Maggie on the shelter's website. The picture of Maggie sent an intuitive current through her, and that confirmed we were destined to meet the pup. Before we left, Deardra tried to show me the website picture, but I wasn't interested. I hoped maybe she had a brother we'd pick instead.

The early morning December sky sprinkled a gentle snow as we pulled away from the house. Deardra's plan was to be the first at the shelter when the doors opened. The entire ride to the shelter was spent coaching me to be a "nice dog" and a "good dog," with her emphasizing "no barking and no growling."

"This puppy is a friend for you, for us; she'll be your sister." I snorted. She stopped the car. I was in the back seat, so she turned around, looking directly into my eyes, and firmly said, "You be a good boy—no barking, no growling!" I could tell by her tone she was serious and meant every word. I realized I'd better be good. She never punished me with harsh or mean actions, so I wasn't afraid of her, but because I loved her, I didn't want to disappoint her. Still, it was going to be extremely hard to behave the way she wanted me to.

She parked on the street and went into the shelter first, leaving me in the car. I could smell fear, anxiety, and a sad confusion coming from the shelter. It triggered bad memories of The Pit. The fear and anxiety hit me from those frightening memories of The Pit. It was a horrible place, and any thoughts of it twisted my stomach. I was lying on the back seat, wondering what happened to Wise Rex and the others I vaguely remembered, when suddenly the car door opened. Deardra snapped the leash on my collar and went over all the instructions again about being a good dog, no barking, etc.

Yeah, yeah. I get it. I wasn't in the mood to hear about my reactions, which she considered personality flaws, and I considered my strengths as a dog.

As we walked across the street, I suddenly felt a rush of air, but it was on the inside of my body. Waldo swooped in long enough to give me an important message: "This puppy is meant to come home with you. It is important for you and Deardra, so accept, be silent, be calm." Waldo knew how difficult it was for me not to be reactive.

The way my dog body was wired was contrary to being calm, especially with memories of The Pit being set off. But it was good to feel Waldo's presence, and I knew this must be very important if he was advising me.

As we went in the door of the shelter, the stronger smell of fear instantly triggered me. The loud barking contained a terrified, melancholy sound that I remembered from my time as a puppy. The combination hit me all at once. I almost started to bark—then in the next instant, I was barking. Deardra gave a sharp tug on the leash, snapping me back into the plan.

Originally, when Deardra went into the shelter, she talked to a man who said she should bring me in to meet the puppy to make sure we got along. When she came back in with me, the man she had spoken to was helping someone else. The woman now at the front desk had her own idea about the home the pup should go to. When Deardra asked to see the puppy, the woman inquired about the home we'd provide. Deardra explained our living situation. With a sour look, the woman harshly stated that a family with children was a better choice for the puppy than a single, working woman.

I felt Deardra's energy drop.

Curtly the woman said, "You can fill out an application, but she's such a beautiful puppy she'll be adopted quickly."

She glared at Deardra and tossed the application on the counter, then turned to walk away. I thought the woman's face resembled the farm bulldog who tried to frighten me with the railroad tracks story.

I could sense Deardra's irritation building, which made me want to bark. She contained her anger and politely said, "Excuse me, ma'am, but as a business owner, I often work from home. I have no children, so my dogs are my fur-faced kids whom I deeply love. The puppy would have a large fenced-in yard. We go for walks daily on mountain trails, and I feed my dogs the best organic dog food. And most importantly, I shower them with affection."

The bulldog-faced woman wasn't interested in what Deardra had said. Instead, she looked over the counter at me. "How old is he?" she asked. She scowled the question as if she had just smelled something bad.

"He's almost two and also a rescue." It was clear the woman didn't want Deardra to have the pup.

"Fill out the paperwork, but by then others will be ahead of you to visit with her."

Deardra patiently replied, "I was here first inquiring about the puppy. You can ask the nice man on the phone." She nodded toward the tall, older guy with kind eyes.

I was ready to leave, pulling the leash and moving toward the door. Obviously, it wasn't meant to be for this puppy to come home with us. I felt a little sad for Deardra, but she'd get over it.

Deardra tugged the leash, instructing me to sit. I could hear frustrated anger building in the back of her throat, and I knew that meant she was about to cry or lose her temper.

She remembered a veterinarian she'd talked to on different occasions where her friend Julia worked. "I think you know who Dr. Avery is," she said to the woman in a low, flat tone. Before the woman could answer Deardra leaned on the counter toward her. "He is one of the original founders of this shelter and is still on the board of directors. I'm sure he wouldn't be pleased to hear someone was working here who was discriminating against single women—especially a single woman who wanted to provide an excellent home for a puppy."

The change was amazing! The woman suddenly became a nice, smiling lady. "Please fill out the application. Then the next step is the visit, and we'll see if your dog gets along with her," she said.

Deardra asked her to place a hold on the pup so we would see her first, which the lady did.

Now all the pressure was on me and my behavior. I had to close my eyes and look away while Deardra was talking to the woman so that I didn't bark or growl, but it was becoming more and more difficult to hold myself back. The constant sounds of dogs barking, crying, growling, and whimpering, coupled with the smell of wee and poop, was too much for me. Noisy people were starting to come in. With my senses overwhelmed, I was teetering on being a bad dog.

Francis told me later that through the window, Deardra caught sight of a little boy getting out of a car across the street with his parents. So she quickly finished the paperwork.

I could feel her panic but didn't know what was happening. She noticed an open visiting room and asked the lady if we could sit in there while we waited for someone to bring the pup in. The lady gave the OK. Deardra pulled the leash short, so I was right next to her as she tried to shield my eyes with her free hand. We walked fast as she softly told me what a good boy I was. We made it inside the room. Her hands were shaking after she closed the door, and she sat down with a sigh of relief.

"I love you, Puppa, but your personality quirks sometimes cause me a lot of stress. The puppy is coming to visit, so please, please try to be a good boy." I heard the pleading in her voice.

What an ordeal! It had only been a short time since we had come in the door, but it felt like it had been hours. This being good was exhausting—and for what? Now I was going to have to share Deardra, my food, and my toys. And I'd have to guard Waldo's things since he wasn't around to do it himself. And who knows what else. All for a stinking girl pup I didn't want.

Josephine softly asked without judgment, "What do you have against girls? Females are extremely important in this dimension and many others. Perhaps this would be a good time for you to shift your energy to develop a more open-minded, optimistic attitude."

Just then the visiting room door opened, and the pup was carried in like royalty. Wow! She was a beautiful puppy. Honey-blonde fur, sweet face, soft eyes. She was oozing with cuteness. Then it hit me; she's going to get all the attention! My mind filled with fearful, anxious thoughts. I'll just be in the background. Puppa the stubborn mule. Who's going to love me when this sweet, beautiful puppy is around? My mind was spinning—Deardra will love her more than me. Next, I'll be here at the shelter begging for a home. But who would adopt me? I'm puppafied. Then I remembered. I had heard about puppy buyers who came to get puppies to take them to new homes. If she makes it to the house, maybe I could figure out a way to get the puppy buyers to come and get her.

My anxiety was building with every fear-filled thought I fed into my mind. Spinning down a dark hole of despair, I heard Francis with a crisp clarity that was front and center. "Negative anticipation brings forth a state of suffocating fear. Fear cannot exist without giving it life through *believing* fictional thoughts. Remain clear on what you're making up versus what is real. Relax in the faith that all is happening as it should. You are safe. You are loved. Release your fear; if unfed, it will release you."

I groaned as I lay down. Deardra was cooing as she cuddled the puppy. I could see the energy she radiated growing stronger as she held the pup. Smiling at me, she asked, "Come see your new friend." As she put the puppy next to me, I sniffed it. Then we looked in each other's eyes. The short message I got from her was this: "The Guides sent me, and Waldo's in on it too." She shifted her gaze to Deardra as she yawned the sweetest yawn. Yep, I'm in for a rough time with all this cuteness. I couldn't help myself when a throaty growl started to build.

Deardra heard me, suddenly standing with lightning speed. She handed the pup to the young woman, "We definitely want her." We started toward the door as she said, "I'm going to take Russell to the car. Then I'll be right back to pay and finalize any paperwork. Thank you so much for bringing her in to visit with us." She secured me on a short leash by wrapping it around her hand as we walked out of the room toward the front door.

We only went a few steps when I detected a rush of fear shoot through Deardra. I could sense her heart pounding. I looked up at her, then turned my head back and instantly knew why she was afraid. There they were—little twin boys, running in the front door, making loud noises, pushing each other like the ones from The Pit. I panicked! A snarling, growling bark bellowed out of me, stifled by Deardra pulling the leash so tight my air was almost cut off. In a loud firm voice, she said, "Excuse me. Excuse me, please." I could hear her panic. She must have been afraid of the little boys too. As we tried to leave the crowded lobby, one of the little boys put his fingers out toward me; terrified, I snapped at his hand. Deardra pulled me up off my front paws away from the boy. We were out the open door in a flash. The little boy was crying, saying I tried to bite him, which I had.

Once outside, Deardra loosened her grip. She gave the leash some slack so I could breathe, allowing me to wee on a nearby tree. She didn't say a word, but I knew I was in enormous trouble. An angry fear radiated from her like a flashing light. When we got in the car, she was so mad that her voice was shaking as she chastised me for trying to bite the little boy. Then she began to cry.

What did she expect? What was I supposed to do? He was going to hurt me or her. She didn't know about The Pit, and I couldn't tell her, but her not knowing caused lots of trouble between us. If I could let her know what had happened in The Pit, she'd understand and be happy to let me protect us from little boys. Besides, I could feel her panic when she saw them too.

As she scolded me, her energy calmed. She told me she cried from frustration combined with relief. She looked at me with teary eyes. "I love you so much, but what am I going to do with you, puppafied Russ? You can't go around biting little boys."

We had tried dog training once, but it didn't work. The dog trainer said that I was too stubborn. He started to get rough with me, saying I needed a tougher hand, but Deardra wasn't going to allow that. She dismissed him, saying she didn't like his style and suggesting that he find another line of work. She was good at speaking her mind, especially if she thought someone was mean and needed to know that certain behavior was unacceptable. After he left, she was still mad, but not at me.

After we sat in the car awhile, she took some deep breaths, patted my head, and then affectionately said with a smile, "You're a puppafied, mulish teddy bear dog, and I love you. Now be a good boy while I go inside to get your new sister."

The car door closed, and I moved to the driver's seat. I waited and thought about The Pit, Waldo, Deardra, Josephine, and Francis and how things were going to change with this new intruder. I couldn't help feeling resentful, anxious, and jealous. Couldn't she have found an ugly puppy so that everyone would want to go the other way because they'd never seen such a homely pup? But no, she had to find Ms. Beautiful!

Then it occurred to me. I was bigger, smarter, and looked like a red teddy bear, which most everybody liked. Deardra says I'm deceptively cute because people think I'm an adorable teddy bear dog. Then when I growl or bark at them, they know different.

So I'll be in charge of everything with this new puppy. Deardra has nothing to worry about. I'll keep Ms. Beautiful in line. I felt a bit better, but I still didn't like the whole thing.

Deardra finally returned to the car, moving me to the back seat as she carefully placed the pup on the other front seat. As a woman walked by our car, I heard her tell her little girl, "You can't get what you want every time, but often you get exactly what's right for you."

I've learned that when I hear phases that stand out, I know it's more reinforcement from the other side.

"Very good!" I heard Francis comment. "Infinite Source speaks to us in many forms. It could be through music, a bit of conversation randomly picked up—reading a line, perhaps a comic, anything that clearly stands out and then resonates with you. This is how you know it was meant for your attention."

"But I still don't like any of it," I shot back.

"Have faith that everything is happening for your greatest good, including the greatest good of all who are involved. Open yourself to possibilities. Remember, stubbornness causes one to be stuck."

"I'll try harder, Francis. I've learned that change is unstoppable, but I'm selective about the change I like or am willing to accept. Maybe I am a bit of a stubborn mule, but I don't see anything wrong with mules—they know their own minds and know what they want. So what could be wrong with that?"

Francis calmly said, "You already know the answer to that question. I'll leave you to reconsider the defeating justifications your mind is entertaining."

As we were driving home with the new intruder, Deardra named her Maggie. Maggie was lying down on the front seat.

Deardra was somewhat happier, at least more than she had been since Waldo became sick. And because of her being happier, I felt better too, but still apprehensive about this new puppy idea.

When we got home, Deardra put Maggie on the ground to wee. I jumped on her, wanting to play, and knocked her down. Deardra shouted at me, "No, Russell! Bad dog!" I put my head down, pouting, as I went up the stairs to the front door. It was going to be a long, difficult road. If only Waldo hadn't died, my life would have been so much better.

After we got inside the house, I tried to settle down, if that was even possible with some strange, stinky new puppy. She was smelling all my toys, my food bowl, and Waldo's stuff, and then she took a wee on the carpet. As Deardra cleaned up the mess, I thought, "See that? Let's take her back."

Later, Deardra sat down next to me. "Maggie is a little puppy," she explained. "You're much bigger, so you can't jump on her. You could hurt her. If you want to play, you have to be gentle."

Ha! I didn't even want her here. Deardra just didn't understand. If I couldn't jump on her, play, and do some wrestling, then what good was it to have a puppy friend? That meant she'd only eat, drink, sleep, wee, and poop! What kind of a friend was that? Just taking up space and boring—that's what kind!

About a week later, Maggie showed some improvement due to my guidance. She didn't know anything, so I was the one who had to teach her about being a good dog. It's something I'd been at for almost two years, which was another reason I was the natural choice for being in charge.

It didn't take long to figure out Maggie and I were opposites. I wanted to chase spots—she wasn't interested. I liked to attack empty boxes and play with the ball—she didn't care about either one. I liked to play tug-of-war, and she didn't get it. Sometimes she would do a little wrestling, but I would have to hold back, or Deardra would scold me for being too rough. I started to think my name was "No, Russell" or "No, Puppa."

It was sort of nice to have some company. It was a bit of a distraction to take my mind off Waldo, but I still missed him every day. He liked to play with the green bone, and Ms. Boring didn't even *like* my green bone.

After a while, Deardra started calling Maggie other names: Maggie Pie, then Mag Pie, then sometimes only Pie. Imagine. A dog called Pie? What next? Was I going to be called Dumpling?

A few weeks later I jumped on Maggie and broke one of her front legs. Dr. Les said it was a stress fracture, and Maggie had to stay quiet for weeks so her leg could heal. I was in more trouble than I'd ever been in my whole life. My name became "*bad dog*" if I went anywhere near Maggie. Maggie's smugness grew with all the doting sympathy she got from Deardra, and she completely ignored me for my sin of breaking her leg. She even called me a dummy when I hit her in the head with my green bone. I thought that Maggie would probably continue to get all the attention, and I would just be Puppa the mule in the background. My anxiety-causing thoughts were mounting again.

"It would be appropriate for you to apologize to Maggie for breaking her leg," Josephine said.

I didn't want to hear that. "What's the big deal? I was just playing. It's not my fault. I didn't break her leg on purpose. She probably put her leg in a weird position so that I'd break it, and then she could be the victim and make me look bad. I bet that's what happened."

Maggie heard me and snorted.

I fell asleep and dreamed of Waldo. After I woke—

17
Realizations

Setting one's intention brings clarity.
—Francis

Francis had some thoughts about my attitude. "Let's recall when you were Pete during the period after the army and how you consistently looked at the negative in most every situation. You would get revved up on negative energy, spreading that energy to anyone who would listen. Your dark thoughts could lower the vibration in a room full of others. You suppressed the guidance you received of how your fear-based thoughts defeated you. The negative energy you created was to fill the void of unhappiness you constructed. Do you recall ever considering how harmful it was to yourself or others?"

"I'm seeing those memories unfold." I watched numerous instances of how I was in a state of fear most of the time. I realized it was parallel to the same energy pattern I expressed in this lifetime.

Josephine asked, "Is that a trait you want to continue to bring forward, or would you prefer to rise above it, in this moment and moments to come?"

"I guess I'd like to rise above the state of fear now. But if that's how I'm wired, won't it be hard to get beyond it?"

With a loving softness, the response came as if on a warm breeze, which highlighted the importance of the next question. Francis asked, "What is your *intention*?

I pondered that. "I'm not sure. I guess to be happy, though it's difficult for me to be positive, whereas negativity seems to come easily. Most of the time, I'm scared."

"Wiring, as you call it, still presents a choice, and that choice contains an opportunity to examine the original cause. Many of the dominant traits you are here to overcome are being revealed to you."

Just then a memory appeared. I observed part of the plan I had designed against the advice of my Spirit Guides. The brief scene gave me some insight into the emotional turmoil I was living.

Francis continued. "As you just witnessed, the difficulty of your choice caused it to be discouraged. And there are more self-imposed complications yet to come. Know that there is another reason, a vitally important reason, that you can't recall at this point why you selected this incarnation as Russell the dog. The time has not come for you to recognize this reason, but it will."

Francis always sounded so peaceful, lacking any judgment. Even so, I felt panicked at the thought of more complications. This sounded to me like more painful problems. "I'm just tired of suffering. Show me what to do; then I'll try to do it."

Josephine answered, "Live to love. Love being alive. To live in a physical body is a constant, ever-changing adjustment for any soul that comes into the temporary beingness of flesh.

Each soul chooses the type of container to be its vehicle. It could be human being, animal being, plant being, other-world being. All forms are perfectly chosen to serve each soul's evolution. And all are expressions of Infinite Source. Openness and compassion for yourself will help you understand the lessons you made a commitment to embrace. Everything presented is an opportunity to increase your awareness in order to rise above your dominant traits."

Some of what I heard seemed vaguely familiar. There was a pause so that I could contemplate, and then she continued.

"When in the physical, many souls have this question: what is my life purpose? The answer is that there are usually two or more life purposes, depending on the soul's agenda. The first purpose is the soul's reason for coming into the physical. The second purpose is anything having to do with the survival of the body—how one goes about meeting physical needs, such as, food, shelter, and warmth. Another part of physical survival involves, emotional security, identity, creative expression, and so on."

"Well, my physical survival as a dog is in Deardra's hands. So how do I figure out my soul's purpose?"

Francis spoke this time. "Well, you know your primary purpose this time is to review your past life as Pete. To know the other reasons of why you are here, examine your weaknesses and strengths. These produce your personality, creating your *personal reality*. Use your strengths to overcome your weaknesses in order to help achieve your highest and greatest good. This reveals a big part of your soul's purpose. Strengths also show the direction a soul has chosen to travel. Everything evolves according to each soul's spiritual objective with limitless, distinctive variations of designed destinies."

"So what's my other life purpose? To overcome stubbornness and fear-driven denial? Or is it to be the first split *personal-reality* dog? Sorry I couldn't resist a little humor."

Josephine answered, "We in spirit appreciate the joy of humor." I sensed they were both amused. She continued. "The opportunities for enlightened growth of your incarnation as Pete are and were overcoming the tenacious traits of negativity and addiction to easy money, expressed as gambling, alcohol, neglect, and anger. You can add stubbornness, fear, and denial. Many of the latter characteristics have presented again in your current life as Russell the dog."

"With each passing day, I have become more and more aware of my flaws," I said. It was almost a relief to recognize my faults.

Josephine continued without judgment. "As Pete, lessons were ignored that would have helped you transform the painful things inside your head and heart," she said. "Those lessons could have served you. As a defense, you developed a high degree of denial to maintain a level of numbness in order not to change. You avoided or rejected the direction your Spirit Guides offered you to change yourself from the inside, and that rejection reverberated on every level, including the unhappiness in your physical life."

I observed multiple scenes of my judgmental words and actions overtaking my mind at a slower, more-detailed pace. Only this time I experienced the negative emotional reactions of the others connected to me. I observed every instance as if it were taking place in the present because it was. I relived every moment again as if time traveling.

"Observing scene after scene, what do you see?" Josephine asked.

"I see myself as Pete pushing my harsh, judgmental ideas on others. I was expecting my views to be accepted as fact instead of as my opinions. I often lacked compassion for those closest to me but easily expressed compassion to homeless strangers. My pattern shows the destructiveness of unforgivingness and the need to constantly judge others and myself. I fed the negative identity that I had become a container for. I used blame as a tool to avoid deeply examining my own actions, which caused many disappointing outcomes brought about by my own decisions." It was agony to observe and then feel emotions that I caused in others. It was, however, incredibly instructive.

Instantly, my ego moved in with a defensive stance. "It's clear to me now, but it wasn't then. I wish I could go back and change it, but I can't," I said.

Francis weighed in. "By reviewing your thoughts, emotions, and actions as Pete, you are expanding your awareness to perhaps not repeat the same patterns."

"I constantly tried to survive the endless suffering that ate me up as Pete. But here I am, reliving it all again. It's no wonder I refused to have my life review. And the worst part is yet to come? You said my life as Pete ended violently. When am I going to relive that nightmare?"

"Almost every soul that comes into the physical has varying degrees of pain to overcome," said Francis. "Even the ones who appear to have everything still experience pain. Pain is a powerful teacher. This knowledge hopefully makes it easier to apply the power of compassion and for you to bring awareness to your thoughts that lead to actions. Perhaps a good place to begin now would be for you to sincerely ask Maggie to forgive you for breaking her leg."

"I've tried, Francis, but honestly I don't feel sorry. I was just playing. It was an accident."

"In this case, it is the end result and not the intention that matters most. Was her leg broken because of your actions?"

"Yes."

"Is the real issue that you are jealous of Maggie, thus disliking her?"

"Probably. Well, OK, yes. I need to work on it, but I don't know how. Those feelings are gripping me like a fist. I want to feel genuinely sorry, along with not being envious of her, but I'm just not there yet."

Josephine asked, "May I suggest an affirmative prayer? Recite it whenever you think of Maggie or the situation with Maggie."

"OK. What is it?" I was tired of the subject.

Josephine gently spoke the words as Francis joined in.

"Forgive me—I am sorry for any harm I caused.

I release you and myself from further animosity.

We are each filled with the serenity of forgiveness.

We are whole, happy, and healthy.

And so it shall be."

After I heard the fluid sound of the prayer, I made a promise: "I will try reciting it with the hope it helps."

"So be it," said Francis. "You are acknowledged for making an effort to embrace higher levels of awareness. Do you remember why you chose to have your life review as a dog being?"

"You said before because dogs feel more from a different perspective?" It was a fact I was experiencing firsthand.

"Yes, but it was also because you couldn't bear to review all the thoughts, beliefs, and actions that led to your death.

Your life as Pete was left unresolved. Do you remember how your lifetime as Pete ended?"

"No, it's a foggy void. I can't seem to remember. Why is that?" I could feel horror rise, shaking me to my core.

"Because your lifetime as Pete ended violently, your soul was not ready at the time to review it. May we remind you—you are one of the exceptions of how you are experiencing your life review. Normally, a life review takes place soon after the soul leaves the physical. Most souls have an agreed-upon agenda in body and out of body. This is decided on a soul-by-soul basis depending on the circumstances and related choices of a particular lifetime. Because each soul has accountability with itself, the conclusions can be painful."

"When will I be ready to review my life ending as Pete? And when will I know the other reasons you mentioned for my being here?" A sinking, panicked sensation clutched my stomach.

Josephine gently responded. "All happens in Divine timing according to what your consciousness is ready to embrace. When Francis and I return, we shall explore how the egoic personality influences choices. It is the repercussions of actions that enhance the education of the soul. Hold in your heart the knowledge that you are safe, watched over, and loved. Rest now. A great deal of learning remains ahead."

I moved from my trance dream state to fully awake. After Francis and Josephine left, I considered what was yet to come. I worried if I could handle it. Then I considered what Josephine said about transforming pain into purpose, and I wondered how I could do that. My exhaustion made it hard for me to think. I needed a break to sort through everything I had witnessed and felt.

I heard Deardra and Pie playing in the sunroom. I moped down the hall from the bedroom to join them. I jumped on the couch and lay down next to Deardra, putting my head on her leg. Normally we weren't allowed on the couches, but she made an exception when she sensed our need for extra love. Deardra stroked my head and said she loved me. The warmth of the sunbeams filling the room help me relax. I was dog-tired and fell into the sweet escape of a peaceful nap.

18

The Snake in Paradise Is a Cat

Expect the unexpected.
—Maggie Pie

A few days later I was lazily napping in the kitchen, dreaming of chasing chipmunks with Waldo. Abruptly I woke to the loud squawking of crows and magpies. At the same time I smelled a strong, pungent odor. Maggie was frantically barking as loud as she could. In a flash I was out the dog door to see what the emergency was. It was a mountain lion! She stood on a nearby boulder just outside the yard, not far from the fence. Swishing her tail, she glared at us like we were her disobedient dinner.

The intensity of our barking screamed danger. We were trying to alert Deardra and also hoping to scare off the menace. The whole of my body was shaking so much that I could hardly stand. "Get away, you feline murderer!" I boldly choked out.

She stared at us with her intelligent, icy, golden eyes. If she was slightly fazed by our display of fierceness, she hid it well.

Maggie and I stood our ground, trembling, barking, giving our best effort to protect ourselves and Deardra, who was unaware of the extreme danger we were facing. She was inside cleaning while she listened to loud music. I knew it was definitely a mountain lion from my experience watching television, which Deardra found funny.

A mountain lion is a highly tuned predatory animal—a stealthy killer. This one was in a heightened state of survival instinct and let us know she had a cub to feed. She spoke to us in a whispered hiss. "It's nothing personal, but I am the superior species with a greater right to live. You're only domestics with no value in supporting the balance of nature. Plus, you pitifully lack sharpened instincts for survival. To be more specific, you have no *real* purpose, so you would be no loss and my easy meal."

We had heard from the neighborhood dogs that a big female was on the prowl and already had killed a medium-sized dog that lived up the road. Deardra also heard the story and told us to run inside if we ever saw a mountain lion. She didn't understand how instinctively every cell of our beings demanded protection of ourselves, our loved ones, and our territory.

We continued frantically barking, as loud as we could, telling her to get away—to find food somewhere else. "You can't take us both. Together we'll take you down or wound you so badly your cub will starve. Leave now!" Our threats weren't working since our strong smell of fear gave us away.

She moved closer, and then I noticed a black mark on the right side of her face. Terror struck my very core. I remembered my past lives and the warning my mother, Tess, had given me about the dark soul that would hunt me.

The murderous cat's tail rapidly swished back and forth as she carefully watched every move I made. She casually said, "I'll take you both. One I'll eat now, and the other I'll wound and eat later. Might as well make it easy for us all. Give up now. Play dead, and then be dead." Amused with her last statement, she stared directly at me, ready to pounce.

At that moment, Deardra began calling us from the deck at the front of the house that wrapped around into the yard. The She Cat bounded off the boulder and disappeared through the trees. We ran to the deck and into the safety of the house.

As we were running toward the house, we heard the She Cat say, "I will eat you domestics another day, and your pet mother too."

Once inside the house, Deardra asked us to sit. "Stop barking so much! Why are you both shaking?" We moved to the sunroom, where she began petting us and sweetly kissed the top of our heads. She sang one of the songs she liked to make up, mostly about us being furry and sweet. Maggie and I slowly stopped shaking as she finished her songs; afterward we each received a few treats. With the day ending, as darkness moved in, the terror of this new menace dominated our thoughts. Our world became tainted with panic. Remembering the black mark on the She Cat's face made me feel I was falling into a dark, bottomless hole. No longer were any of us safe. And it was because of me. I had brought this dangerous murderer here.

I told Francis and Josephine I would be courageous, but things seemed crazier every day. Now a mountain lion with a black mark! How did this fit into the plan of why I was here? I put the question out and received no response.

I had other problems too. Maggie Pie was getting bigger almost by the day. If this kept up, she would be bigger than me in no time!

Deardra doesn't like that I'm always jumping on Pie. She constantly tells me to stop beating Maggie up. Then she often comments, "One day, Puppa, Mag Pie might be bigger than you; then she'll start beating you up. That's how karma works."

I couldn't allow Pie to become the boss or imagine that nightmare. However, the possibility was looming, so I decided if she does get bigger than me, I'll just have to be tougher. Deardra won't like that, but I must always be the boss.

"You have much to *relearn* about living under the control of your ego," Francis said. "Currently, your mind is occupied with the defeating energy of fear, which clouds your thinking. Start with the intention of what you want to happen and then think of ways to create that outcome. A clue for a starting point is to rise above your ego's need to control another. As an example, Maggie becomes bigger and then moves for dominance. If, you begin now, you can establish a respectful relationship by *sincerely* asking her to forgive you for breaking her leg. The outcome could be vastly different from what you fear, even desirable."

"Not likely," I said with a snort. "I have apologized, and she just calls me a dummy."

Josephine was as tender as always. "Your apology was not sincere; it should be heartfelt. You can accomplish this by rising above the jealous, negative emotions your ego harbors. Many months have passed since you broke her leg, causing resentment to build in Maggie by your lack of a timely apology. Do you perceive yourself as being resistant to the unchangeable truth, which is that you broke her leg?"

"I suppose I am."

"Here are two easy questions. What does resistance produce? And what does stubbornness cause?" Josephine asked them as if they were part of a pop quiz.

I answered with a slightly insulted tone. "I already know this. Resistance causes suffering—and stubbornness means to be stuck. I don't want to be stuck or cause any more pain for anyone, especially me. I've had enough suffering lately."

Josephine praised me. "Very good. You *know* the answers, but knowing is not *doing*. What will you *do* to move your knowledge from thought into action?"

"I'm not sure," I answered, my mind going to more pressing things. "And what about the She Cat? She has the black mark." I began to shake just thinking about her.

"She has her own agenda as a mountain lion, with the added purpose to impose revenge upon you," Francis said casually.

I couldn't believe what I was hearing. "What? You aren't concerned? On top of the intensity of my life review, a vindictive mountain lion who wants to eat me has been added to complicate the whole thing. And you don't care? What about Maggie? Does the She Cat's revenge include Pie, or am I just the lucky one?"

"Everything is happening exactly as it should," Francis stated, with almost a bored tone.

"Is this a sick joke you two are playing on me?" New heights of panic gripped me. "What are you talking about? That gigantic, overgrown cat is a killer! And why don't you care? She wants to kill us—well, OK—mostly me. Won't that put a crimp in my life review plan?"

Francis and Josephine were still unfazed, even casual. Francis said, "Perhaps a positive affirmation will help. When you feel scared, resistant, or negative, repeat this phrase: I have a constant flow of peace and guidance and the understanding to go in the house when there is danger. And so it is.

Repeat that while focusing on your breath."

"OK, *you* have a constant flow of peace and understanding, and so it is." Considering my terrified state, I was amazed at my attempt to be clever.

Josephine added, "Humor is important. I'm glad to see you haven't lost your sense of it. You were quite the class clown when you were Pete."

"What about the killer She Cat?" Now I was begging for some concern.

Francis said, "Remain alert. Next time ignore her by going inside the house, and Maggie will follow."

I was shocked at the indifference. I felt abandoned. "You don't care if I get eaten?" I asked with a whimper.

"Again, all is happening as it should," Francis repeated. "You have choices. Everything is a cause-and-effect relationship, with opportunities to demonstrate what you have learned."

I couldn't handle anymore. I felt defeated—I sighed, exhaustion taking over. "I'm very tired. I'll try the affirmation, but at this point, I can't think." The energy shifted, the encounter was over, but I knew the conversation wasn't. My mind was racing as I tried to fall asleep. My emotions were raw. Maybe I should apologize to Pie? I wished I could run away, but I had nowhere to go. I was sure I had entered a level of hell where no one was going to care if I got eaten by the She Cat.

19
Surprise Love Encounters

In this life I have met many kindred spirits, but only one soul mate.
—Deardra

On a warm Saturday in early May, Deardra led Maggie and me into the bedroom. As she closed the door, she told us—but mostly me—to be nice. We knew this meant someone new was coming to the house. It's no secret that I still didn't like little boys, especially on bikes. I often didn't like men either because, the way I see it, many are just little boys in grown-up bodies.

Pie likes everybody except me. And for sure, she likes anyone who pets her or makes a big fuss over how beautiful she is. She is a beautiful dog, but beauty on the outside doesn't mean beauty on the inside. I'm the one who has to live with her biting my head. Plus, she gets bossier every day.

We heard the front door open, followed by the sound of a man's voice coming up the stairs. Of course we started barking from the bedroom. After all, it was our job to protect Deardra and our house.

I heard her apologetically say, "He barks at everyone, I know I mentioned this on the phone, but when I bring him out, it's best to stand still and let him approach you. He'll bark at you, act very skittish, bark some more, and then ignore you for a while and maybe bark at you now and then."

Next, we heard Deardra walking down the hall. Slowly opening the door, she looked directly at me and said, "Be nice. No barking."

I pushed past her, and Pie followed. We ran down the hall, with Deardra quickly catching up. I came around the corner, and there he was, standing in the sunroom with a big bright smile. An odd feeling came over me—I didn't want to bark. I walked up to him as he slightly extended his hand. I sniffed his fingers and sat down. I looked up at him as if he were a long-lost friend. This had never happened to me before.

He laughed and said to Deardra, "He seems OK to me. I was expecting a mean junkyard dog. He looks like a red teddy bear, just like you described."

Deardra was stunned! She said she couldn't believe my docile behavior. "I've never seen him respond that way to anyone," she added. With a mischievous look, she laughed and asked, "Do you have a pork chop in your pocket?"

He also laughed. "No, and I will defer to being a gentleman by not answering that question with what I could say."

She blushed as they both laughed.

I was also confused. I couldn't put my paw on why I liked him. It made no sense. He smelled like cats, yet I still didn't want to bark at him—at all.

His name was Heath. I felt I knew him—that in some distant way, we knew each other. Not as we were here, in this moment, but sometime before, or maybe a time to come. The feeling wasn't as strong as when I first met Deardra, but I felt it just the same. Whatever the connection was, I couldn't grasp it.

I heard Josephine say, "Perhaps the details don't matter."

I felt all was well, with a sense of completeness. So I enthusiastically brought him my green bone. He accepted it and then threw it for me to retrieve. We were off to a good start; he liked my green bone.

Heath paid lots of attention to me and Pie while Deardra cooked dinner. Pie was always pushing her big self in front of me so she could be closer to get more pets. He tried to give us equal amounts of affection, but I knew he felt as drawn to me as I was to him.

Deardra's eyes lit up when she looked at Heath. His bright smile and blue eyes warmed the whole room as he gazed at Deardra. They talked, laughed, ate dinner, listened to music, and essentially ignored us. But I didn't mind because, somehow, I knew he was the one Deardra had been waiting for.

Our first date with Heath went well. Later that evening, after Heath had gone home, I found myself wishing he would stay with us always. And Pie did too.

20

Everything Is Constantly Changing—Best to Pay Attention

Transition requires a flexible mind.
—Josephine

Now Maggie Pie is officially bigger than me, making my life miserable when she's awake. The big galoot bites my head, beats me up, and won't let me off the deck into the yard so I can wee or poop. If Deardra knew, she wouldn't let it go on, but when she leaves, Pie becomes the self-appointed bully in charge.

Ms. Long Memory Maggie Pie can't get beyond the broken leg thing, along with how I used to beat her up when she was a puppy. Her broken leg was an accident; the beating-up stuff was playing. I've apologized many times. She just glares at me and always calls me a dummy. I've tried the "heartfelt apology" Francis and Josephine talked about, but Pie and I both know I don't mean it. It's difficult to be sincerely sorry when I believe that I was just playing and wasn't trying to hurt her.

Francis was clear. "Denial is an obstacle that brings forth a test to solve the resulting challenges. The source of denial is based in the ego. A lesson takes as long as you decide it will take. But be aware, the longer the duration of a lesson, the more the complications that may occur."

"I guess I am a mule. Deardra says stubbornness and bad decisions usually go together. I'll try harder, Francis, but denial is easy. It temporarily keeps me numb. I'm overwhelmed most of the time just being a dog. Then when I remember the other things I'm supposed to accomplish—well, it really shakes me up."

I sighed, pausing. After I collected my thoughts, I continued. "I don't like it when Deardra says that Maggie is sweet as pie and then follows that with a statement about Russell being puppafied. She calls me 'Puppa' more than 'Russell.' I don't know if I like it—being called Puppa. She does say it lovingly, with a sweet-sounding giggle. The nickname Puppa seems to bring her joy, so I guess I'm OK with it."

"To take things in the spirit in which they are meant brings clarity, keeping the mind aligned with what is accurate," Francis said. "A negative attitude leads to more layers of potential complication, which can distort the original lesson."

The whole subject made me irritable. "I'm working on it, Francis."

I was ready for a nap, but Ms. Meany Maggie chased me off my favorite spot on the deck. So instead, I slept under one of my favorite trees in the yard.

Deardra was spending more time with Heath, making her happier than before he came. Sometimes she would drive away and come home hours later with the scent of Heath and his cats all over her. I wondered what they were doing. Rolling all over each other? Then Heath started spending more time at our house. He liked the serenity of the mountains and was falling in love with Deardra, as she was with him.

"My mom thought I'd end up in the mountains," he said with a smile one evening as he and Deardra sat on the deck swing.

"Your mom's an intuitive lady. I look forward to meeting her someday." She smiled with a deep sense about the direction things were going with Heath. I could sense her heart expanding with love.

Josephine began to tell me about Heath's mom. "Lillian is remarkable. This is true of both his parents. Together they chose to bring five souls into the physical, and they encountered extreme challenges, especially for Lillian. Heath's father, Joseph, had an easy sense of humor, was kind, and tried not to offend anyone. He was liked by most everyone. However, his life in the physical was quick, ending when he was thirty-six. Lillian, who was twenty-nine, was left to raise their five children—four boys and one girl. The youngest boy and girl were twins. All were under the age of ten. This was a daunting mission for a young widow in 1959, but it actually would have been challenging in any three-dimensional time frame. Her spirit was determined to persevere, so she did her best to navigate a very complicated path. Later, she became involved with a man who drank too much, and they had a daughter together. She never again found a love close to the depth she and Joseph shared. He was the love of her life and many lifetimes before. As the years passed, her heart continued to yearn for him. What gave her comfort was an unwavering awareness that they would be together again."

Immediately I felt sad for Heath. "Why did it happen that way?"

Josephine was clear. "It is easy to question the spiritual path chosen by a soul, and it is sometimes difficult to accept the sacred contract each soul designs with Infinite Source. Remember, the soul is not harmed by what takes place in the physical; it is only enhanced by the immense growth that is attained."

Deardra and Heath started to kiss. Even though I had deep feelings for Heath, jealousy set in. Deardra didn't pay as much attention to us when Heath was around. I further allowed negativity to take over my mind. What if Heath moved in and lived here? Then what? Would we get any affection at all? What about his cats? Would they live here too? I draw the line at cats living with me and Pie. And he'd probably get our portion of Deardra's food that she adds to our dry dog food. This would be the same as him eating *our* food. My anxiety grew with each fearful thought.

Deardra seemed to read my mind. She came over to where I was lying and began to pet me with reassurance that radiated from her heart center through her hands. After a while she moved to Pie, showering her with the same loving affection. It was important to her that everything was equal for us pups. We appreciated her efforts, as we did keep track and felt bad or slighted if one received something the other didn't.

As she was petting Maggie, a wonderful thing happened. Heath came directly over to me and scratched my head with genuine love. I sensed he had some awareness of our having been together before. In that moment, I knew I no longer needed to be jealous. I slowly drifted into a deep, satisfying slumber, aware that many changes were to come, but I was at peace with the idea.

After about a month, Heath started staying all night when he came to see us. Unfortunately, he made some big changes that Pie, and I didn't like. We had always slept on the bed with Deardra, but that didn't leave enough room for Heath, especially because Pie was such a big galoot. Heath came back with big cushy dog beds meant for sleeping on the floor. Not good! Really? Now he's treating us like we're dogs. Of course, we are dogs, but that doesn't mean we have to be treated as such. We've heard about how some dogs live, and it's not how we want to live.

Well, Maggie and I didn't like the change. I thought that maybe he should sleep on the dog beds and we should continue to sleep on the bed. After all, we were here first. Pie agreed, but we knew that wasn't something Deardra would consider. After a few nights, I did get used to my dog bed since it was cushy, soft, and nice to sleep on. But Pie wasn't having it. In protest, she tried to sleep under the bed. This didn't work because of her size. She'd get stuck. Then Heath and Deardra would have to pull her out. After that, she slept on the floor next to her giant-sized dog bed because she was even too big for that. After Pie made it plain, she wasn't going to use the dog bed, Heath eventually took it away, making Pie an official floor sleeper. This made her even more moody, so of course, she took it out on me. She continued to resent not being able to sleep on the bed and grumbled about it. She didn't want to be treated like a common dog instead of a special girl. However, I didn't mind. I had a soft, comfortable bed of my own to sleep on near Deardra and Heath, who were falling deeper in love each day.

21

Edmond

The karmic wheel is always turning.
—Francis

A ten-minute walk down the road from our house was a beautiful place with water. Deardra and Heath packed a picnic lunch, which included treats for us, and off we went for a long hike in the woods. For Maggie and me, it was our number one favorite place to go, with so many new smells, animal beings to chase, and water to wade in.

After an exciting day, we got home late in the afternoon, tired from running, playing, small-animal chasing, and other fun things. Pie got in trouble on the hike for disappearing. For once I wasn't the bad dog, so I gave her one of the disgusted crusty looks she liked to give me when I got in trouble. She didn't like it, saying I shouldn't look at her or she'd bite my head.

I looked away and then said, "Ms. Touchy can dish it out, but she can't take it." Then she bit my head. It was just another day in my life with the head-biting bully, known as Maggie Pie. No wonder I have a hard time sincerely apologizing; she's always mean to me.

By the end of the day, I was more than ready to settle on my soft dog bed, which smelled especially good because it smelled like me. As I was falling asleep, a memory scene began to form with crystal clear clarity. I thought it was one of Pete's memories vividly unfolding, but to my surprise it wasn't. I was experiencing, and at the same time witnessing, the lifetime right before I was Pete.

"Watch for repeating traits," Francis said.

It was March 1887. I was seventeen years old with a headful of dreams, hell-bent on finding gold. I intended to find my way to Colorado and strike it rich.

I was born in Pittsburgh, Pennsylvania, to a family of seven kids. I was the fifth child. My father was a dreamer who worked in a mill twelve to fourteen hours a day for six, sometimes seven, days a week. It was a punishing, harsh life with few pleasures.

My mother was overwhelmed by having so many kids, so she took to nipping at a gin bottle here and there, trying to hide it without success. Still she was a kind woman with a feisty streak, as my father would say.

Both my parents were immigrants. My mother was Scottish. My father Irish. He was a sailor who found himself in Scotland. He fell in love with a "real beauty" who would later be my mother. They married with the hopes of making a life in America. It was 1860 when they left Ireland on a ship with their first three children. I was born here, in America. My name, Edmond O'Dell.

My father loved stories of buried treasure and gold mining. The possibility of the instant riches that came with such a find intoxicated him. He had often dreamed of someday finding treasure that would transform our lives to living in grand style. Then he'd be what he always wanted to be: the hero.

I reveled in hearing him tell the tales of treasure hunting. But my favorites were about mining. Stories of "hitting it big" were mostly reported from newspapers, but some tales he would read to us from short story books he got from a friend of better means. My mother taught my father to read. She liked to say with pride, "It wasn't a difficult task, due to his good brains, and he knew his letters to start."

All that mattered to me was to go West in search of my share of the gold. I often daydreamed of the day I'd go home, with gold coins falling from my pockets, to provide my family with the comfort of living in grand style. That would prove to my father that I was his best son.

My mother liked to say that we were two peas in a pod because, of all the kids, I looked and acted the most like him. We were both dreamers who shared the same dream—with one big difference. I could chase riches while he was stuck in a life he mostly regretted. Many times he talked to me about the importance of freedom. He encouraged me to strike out on my own. He said that it was my only hope to escape a hellish life of slaving for greedy mill owners who only cared about their own wealth. He believed their never-ending lust for money caused them to lose compassion for those less fortunate. He liked to say that their hearts were made of cold stone, without a care for anyone else. Then, on Sundays, we'd watch the mill owners place a few coins in the collection plate for their cheaply bought piety.

When I finally left home, I barely had enough money to

survive for a few weeks. Even so, I had my mother's brains and my father's dreams of gold, which were now mine.

On the day I left, he hugged me and said, "Go make me proud, son. Make us rich so we can live in fine style. The good Lord is with you, Edmond." His eyes twinkled with the hope I might accomplish our shared dream.

I tried to hold back my tears and said I'd do my best.

"That's all a man can do." Choking up, his eyes filled with tears, and he said it again: "Make me proud, Edmond."

After I bid farewell to my brothers and sisters, I wondered if I'd ever see any of my family again. Deep down, I knew I probably wouldn't.

My mom was sick with grief to see me leave. We said our goodbyes last. "Be your own man, son. Don't live your pa's dreams. Live your own. Gold fever is a sickness, only causing darkness in the end." She blew her nose, wiped her tears, and with a deep breath she hugged me. "I just want to see you again. I don't care if you're as rich as a king or as poor as a church mouse. Come back to me, my son."

I couldn't recall her crying so much, which made it harder for me to hold back my tears, so I quickly got on my horse. As they all said goodbye, I realized how much I loved each one of them. Slowly I rode off, looking over my shoulder. I saw my dad hug my mom to comfort her. Her voice cracked when she yelled, "May God bless you and watch over you, my son." I turned the corner, we lost sight of one another, and my heart broke. Neighbors and friends, I'd known all my life waved and called out their good wishes as I passed. Later that night I cried until I had no more tears, and sleep overtook me.

After a few months of working mostly odd jobs to survive, I met a man named Luke Fitzpatrick. He was living in a small ranching town, a few hundred miles from the Colorado-Kansas border. His hazel green eyes danced with delight when he told his stories of gold and silver strikes. They were strikes that made overnight millionaires of those who had enough grit to work the hard, backbreaking hours required by mining. He was saving up for what he called a "grubstake" to work his gold mining claim when he found it.

He said he almost had enough to take him the rest of the way to the Colorado mountains, where he was sure he'd find his part of the gold. Excitedly, he repeated stories about gold just lying on the ground. He told how a man could just walk along a Colorado mountain stream, finding enough gold by the end of a day to live for weeks, maybe even months.

I had heard the same stories as gold and silver strikes became more common. Part of me felt it was too good to believe, yet part of me supposed the stories of gold would be true for me if I didn't give up.

Luke said he was around thirty-nine, give or take a year or so. I thought he was much older. He wasn't sure of his age because when he was a small boy, the local church burned to the ground with all the birth, death, and baptism records. His parents and two sisters died from diphtheria when he was about four. He was spared and believed it was God's will, but he carried a bitterness for the unfair loss of his family.

A neighboring family that lived outside of town took him in. They didn't know his family, except by sight, and had lost their son to the same sickness. Luke said they were good, God-fearing people. As he grew into a young man, all he wanted was to follow the stories and go West to find gold.

I asked him about silver. He said it was OK, but for him, there was nothing like gold.

I quickly grew attached to Luke, thinking of him as a second father. It helped fill the loneliness I suffered from missing my own family. We jabbered on at night, dreaming how we'd find side-by-side claims so we could watch each other's backs. Lawlessness was a way of life in mining towns, with the lust for gold so strong that men would kill for it. Gold fever was a powerful, irresistible force that consumed many, and it made us no different except that we were honest.

Then the unthinkable happened.

One night, some months after I met Luke, he left camp, deciding he wanted to get drunk. Later he was dragged out of the Kansas saloon, where he'd crossed the wrong sort. I woke before midnight, worried he wasn't back from town, so I decided to look for him. After I searched almost the entire town, I found him badly beaten, laid up in the mud between the livery stable and hotel. I picked his head up, gently resting it in my lap. I called his name as I attempted to revive him. He slowly opened his eyes. When he recognized me, he asked me to take off his left boot. Inside his boot was a dirty rag made into a pouch with the money he'd saved for the dream he wouldn't see. He gasped, barely able to breathe, and said, "They beat me bad, but they was too drunk and stupid to think about robbing me." I put his money pouch in his hand. He clutched the money to his chest as he groaned in pain. His mouth bled as he whispered, "You take it, boy. My time is done." He asked if I could see the bright light coming closer.

I cried like a baby. Luke was all I had in this God-deserted place. Holding his head, I told him I'd ride to the next town to get him a doctor with the money. I desperately pleaded with him not to die. He smiled, his mouth and teeth covered in blood. I could barely hear him say his last words. "You're a good boy. Forget my lies of gold. Don't end up like me, boy, dreaming fools' dreams. I gave up everything—my wife and two little ones—for gold fever. Don't let the fever take you too, boy." He writhed in pain, then closed his eyes, breathing his last breath.

I sobbed when I put my head to his and said my goodbyes. I told him how much I'd miss him and never forget him. I heard voices, so I pulled his body into the livery stable, where I gently placed him on some hay near a horse stall.

Stunned with the shock of how fast everything had changed, I had the impression that the world seemed smaller—I felt smaller. Because it was dangerous to be alone on the streets that time of night, with only the bad sort prowling around, I decided to stay with Luke in the stable. I couldn't sleep. My heart pounded with grief and worry about what I was going to do without Luke.

Right before sunrise, I made my way back to camp, unable to see much through my tears. Exhausted, I fell in a sitting position, then remembered the pouch Luke had given me. I opened it, not expecting to find much. I couldn't believe my eyes when I found he'd saved forty-six dollars! God bless him! I cried more, thanking him and God for the help, but I felt lonelier than I ever imagined possible. I thought of my dad back home and what he might do or say. I imagined he'd say, "Keep going, son. The gold is waiting."

The next morning, I bought some supplies and paid the undertaker three dollars to bury Luke. He wanted to know how I—then two shots fired—folks running, women and kids screaming, men yelling, all running for cover. I decided it was time to leave and jumped on my horse. I yelled at the undertaker to make sure Luke got a good burial, assuring him I'd be back to check on his honesty. No way in hell did I have any intention of ever coming back to that godforsaken place. Kansas wasn't going to see the likes of me again.

On my way to the mountains, I'd never cast my eyes on a sky so blue. From the high places above Denver you could see for miles. When I looked east, I thought I could see Kansas and probably did, according to most folks. Then there were the Rocky Mountains—for me, it was love at first sight. There are few words to describe the beauty of the Rockies; "magnificent" is the one I settled on. The air was dry, with a crispness I found refreshing after having grown up in a humid climate where winter stays a long time.

Eight months after leaving home, I was riding my horse down the main street of Idaho Springs, Colorado. It was a loud, wild town made up mostly of prospectors and miners with their horses, mules, and wagons. Each was kicking up its share of dirt and noise on the dusty main street. It smelled of horse dung, human waste, sweat, and food cooking. Life in a mining town was a mass of slightly ordered, confused chaos. I found my way to a saloon. This is where a man could get the latest news of gold strikes, plus information on the dangers of the area.

I had thirty-nine dollars left of Luke's money, along with two dollars of my own that I had managed to save. I missed my family and Luke, wishing he was there with me.

At the general store I bought more supplies: a bigger tent, food, gold panning equipment, a pack mule—all the essentials a gold miner needed. I prospected for a few days, then staked a claim on Clear Creek. A week or so later, gold panning started to pay off, which allowed me to send some money home.

About a month later a stranger showed up. He acted friendly enough, but there was something about him that made the hair on the back of my neck stand up. There was a strange, dark mark on the right side of his temple that made me very uneasy. He reeked of whiskey, tobacco, and the stink that comes from not bathing for weeks or maybe months.

After a few minutes of small talk, I wanted him gone and asked him to leave. He pulled a gun, declaring I was on *his* claim. A neighboring miner called to me. It surprised the thief. I threw my hot coffee in his face, followed by a few well-placed punches that didn't faze him much. So I pulled my pistol as the final way to convince him to leave. As he walked away, he turned back toward me with a small gun he had hidden. Unfortunately for both of us, I had to shoot him. I checked to see if he was still alive; he wasn't. I'd never killed a man before. I felt sick. It was my intention to never kill anybody, but he had given me no choice. It was him or me. I played the scene over and over in my head. His face haunted me for the rest of my life as Edmond.

I asked Francis and Josephine to stop the memory vision. "Why am I hunted in every lifetime by this seething murderer?"

Josephine answered, "You are pursued by a shadow soul. You will learn why you are hunted by one so darkened with hate. However, it is not yet time for you to know."

Frustration quickly took hold. After a few breaths, I decided to trust Josephine and Francis. Accepting their word, I said nothing.

"Very good," Francis commented. "You are making progress."

"Yes," Josephine agreed. "Trust leads to patience; patience brings wisdom."

I began to experience Edmond's life unfold once again.

Later that same month, I shot a grizzly bear that had ransacked my camp. One snowy afternoon, I watched him in the distance. As he got closer, he picked up speed. Standing on his hind legs, he closed in on me and my dog, Duke. Duke was a large, scraggly stray who had decided to adopt me as his master when I came to town. He was tough, but not tough enough to tangle with a hungry grizzly. When I was finally able to take a shot at the huge bear, I only wounded it. Duke and I tracked it for more than half a day to put it out of its misery but had no luck finding the wounded beast. More snow was moving in, so I headed for town. I had twinges of guilt for not cleanly killing the menace and prayed that the Lord would take it so that it didn't suffer long.

My efforts from gold panning began to pay off, providing me with a tidy amount. When winter came, I rented a room in town at a boarding house a short ride from my claim. I met a pretty brunette girl named Sofie. I wanted to marry her, but her father wanted me to have a house for his girl to live in before he would give his blessing. A year later I bought a small house, and my dream came true. Sofie and I married. Nine months later our baby girl, Beth, was born.

After Beth came, Sofie wanted me to stop chasing gold, suggesting I go to school in Denver to become a lawyer. We had saved some money from the gold I found panning, so we could afford to leave. But for me, it wasn't enough. I wanted to strike it rich.

She passionately said, "Gold is a fool's folly, and I don't want our daughter to grow up in a wild place like Idaho Springs. This is no place for a girl."

I wanted better for my little Beth and Sofie too. Even so, I had gold fever bad. But I didn't want to admit it, so I told Sofie I'd think about leaving while harboring doubts that I would pull it off.

Gold fever is a gambler's sickness—turn one more shovel of dirt, and you can hit it big. But obsession can become bigger than dreams, turning into a sickness. It's a gnawing need. An itch you can't scratch. A greed so deep you think it's seeped into every part of you.

It was May when I promised Sofie that if I didn't hit it big by the following May, we'd leave for Denver. I also agreed to become a lawyer. She said she didn't want us to wait that long, feeling it might be too late. "Too late for what?" I asked.

"I don't know," she answered with a faraway look, as her light brown eyes filled with tears. "Your fever for gold is more important to you than me and Beth." The hurt she felt echoed in her voice.

"That's not true," I protested. "You knew I was a gold miner when you married me. I've made enough and more to get us this far. I've got things to prove as a man, to myself, to you, and to others. If I leave now, it's the same as saying I was wrong all this time to be gold hunting. I owe it to my dad to try my best. And I can't die not knowing if I would have hit it big."

She answered with a soft tone. Her tear-filled eyes looked deeply into mine. "You've already hit it big; you have us. No one will ever love you more." She let out a small gasp. "Wake from your gold fever before it's too late," she said. She began sobbing, and then Beth started crying too.

"I can't take all this crying," I shouted, but it pained me to hurt her. "We'll leave in one year's time and not before." I slammed the door, and headed for the creek. I had work to do if I only had a year.

I felt ashamed I wasn't more tender with Sofie. She deserved my patience, as she truly loved me and I her, but I had things to prove as a man. And besides, a man doesn't let his wife decide his fate. A thought crept in; I was also determining her and Beth's fate. It was a consideration I didn't want to think about, so I quickly pushed it aside.

Although I denied it to myself, she was right; gold fever had taken me. Luke's last words rang in my head. Emotion welled up from my chest into my throat. I decided I needed a drink.

The next scene was extremely painful. It was February, and I was at the Georgetown cemetery lying on the graves of my pregnant Sofie and my three-year-old Beth. I sobbed and cursed God, cursed myself, and prayed for God's forgiveness. I prayed that I'd die. Pulling out my pistol, I held it to my head. I cocked it—then dropped the gun. I screamed out, begging for someone to kill me.

It was influenza that took my Sofie and Beth. But it was really the gold fever that I had allowed to take everything from me—every single thing worth living for. I didn't even know who I was without my dreams of striking it rich. I thought of my mom when she told me to discover and follow my own dreams. It was too late. All I had worth living for was gone—gone because I had made every decision based on my obsession for gold.

I did shoot myself dead in the graveyard that night. I couldn't go on—I couldn't endure the painful memories of my little girl's smile or the sound of her sweet laugh. I remembered her bright green eyes as she looked up at me for the last time. And I grieved for the unborn child I would never see. I felt Sofie's face come to mine and leave a gentle kiss on my lips. I couldn't bear knowing they were in the cold, dark ground because of my choices that had determined their fate. The guilt was unbearable. There was no reason for me to go on when I had nothing to live for. So I had made my choice to end my life as Edmond.

—∞—

As I left the memory, I realized Beth came back to me as Pete's youngest daughter, Annette. The parallel made sense, as Annette never seemed to trust my judgment.

Francis gently spoke. "Soul agreements play out. The highest outcome is when the souls involved embrace the highest frequency of love. This overcomes the slower frequencies of harm."

I cried from the immense pain of reliving Edmond's life.

Then, as I calmed down, I shared what I hoped were meaningful observations.

"I now see I hadn't forgiven myself for how I played out my life as Edmond because deep in my soul I didn't fully embrace the errors as errors. The choices I made caused the repercussions that affected Sofie and my daughter, Beth. The anger, stubbornness, addiction, and self-inflicted death I chose as Edmond bled over into my life as Pete. Again, the repercussions of my actions played out on those around me."

Choked with sorrow, I thought for a while before I continued. "I clearly see as Edmond, and later Pete, that all I ever wanted was for someone to truly love me. So that I could feel I was worth something. I know now that I shouldn't depend on the love received from another—or materialism, desired or achieved—to define my self-worth. Sofie loved me, but it wasn't enough because my ego had to be right. My self-respect was dependent on material wealth rather than the intangible richness I possessed in my life as Edmond. My wealth was being loved and giving love."

Josephine added with kindness, "Yes, you are correct. The ego identity forms the personality, which can stifle all in its path, including love. There are levels of love, such as love felt but not expressed. Or love given but not received. As Edmond, your love for Sofie was felt, but it was not fully expressed due to your ego's craving to be fed with gold. She fully gave you her love, but under your ego's influence you were unable to completely receive it. What you feed, you become, and what you don't overcome becomes your destiny. When a soul chooses to end a lifetime, what is unresolved persists to the next incarnation. Let us observe."

22

Tenacious Traits

When in the school of karma, every incarnation is part of the soul's journey, during which it reveals itself.
—Francis

Instantly, I was Pete again—this time in Germany. Full of beer, I boasted to my army buddies how I was going to strike it rich mining for gold in Colorado. They laughed and tried to discourage my dream with practicalities, such as the low price of gold. They had no vision, so I assured them the price of gold would rise again, and when it did, I'd be ready with my claim. Logic had no effect on my reality. My mind was made up; I was going to get rich mining.

The trait I brought forward from my life as Edmond was unmistakably persistent. The tenacity of the trait repeating again alarmed me in an eerie sort of way. Even in the face of 1950s reality, I still wanted to *strike it rich*. This was another clear example of how much I depended on denial to justify what I was determined to do, whether it made sense or not. My ego still craved both the need to be right and the prospect of easy money.

It was 1953. I had one year left in the army. From the

observer's perspective, I noticed my idealistic dreams built the stage for my hard lessons to play out again. As a starving ego, desperate in my search for something to hang on to, it was the dream of wealth I chose to cling to. I imagined money would fill the empty places inside me that I defensively guarded.

After leaving the army, I tried convincing my dad to move the family from New England to Colorado. I was surprised to see that my dad in this lifetime had been Luke in my last life as Edmond.

I had to marry eighteen-year-old Gretchen, whom I had gotten pregnant after I returned home from the army. The only thing we had in common was that we both had brown hair and brown eyes. She didn't want to marry me, but under the circumstances she had little choice in 1955. And truthfully, I didn't really want to marry her either. She was from a comfortable, upper-middle-class family that had waited on her as if she were a queen. She had never been taught to cook or clean; nor did she want to learn, thinking it was beneath her.

She looked down on my family, which was considered lower-middle-class. The last thing she wanted was to move to Colorado, so far away from her indulgent family. She often commented that my parents were ignorant because my mother only went through the fourth grade before she was put to work in the factory. My father had gone as far as the eighth grade. But to me, her ignorance of kindness was glaring.

My plan as Pete was to move the family to Colorado, graduate from the Colorado School of Mines, make millions mining gold, and after a few years never have to work again.

I often daydreamed of me driving around in a Rolls Royce, doing as I pleased.

I had it all figured out. On the weekends my dad and I would prospect for gold. As soon as the price of gold went up, we'd be ready with a claim we would discover on our weekend trips. It was a pipe dream, a long shot. I had to believe it might come true since it was the only dream I had.

From this new viewpoint, knowing my dad had been Luke, I understood why we were together again. We shared part of the same lesson plan concerning dominant traits yet to be resolved.

In March of 1956, my beautiful baby girl, DeDe, was born. Gretchen had a hard pregnancy for many reasons; the biggest one was that she didn't want the baby. Everyone said that after the baby came, the natural bonding between mother and child would occur, and she would do better—but she didn't. Gretchen barely functioned, not able to take care of our daughter or herself. Thankfully, while I was at work or school, my mother helped to look after the girls.

I pressured Gretchen to go back to work when DeDe was three months old. She resisted, asserting that she wanted to stay home with the baby. But when she was home, all she did was lie on the couch. One day a neighbor caught me in the hallway of the apartment building we lived in. She voiced her concern about DeDe crying for long periods before she would hear Gretchen move around. It broke my heart to think Gretchen was neglecting DeDe or only providing minimal care for her. When I confronted her about her negligence, she said, "It's not that bad." This was one of her favorite denial phrases to minimize her lazy, uncaring behavior.

When DeDe was two years old, we packed up our possessions and moved the family to Colorado. The family consisted of Gretchen, Mom, Dad, two brothers, and a sister.

After the move, Gretchen continued to fall deeper into depression and was barely able to function enough to go to work. She resented working, so when she came home, she would be on the couch or in bed, expecting to be waited on while dictating orders. Usually the only time she would get up was to go to the bathroom. Her irritability was constant, especially with me and DeDe. Sometimes she would hit DeDe for no reason. She also took pleasure in starting trouble with my family, which lived next door. Still, provoking a fight with me seemed to be her favorite pastime, and the fights were typically full of verbally abusive rants. There was little happiness for any of us. Gretchen made sure of that.

In 1960, my second beautiful daughter, Annette, was born. At first, I was disappointed she wasn't a boy. That was mostly because every man is supposed to want a son, and I was no different. But I loved her just the same. I made the mistake of mentioning to Gretchen my initial disappointment. She used this in her arsenal as a club to beat me with, and she never let me forget it.

As DeDe grew, I told her many times, "We're going to be rich and buy a Rolls Royce." She would look at me with her blue eyes and ask, "When are we going to be rich, Daddy?" Even then it was clear to me—I was a man of many words, followed by very few actions to make my unrealistic dreams come true. But it was my escape, my only reason to keep going.

"When me and Grandpa strike it rich gold mining," I replied to her, trying to sound confident. However, my answer contained less belief than I once had because deep inside I didn't think I deserved it. Even so, there was a hunger driving me to prove I was worthy—to show I was right even though deep down I knew I was wrong.

It was easy to see; DeDe didn't believe me. Perhaps because of her young age. Or maybe she could see something I didn't.

―⚬⚬―

Francis asked, "Do you see the repetitive patterns of your ego's tenacious traits?"

It was astounding how clear it was. I felt discouraged as I answered, "Yes, I see it. How can I break an ingrained repetitive pattern that is so strong that it seems to have a life of its own?"

Francis answered, "The light of awareness you shine upon the trait is how your soul can rise above a destructive pattern."

"I assume this came up in my life review as Edmond?"

"It did. In your case, the addiction for easy money and gambling are a few of the characteristics you brought forth to rise above as Pete. As we have stated before, it is each soul that decides the difficulty or ease of a lesson plan, a plan with many tests and occasions to demonstrate whether the soul has truly completed a lesson. This is what has transpired in your case."

"I feel like a slow learner. Can't you make me smarter so that I don't continue replaying the same personality patterns?"

I sensed a lightness come forth from Francis. "A lesson takes as long as it takes, without judgment about the speed of learning or the depth of intelligence. You have more identity complexities than some and far fewer than others."

"You said identity. Is that the same as personality?"

"These are separate sides of the same butterfly. Your chosen identity forms the personality, and the personality temperament shapes the identity. Both are part of the ego's anatomy."

Josephine gently added, "Be confident in your development. You are right where you're supposed to be, or we would be examining different traits. You clearly see what you've brought forward. But do you know why?"

I wanted to get this right. "Is it because my ego-self could not release the idea of money dictating my self-worth? I'm ashamed to say that I also enjoyed the addiction, even to the detriment of myself and the ones I loved. Clearly, my selfishness grew into narcissism, which was used as a tool to empower my addiction."

Francis and Josephine both praised me. "Very good! You are correct!"

Josephine continued. "This is why you did not attain your dream of becoming rich. It would have been an obstacle to your soul's advancement. A great deal of responsibility comes with having material wealth. It can easily corrupt the ego and create new karma or magnify old karma, as happened in your previous life as Octavia. Material wealth is one of the greatest tests of a soul's advancement. Greed easily grows to feed a hungry ego. The ego begs to be contained by the soul and at the same time resists."

I had to ask it: "Why is greed such an overpowering need for some—even when they have the knowledge that greed continues to be the downfall of humanity?"

Francis answered, "There is a collective consciousness for each part of the whole. On the earth plane, each half is known as male and female. Together, the combination of the two brings forth a larger collective consciousness. Each half balances the other half's strengths and weaknesses. The male ego is generally tested on a larger scale, because it is generally more susceptible to the darker side of the ego self, especially greed. Specifically, I'm referring to a certain type of male who finds it difficult to resist slower frequency impulses of the ego.

Yet some females are also challenged by the ego and the intoxication of greed. However, generally speaking, because women bring forth life, they are more likely to have a reverence *for* life. In most cases, a female's nature is more constructive than destructive. Feminine energy is the grounding force for the masculine. Even so, certain types of males resent being held back from the darker side of the ego identity. For this reason, the power of the feminine has been suppressed. However, for humanity to survive, the wisdom of the feminine can no longer be silenced. As you can see, the power of greed is a tenacious trait of the individual and collective consciousness of humanity that must be overcome."

Josephine added, "It has been said that greed is the original sin. The fatal flaw of humanity. Whether a person is entrapped by greed is, however, one of the ultimate tests, as the frequency of greed can lower higher levels of consciousness. It is one of the lowest vibrations of conscious awareness."

I quickly asked, "Is there a lower vibration?" Then I tried to guess: 'Is it hate?'"

Francis answered, "Yes. Hate is based in condemning fear. From condemnation, fear thrives, producing the malignancies of hatred, aggression, prejudice, and killing—all of these feed the desire to destroy. To condemn or fear another for that person's skin color, religious beliefs, or any other trait is a tragic error."

There was a slight pause before Francis began again. "For greed to survive and thrive, it must silence the conscience since it cannot grow in the presence of accountability, compassion, or love. So the ego silences the principals of right and wrong, bringing forth what is known as sociopathic behavior, which basically means acting without conscience. Then the power of destructive domination produces the co-frequency of narcissism. At this point, greed becomes a mental illness, as some Native Americans believed it to be."

Josephine added, "One of the most harmful parts of the progression of greed comes from its insatiable need to survive. At this point, it becomes a parasitic entity, aggressively in search of a host, without boundaries of decency or concern. So ravenous is someone who is infected with greed, they will feed off the labor and suffering of others. Slavery is a tragic example of greed, and how it exploits every *form* of being, including the miraculous life force of this planet. When reverence for life is lost, even the act of killing the planet, including all forms of life, is not enough to dissuade the parasite from its destructive path. It is important to remember that the nature of a parasite is to eventually kill the host."

It seemed an obvious question, but I had to ask, "Why doesn't Infinite Source stop it?"

Francis simply said, "It is the ultimate test of free will—of the ego identity, which is for the benefit of both the individual and collective consciousness. Remember, each action *reveals* the soul's level of awareness. Fundamentally, it is the soul's desire not to create harm, but if the ego acts against that desire, karma can accumulate over many lifetimes. Eventually the soul will prevail, but not until much suffering is caused and received from the actions born of the ego. It is one of the primary reasons humanity has previously destroyed itself five times."

"So this is the sixth try for human beings to get it right?" The thought made me shiver.

Josephine stated, "On planet Earth, in this dimension, yes. That is correct. Presently, the collective consciousness of compassion and higher frequency thought is growing. However, it must increase at a faster rate with more accountability, or there will be a seventh effort for humanity to collectively attempt to advance beyond the tenacious trait of greed."

Josephine lovingly suggested, "Let us shift our attention back to you and the lessons of Pete's soul."

I tried to process what my limited mind could grasp. I was considering everything I had just learned when Francis asked me, "Is there more you would like to add?"

My mind raced to sort through my thoughts. I began with some hesitation. "I've learned that I didn't *have to* be greedily craving gold. It is important to have self-esteem and self-respect, but I had very little of either, and I mistook selfishness for these. I have learned genuine love is giving that is completely free of the expectation of getting. As Pete, it was hard for me to give of myself because I was resistant to rising above my perfectionistic expectations of what others should be or do for me. This allowed my ego identity to be in charge, putting the most importance on what I wanted or what I would get."

Josephine sounded enthusiastic. "Very good! Remember, as Pete you were a good man in many ways—sometimes holding the higher frequencies of charity, empathy, and concern for those less fortunate. Ego-based arrogance created the coldness you expressed as Octavia because of your belief that the wealthy were superior. It was a belief held by her family, who missed the greater responsibility and the many integrity tests that come with the power of material wealth. Consistently, you felt or acted superior to those of a different class, race, or religion. Octavia believed that owning slaves was acceptable while she also professed to be a Christian. Jesus did not teach harm or exploitation of others. His message was compassionate acceptance, leading to charity for all. Then, as Brother Gabriel and Edmond, you were compassionate with those less fortunate. However, as Pete, that did not carry over to those of different skin colors or religions, did it?"

A scene unfolded before me. I watched myself, as Pete, spread venomous hate about anyone who wasn't white or Christian. The hundreds of times I expressed white supremacy beliefs were compressed into a few moments. It was another facet of the same superiority trait I had expressed as Octavia. It was not as severe, but still there. I could see how wrong that was, and I felt a deep shame. My hatred was based on fear. It was the fear of accepting others who were different—others who had values that seemed in conflict with my own. But now, with clarity, I observed that everyone is a soul in a body, here to pursue that soul's unique spiritual evolution. And most importantly, everyone wants to be loved.

Next, I observed myself easily using threats, criticism, and physical abuse—combined with humiliation—in an effort to control the behaviors of my daughters, depressed wife, and immediate family. I extended this at times to anyone I wanted to control or manipulate to get my way. Though this wasn't my behavior a majority of the time, it was expressed enough times to create lingering negative energy.

As I observed, my emotions were extreme embarrassment and shame. Drained from everything I had just relived, sleep called to me.

"You are doing very well," Josephine said with a tone of loving praise. "Do not be a container for shame. Instead, embrace self-forgiveness. The energy of pain is more useful when turned to purpose. Forgive yourself for falling into the frailties made evident through ego tests. These tests come to help you overcome and resolve your tenacious traits. I remind you again—a soul chooses the physical to feel, learn, experience, and then *demonstrate* what it has learned. This is all for the purpose of evolving the soul to higher and more expansive levels. You are in the process of accomplishing that."

An intense emotional aching engulfed my insides. I blurted out, "I'm lost. I don't know how to handle all this. Who or what am I?"

Francis serenely said, "You are an evolving soul, in a body, having a physical experience."

"What about Pete and Octavia, Brother Gabriel, Edmond, and the countless others I've been? And what about me now, Russell the dog? What happens to all of us?"

Francis answered, "Each personality or personal reality is part of your soul. Each incarnation is an instrument for learning, adding to your spiritual evolution. Remember, you are here to demonstrate what you have learned and what you have yet to learn. Trust everything is as it should be. You are progressing well. We shall leave you for a short time so that you may consider and embrace all we have reviewed thus far."

I heard something as my eyes opened. I sat up and noticed it was just Pie, digging a hole at my favorite spot in the yard. Unphased, I lay back down, somewhat soothed to know I was making progress. I was grateful that Francis and Josephine were going to give me a break. I had much to consider. At that moment, I wasn't aware of the horror yet to come.

23

Pie Has Issues

Speak your truth with kindness.
—Heath

I was peacefully sleeping when loud, frantic barking frightened me awake. I shot to my feet. It was Pie playing a trick on me as she barked a few inches from my head. She said she was tired of my *stupors* and demanded to know what was wrong with me.

"What if I had been the She Cat sneaking up on you? She would start eating you before you'd wake up! What's wrong with you, Puppa?" She had started to call me Puppa lately, with a tone of mockery, but it was better than "dummy."

"Relax, Pie! I'm busy with important things you couldn't understand. If the She Cat comes back, I'll be ready." I was so tired from all the pieces and parts of reviewing my life as Pete that I was appreciating my well-deserved nap. I resented being interrupted by a blonde, overgrown, critical, head-biting bully.

Pie quickly turned her head with a look of indignation. "I heard that dummy, Puppa."

Pie shared her point of view with one of her Guides, which for some reason I was able to hear. I knew all beings had Spirit

Guides, but I never thought about Pie having one since she was so mean to me all the time.

"Puppafied Russell has made my life miserable from the beginning. He's a high maintenance, hyperactive, strange excuse for a dog. He gets most of the attention from Deardra because she's constantly having to do damage control due to his erratic, peculiar behavior, which no one can figure out. I love Deardra, and I know I'm supposed to be with her, but Puppa makes it difficult for me to enjoy my life and get the affection I deserve from her. And he's red. I don't like red dogs. They're not as good as white ones. Plus, he broke my leg when I was a little puppy and never sincerely apologized. Do I have resentment toward Puppa? Absolutely! Only a saint wouldn't!"

I defensively chimed in: "It was an accident."

A moment later, I heard her continue on with disgust as she watched me pounce on a huge bug.

"He's constantly aggravating me with his strangeness. Look at him—he's jumping on a beetle as if it's worthy of his attention. When I was a little pup, he would tell me he was going to get the puppy buyers to come and take me away. I was too young to know he had no way of doing that. So I was afraid every time a car went down the road until I realized he made it up just to scare me because he was jealous."

"Maybe I am jealous—because Deardra loves you in a sweeter way than she loves me. She never calls you a mule. Or says 'no' to you several times a day. And on top of it all, you don't like to play. Waldo played all the time until he got sick. All you want to do is be Miss Boring Prissy Princess Pie."

We heard something and stopped to listen—it was just Deardra starting to vacuum.

Maggie Pie went on. "Deardra has to tell you 'no' so much because you're always doing ridiculous or bad-dog things."

I snorted and said, "At least I'm having fun. All you do is try to figure out ways to make me miserable because of the broken leg thing." It felt good to say how I felt, but I wondered what she'd do to me later.

Pie continued to talk to her Guide. "One of the most annoying things he does is pass out, as if he's in some kind of trance. It's dangerous for us all when he's not aware of what's going on around him. It's only a matter of time until the She Cat comes back. He can't do his job as a dog if he's out of it. Deardra and Heath think he's funny and amusing, which only adds to my irritation. I don't get the recognition or attention I deserve because puppafied Russell is so high maintenance."

Then I heard Pie's Guide remind her of the power of compassion, forgiveness, and equality of all souls in the eyes of Infinite Source, no matter the color or other differences that can be used as excuses to justify an attitude of superiority. "Be a container for respectful, kind energy." That was the last part of the message I heard her receive from her Guide. Maggie just glared at me. I heard no more after that, so I settled down in the nice cool dirt for a peaceful nap.

24
Life in the Physical Is a Temporary Status

Life is an amazing, wonderful adventure full of twists and turns, anguish and elation. Navigate it well and know it is as temporary as the sunrise.
—Josephine and Francis

The day started in the usual way. After I woke up, I did my full body rub on the carpet, carefully concentrating on the shaggy red hair on my head and face. I sneezed twice, then looked around to see what everyone was doing.

Deardra and Heath laughed at the way my hair was sticking up. And they said that not one of my hairs was going in the same direction. Then Deardra sang the morning song, with belly scratches to follow.

The day was starting off well except there was an odd feeling—I'm not sure how to describe it—almost as if something was out of place, causing a thick heaviness in the air. Pie felt it too, giving her an uneasy, restless feeling. The morning went on as usual, but the strange feeling lingered. I wondered if Francis and Josephine were lining up a major review for me. I hoped not; I was still reeling from the last one.

Everything else was the same. Heath and Deardra both left for work at the usual time, but that heavy dark energy hung in the air.

From the time they drive away, we begin waiting for their return. Being a dog requires almost constant waiting. After we've waited all day, they finally arrive home. We're so happy to see them, we're barking and jumping around with excitement and we can tell they're happy to see us too. Occasionally, they'll came home preoccupied and barely pay any attention to us. Luckily this doesn't happen very often, but when it does, we feel rejected, disappointed, and unloved.

As the day progressed, the strange aura strengthened, expanding into an ominous feeling of dread. It was a chilly mid-October afternoon just before dusk. It was the time of day when the sun hits the leaves and the pine needles begin to shimmer. Josephine called it "the glistening time." But even the light and breath of the trees seemed veiled with the menacing feeling.

Deardra and Heath were in a hurry when they came home. After quickly feeding us, they went out the back door to the next-door neighbor's house.

The sinking feeling had grown, consuming us in anxiety. Pie had thought it would be gone in the morning, thinking it could be from the elk poop we had eaten on our walk the day before. Sometimes she'd talk nice to me if she felt unsettled or frightened. It was one of the few times she wouldn't call me names or bite my head.

The first thing we heard in the distance was the sound of crows, blue jays, and magpies—all squawking and screeching as they sounded the danger alarm. Squirrels, chipmunks, and all manner of beings quickly scurried to safety. Immediately, we were on all fours sniffing the air for clues. We watched closely as the crows squawked and dove as they flew above the nearing menace. Then, with the swiftness of a lightning flash, we realized what it was we'd been sensing all day.

We smelled her before we could see her. The She Cat was coming! The instant her stench reached our nostrils, we started frantically barking. A few moments later we watched her brazenly run along the edge of our one-lane dirt road. She entered our territory moving with a fast, focused purpose. Then in one quick stride, she leaped on top of the rock outcropping closest to the deck. This was different from the rocks she'd used before; these were closer to the deck on the side with the sliding glass door that went into the sunroom. For a second, the light hit the black mark on the right side of her face, making it stand out, almost spotlighting it. With the sight of that mark, terror shot through me like a hot knife.

She appeared relaxed, but deliberate, as an experienced killer with nothing to fear. She was at the top of the food chain, and by her confident, arrogant aura, she acted like she knew it.

I heard Josephine quickly say, "Run inside Russell so Maggie will follow."

Then Francis urgently said, "Be quick! Go inside the house!"

I was frozen by an instinctual dog need to protect and defend. And I wasn't going to let the She Cat run us out of our territory.

Again, Francis and Josephine strongly urged me to get Maggie and go inside. However, at that point I was paralyzed with fear—afraid to turn my back on the hungry mountain lion.

From her close vantage point, standing on the rock outcropping with her tail twitching, she began toying with us. "I see you domestics are still here. I came to kill my easy meals," she hissed. "Have you been waiting for me? Who should I take first? The red shaggy bigmouth or the blonde, bigger, prissy weakling?" Her tail moved quicker the more her agitation grew. "You are both pathetically weak and present no challenge to me, but I'm hungry and have a cub to feed, so you'll do," she growled.

We used the full spectrum of expression at our disposal with our frantic barking, growling, and body and tail movements. Our reaction included the emanation of our smells, which warned her of our pending attack but also revealed our fear. We warned her. "Get away! With both of us together against you, you don't have a chance! You'll be the one to die, and your cub will starve!"

She seemed amused, then hissed and said, "I think I'll take the red, scraggly loudmouth first."

Her hypnotic yellow eyes drilled into me as her ears flattened. In a flash, she leaped from the rocks, landed on the deck, and attacked me as I tried to fight her off. Growling while she attacked me, she knocked me off my feet, grabbing the back of my neck and the upper part of my head in her mouth. She was much faster, stronger, and more vicious than I could have imagined. I smelled her sickening breath and felt her warm, disgusting slobber. I also smelled blood—it was mine. I tried biting her when she first came on me, but it was impossible to get an angle or a grip. I cried out from the pain and terror of the She Cat tearing me to pieces. I flashed on an image of Savage trying to attack me in The Pit. Everything was going dark, and then a bright light appeared in the far distance. My life was rapidly ending—why hadn't I gone into the house?

At the moment of the attack, Maggie Pie lunged at the She Cat with everything she had. Releasing me, the She Cat turned on Maggie, who was snarling and growling at the much bigger cat monster. With flattened ears, the She Cat growled, then swiped at Pie, connecting—she clawed Pie's chest, causing her to yelp. Maggie showed amazing courage to even consider fighting the She Cat.

In the chaos of the attack, we didn't hear Deardra and Heath come in the back door from the neighbor's house, and neither did the She Cat. Deardra opened the sliding glass door and yelled. At the same time, Heath came toward the She Cat with a fireplace poker and also yelled. It all seemed to happen at once. Stunned for a second, the surprised cat leaped over the side of the deck just as Heath took a swing, barely missing her.

In her panic to get away, the She Cat jumped, missing the rocks she had used earlier, and fell straight down several feet. As she hit the ground, she hurt one of her front paws. Then a most amazing thing happened. A huge elk with a big rack came from behind the rock outcropping and gored the She Cat as she faltered to get her footing. His head down, he continued his attack, pushing and swiping at her with his antlers. Completely taken off guard by the elk's attack, she let out a scream, then turned to swipe at him with her razor-sharp claws. For a split second she looked at him in amazement, and then she took off limping as she ran. At that point she also had a puncture wound from the elk. Even wounded, the She Cat was fast!

I was on my side, my head slightly hanging over the edge of the deck, so I was able to see the amazing site of an elk striking at a mountain lion. The huge elk looked up at me and caught my eye. It was Josephine! With a wink, she bounded off into the trees, chasing the She Cat. Josephine had protected me again—I started to drift.

Everything from start to finish probably happened in a minute or two, but to me it felt like hours.

Heath and Deardra went into action to save us. Deardra was crying and kept repeating "Oh, my God" over and over. They rapidly checked our wounds.

I was slipping in and out of consciousness from the pain. My mind wandered. I recalled Francis talking about the different types of Guides. Josephine was my protection Guide, and Francis was my wisdom Guide, but both were my teaching Guides. I was grateful for them, but the pain was taking my breath away. I wondered why they let this happen.

I kept thinking that I couldn't leave. If I did, I wouldn't be able to complete my purpose for being in this lifetime,

Pie had blood on her head, face, mouth, and chest. She was shaking from the fight of her life, panting heavily while she made an unusual whining whimper. We were all shaking. Heath said that I was bleeding badly. My blood felt cold against my skin. I couldn't move. I was in and out of consciousness, only partially knowing what was going on.

Deardra was crying while examining my wounds and was wanting to call 911. Heath reminded her that 911 was just for people. She said she couldn't think, and we had to get in the car and get to the Vet now. Heath finished checking Pie to see where the blood was coming from, and he said he thought that she wasn't badly hurt. Deardra got the keys, and Heath said, "Let's go."

I was amazed! Maggie Pie tried to save me! She *did* save me! Overcome with emotion, I thanked her.

With a tender concern, she watched me, acknowledging my thanks. She softly said that she would miss me if I were to leave.

With true sincerity, I said, "I'm sorry for breaking your leg, Maggie Pie. I hope you can forgive me."

Looking into my eyes, she said, "I forgive you, Russell." I could tell she was relieved by my apology, and so was I. Shock was overtaking me, I was so cold. Whimpering, I tightly gripped my life as I felt my consciousness slipping away.

All the pain, remorse, fear, and devastation came rushing in at once. My mind shot from thought to thought. I should have been smarter and tougher, but mostly I should have listened to Josephine and Francis and gone inside. Maybe I was a dummy. Maybe I didn't deserve to live and should die. The stabbing pain in my neck, ear, and head took my breath away. It was all too much to handle. As everything faded into black, the distant Light was returning. I thought about how much I would miss Deardra, Heath, and Maggie.

I woke as Heath carried me down the stairs. Then he gently placed me in the back of the car. Deardra helped, and they got Maggie in the front seat. Deardra was crying, and I think Heath was too. Suddenly we were moving fast. Deardra was in the back seat holding me. She pressed a towel tightly against my head and neck wounds. They kept saying, "Hold on, Puppa. You're going to be all right, and you too, Pie. We love you both. Don't leave us, Russell."

I was floating—dreaming I was in a tunnel with a bright light at the end that was coming closer. I was beginning to rise above my body when I caught a glimpse of Waldo.

Francis entered with a loving, compassionate presence that brought me comfort. Softly, he asked, "Do you want to stay?"

It was an opportunity to take the easy way out. Part of me wanted to leave. I wanted to go into the beautiful, peaceful, healing Light off in the distance of my dream. But I knew it wasn't a dream, it was real. I was dying. This was another defining moment that had presented itself, and I needed to make a choice. Even in my unconscious state, the pain was almost unbearable, which was pushing me toward leaving.

In part of my dream state , I wondered if the She Cat's saliva had poisoned me. Her attack had become a part of me, so it was a type of poisoning that would be with me always. Then I thought about Deardra and how she was an important part of the reason for my being in this body. Then I realized that I wanted to finish my life review as Pete.

With an unshakable certainty, I answered Francis: "I want to stay. I haven't accomplished what I came here to do—I'll see it through to the end."

I heard Francis and Josephine at the same time both say, "Excellent."

Josephine lovingly said, "You have come far, my sweet one. And you have further to go, but you are evolving."

I felt encouraged to know I was making progress. But even so, I had to ask: "Why did you let this happen? Why didn't you and Francis stop the She Cat from attacking me?"

Francis explained, "When the She Cat originally appeared, you were advised to go inside, to avoid a fight you could not win. We did not supersede your free will; we honored it. Josephine shared the elk's body to make a lasting impression on the She Cat not to return. It was not your time to go unless you wanted it to be. You would *not* have died unless that was your choice."

It was true. I was given a different way to handle the She Cat, but my stubborn nature had gotten the best of me again. I faded away, losing all awareness.

When I woke, I was heavily drugged and mercifully feeling less pain. Dr. Les had skillfully worked to save my life. In any event, I knew I was going to live because I had already made my choice to stay.

I heard Dr. Les tell Heath and Deardra that a quarter of an inch is what stood between my artery being hit, which would have ended my life. He put a total of fifty-eight stitches in my wounds and said it was a miracle I was still alive.

Dr. Les had a concerned look on his face as he said to Heath and Deardra, "It's rare for a dog to survive a mountain lion attack this severe, but I think he'll recover. The next twenty-four hours will tell. There's a chance the mountain lion will come back. You need to figure out what you'll do if that happens. Let's report this to the Department of Wildlife and see what they suggest."

Because Josephine had chased her off, I thought the She Cat wouldn't come back for me. But what about Pie? Would she come back for Pie, Deardra, or Heath for some kind of twisted revenge?

I heard Heath and Deardra tell Dr. Les that they didn't want to hurt the mountain lion, but they would have done whatever was necessary to save me and Maggie.

I wish they would have killed her! I was terrified that she'd come back. I kept seeing the black mark that my mother warned me about in The Pit and that had appeared in my other incarnations. If the She Cat was dead, then we could all live without the fear of her returning.

Deardra and Heath also told Dr. Les about the elk attacking the She Cat. He acted as if he didn't believe them. "A stressful situation can cause things to appear different than they really are," he said.

Physically, Pie checked out with minimal injuries. She had a cut on the side of her face, a broken tooth, and a gash on her chest below her throat that required ten stiches. Pie was shaking when she told me, "I'm glad the She Cat didn't kill us." She whimpered as Dr. Les finished her stitches.

With amazement, Maggie described to me the elk attacking the She Cat. I sent a thank-you to Josephine. Maggie said she would tell me more later. I had heard Josephine tell the She Cat as she chased her, "Leave now and live. *Never* come back here again!"

It was hard for me to accept, but I understood it was my free will and stubbornness that had allowed the She Cat to harm me and Maggie. I was grateful to have Francis and Josephine to watch over me and continue to protect and guide me. It was all so that I could accomplish my reason for being here as Russell the dog. In spite of all I had suffered on this journey, I knew that I was watched over and loved.

Together, we all cried at Dr. Les's office. Maggie and I mostly cried on the inside, coupled with high-pitched whimpering and whining. Deardra and Heath held each other and released many tears. But the crying was more than a release; it was also a deep grieving of near death and the knowledge that nothing was going to be the same in the House of Stone and Light or in our peaceful world of trees, birds, and other animal beings.

I stayed at Dr. Les's animal hospital overnight. While I was there, I kept wondering why I hadn't been stronger or smarter. Why didn't I listen to Francis and Josephine and run in the house when the She Cat first appeared? I constantly replayed the attack in my mind and tried to make sense of it. Awake or asleep, the She Cat's face with the black mark was there, stuck in my mind like a thorn. I feared it would never go away. Why was I so arrogant? Perhaps this all could have been avoided if I had been smarter. Instead, I put us all in danger.

Francis was aware of my reoccurring thoughts of regret. He lovingly provided more instruction. "Shame is how one becomes lost in being wounded. It can lead to obsessive wondering and questioning: Why wasn't I smarter? Why did this happen to me? Why didn't I stop it, start it, or run? The questions that come from possibilities are endless, and they all feed the expansion of shame. This produces self-defeating energy and is just another form of fear. If Infinite Source appeared before you and answered all your questions, it would not change the result. The explanation would only give the mind more to fixate on. This would continue feeding the wounded self, serving to keep the wound open."

My mind was foggy from the drugs and pain, but the words felt right.

Josephine gently continued. "Shame cannot survive in the presence of compassion. Self-compassion or any expression of compassion is the first step to forgiving. Shame cannot grow in the presence of forgiveness, but often self-forgiveness is elusive because compassion for one's self has not authentically taken place. Review, as an observer, what might have been done differently; if there's something, accept it without shame. View it as learning and store it in the memory consciousness for future use. Make an affirmative statement such as "lesson learned," and then move forward. If nothing was to be done differently, accept the unchangeable reality and shift to acceptance. All is instructional. Do not make an identity out of being a victim."

"It's difficult for me to have self-compassion when I feel bad about myself for not doing better. Look how far I've come and how much I've learned, but yet I still failed this test."

Josephine stated, "You have not failed, only learned. Be aware that your mind, when obsessive, should be redirected. Choose instead to be the objective observer; this perspective helps to bring clarity. When the event memory arises, give it no power. If not fed, it will lessen in time. Accept, release, and embrace with the intention of rising above the unchangeable reality. Then return to the position of the observer, and see yourself as the victor, not the victim. You can rise above it. It takes consistent effort, as it is difficult, but you will be successful with the commitment of persistence. With rising above this event, there are many gifts."

That caught my attention. "Like what?" I almost didn't believe that was possible.

I could feel Josephine's encouragement as she answered, "Expansive, lasting gifts such as confidence, strength, tenacity, self-respect, courage, and steadfast faith."

Francis said, "Self-compassion means caring enough for one's self to move beyond what is unchangeable. It means selecting the energy of *constructive* thought and action rather than destructive energy. By doing so, you are feeding the Light of your soul, not diminishing it."

"I'm sorry, but I feel diminished and beaten."

Francis declared, "Be gentle with yourself. How you respond to circumstances is revealing. If you lack forgiveness, the ego/personality keeps you small and encapsulated in fear. Again, you can get beyond it by setting your intention to see yourself as the victor, not the victim. Consider that this incarnation and all incarnations are temporary. Explore the lessons, embrace them, and move on. It is important to remember that you chose to stay."

The wisdom Francis and Josephine lovingly shared was deeply soothing. I welcomed the peaceful sleep that followed.

The next afternoon, on the way home, I hoped Maggie Pie would remember forgiving me and never call me names or bite my head again. When Heath and Deardra brought me in the house, it was equal to entering a dimension of heaven. I felt even more loved and appreciated than before. Pie and I were treated like heroes, which was wonderful! But it was Pie, Heath, and Deardra who were the heroes for saving my life.

The transformation of Pie's attitude was incredible. We now shared the trauma bond of surviving a mountain lion attack together. And I was sincerely able to apologize to Maggie. I decided to count this as a gift that resulted from something horrible.

But I still didn't feel completely safe. How could I? The She Cat had the same black mark as the coach driver from my lifetime as Octavia; the monk I had killed as Brother

Gabriel; the claim jumper, whose life I had ended when I was Edmond; and Savage, who had tried to kill me at The Pit.

I put the question out to Josephine and Francis: "Who is this dark soul who haunts my lifetimes and hunts me without mercy? Why can't I be victorious over this dark entity?"

Francis answered with deep compassion: "The dark soul who haunts you is the shadow side of your own soul. It is *you*."

When I heard those words, they took my breath away. I was shocked and couldn't believe it. "What?"

"In a lower frequency, you express harmful actions, words, and deeds. Until each soul recognizes, then accepts, the shadow side of itself, full integration of polarities cannot be accomplished. The shadow side should not be indulged or its darkness fed. However, if the shadow side is not accepted, then avoided, this brings forth more denial, separation, and pain."

It reminded me of a passage Deardra had read to us the day before the attack. It was from Mother Teresa. "Mother Teresa says she became a nun when she realized there was a little of Hitler in each of us." Deardra closed the book and asked Heath, "What do you think of that quote?" Both looked out the window and contemplated, and then they talked about the meaning. They didn't know they were participating in my teaching. Or perhaps, as part of some distant plan, they did.

The revelation that the evil shadow soul was me snapped me back into the moment. I couldn't believe it! "That was me? A part of me? An evil, seething murderer?" I felt ashamed, humiliated, and made a fool of. I resentfully said, "So now I'm the villain, and I've been attacking and trying to kill myself over these different incarnations with a black mark on my face so that I could accept myself?" I was angry and yelled. "This is a cruel deception! You both knew all along. And yet you let me struggle and squirm in the pain of fear. What kind of trickery is this? I thought you loved me."

There was silence for what seemed like hours. They were probably waiting for me to reconsider my reaction, which I started to do.

Josephine spoke first. "To embrace the shadow side is part of every soul's evolution. With free will, you choose to interpret each situation as you wish. You are choosing the egoic need to make others wrong for a truth you don't like at the moment. But truth it is."

Francis added, "You have evolved beyond this reaction if you're willing to step away from your ego and embrace what you have learned. Everything is happening as it should and is an opportunity for you to live and demonstrate what you know."

I still felt slightly betrayed. Or should I say my ego did. I started to calm down and accept this new truth but asked, "Didn't you both know ahead of time I'd choose my ego?"

"No. We can't and don't know what you're going to choose. Consider what you have learned." Francis paused. It struck me how Francis and Josephine always sounded the same: peaceful, nonjudgmental, and compassionate.

Francis gently continued. "This is your courageous journey. Your spiritual adventure on the earth plane. And it comes with the responsibility and repercussions of free will. Remember, each choice reveals what lessons you need to learn based on what you select. Your shadow side needs to be accepted as part of you to be integrated. It played a part in your violent ending as Edmond and then again as Pete. But it is best to leave this subject for now. We will be examining it further when the time is right."

At first, I felt my prideful ego didn't want to let go. As I thought about it and felt more grounded, I quietly said, "I'm sorry I went down the black hole of fear. I *do* know more, but I'm still prone to react before considering what I've learned."

Again they both reassured me of how well I was progressing and advised me to rest. With my next breath, they were gone, leaving me with a great deal to consider.

And I did consider what Francis and Josephine had taught me about the importance of not choosing negativity—not feeding fear and not believing the fiction my mind made up to nourish the fear. I needed to trust their love and guidance, which included trusting their word. They said that the She Cat wouldn't return and that I must integrate the shadow side of my soul. Somehow, I had to embrace seeing the entire picture and use it as an anchor to rise above the repetitive fear my mind liked to latch on to.

The truth about my shadow side brought me some peace, mixed with a painful confusion. I thought of Josephine, as the elk, attacking the She Cat, and I lovingly thanked her again for the protection she gave me. Together, Josephine and Francis made it possible for me to continue on my soul's mission.

I gazed out the windows of the sunroom and watched the birds eating. Listening to the trees breathing, I felt relief. The warmth of the sun shining on my wounded body felt healing. I drowsily listened to the Michael Tomlinson song "Beating of My Heart." The lyrics that were relevant to me rang with a crispness in my ears.

"How can life turn out so different
Than you thought
You never do really know
The kind of dream you want to hold onto
And what you want to leave behind you
I see most everything so different
Than I once did
I wonder who I really was
I guess it's just a part of living
In the world
How do you learn to follow love
And still hold dear to what you let go of
Oh, breathe it in and let it out again
Out here I fell out of time"
Got lost in the skin I thought was mine
Now I am the seed again."

I felt peaceful as Pie lay down next to me, and together we fell asleep. Waldo was waiting for me in my dream, and we blissfully ran through shimmering flowers.

25

Shared Soul Memories

Love can attain what the mind cannot imagine.
—Josephine

In the middle of the night, I felt a memory vision of Pete was about to start. Josephine gently explained how this one would be different. "This will be a shared recollection. You will be witnessing memories of yourself as Pete, but through the eyes of your oldest daughter, DeDe."

The shared memory began with me standing over her and her little sister, calling them brats. Then I shouted at Annette to stop being so miserable. "Why can't you be more like your sister?"

Gretchen yelled from her usual lying position on the couch, "They're both ungrateful brats!"

I could *feel* DeDe was frightened by what was escalating and usually ended in one or both of them being punished. She felt terrible that I compared her and her little sister and recognized, even at her young age, that it was my hurtful attempt to control Annette's behavior. I could see how I was constantly trying to mold their personalities to my liking. Both the girls were accustomed to the name-calling and the hitting that Gretchen and I so generously dished out. By this time, DeDe was getting used to the abuse, after having endured it four years longer than Annette. My heart hurt from reliving the pain I caused my precious little girls, particularly since it was through the eyes and heart of DeDe.

A new shared scene emerged in DeDe's mind. It was the day we went to visit one of my classmates, Clark. She recalled how much she liked Clark's wife; whose name was Emily. Emily was kind and lighthearted, and she enjoyed playing a game with the girls. DeDe considered how she couldn't recall her mother having ever played with them.

DeDe's memory of when it was time to go home was heartbreaking. She cried and begged Emily to let her and Annette stay. The desperation she felt in that moment rang inside her again. "Please be our new parents. They're mean to us. Please, please let us stay here. They're always yelling at us or hitting us."

Emily was shocked and touched. Her eyes filled with tears. "I'm sorry, honey. You have to go home. It's time for you and Annette to gather your things and go outside with your mommy and daddy."

At three years old, Annette happily played with a toy and didn't realize what was going on. DeDe felt rejected and cried harder. Emily quietly gathered DeDe's and Annette's things. Kneeling down, she softly looked into DeDe's eyes. Taking her hands, she said, "You're both going to be OK. Right now, at seven years old, it's hard to see that. You can come back and visit us whenever you want."

But DeDe sensed how Emily doubted her own words. Emily kissed DeDe and Annette on the cheeks and commented on what beautiful little girls they were. Holding their hands, she led them outside.

All of a sudden, the scene jumped to where I could feel *Emily's* feelings and hear her thoughts too. Her emotions ran a gamut of sadness, anger, and helplessness at not being able to rescue these sweet little girls. I could see how difficult it was for Emily to say goodbye to Gretchen and me. She wanted to yell at us—tell us we were awful parents. She wished she could love our daughters the way she thought they deserved to be loved. Instead, she quickly shook our hands, said goodbye, and kissed the girls one more time. I now watched her as she went inside, where the dam of tears, which she had tightly held, broke. She cried for our sweet girls. Part of me felt a great respect for Emily; another part of me wondered if she had ever had her own children to love.

Next, I watched a scene that took place about four days later. When I was Pete, I loved being on campus, but not on this day when I ran into Clark. He said that DeDe had asked Emily to be the girl's new mom. My heart jumped into my throat. I felt my face flush with embarrassment. Clark told me what DeDe said about Gretchen and me. This time my heart broke.

Then I viewed myself asking DeDe about it, as she also remembered my question. It deeply hurt when DeDe told me it was true. She rocked her Thumbelina doll. "Yes, Daddy, I wanted to stay with them. You and Mommy are mean to us." Tears stung my eyes. I hugged her, saying I was sorry over and over. I told her things would get better, and they did for a few days.

Francis interjected. "Through the years, DeDe sometimes reflected on the desperation she felt that day. She wanted to escape—to rescue her little sister from the abusive instability you and Gretchen had created."

"Why was I so blind? I was a bad father, but why didn't I see it then? I knew I could do better, but I didn't know how without the cooperation of their mother. If I could do it all again, I would try harder. What was wrong with me, Francis?"

"That is a question I would like you to answer when you are ready. Shall we continue to observe?"

Many scenes unfolded. Each one clearly showed everything the girls did Gretchen and I considered an inconvenience or aggravation. Gretchen was horrible most of the time, but with a few glimmers of right action that produced hope. The girls found her occasional good behavior confusing, never knowing what to expect from their mother. If it wasn't for my mother taking care of DeDe and Annette, I doubt they would have ever felt loved. I tried, but I wasn't around much because of school and work.

Annette was only three, unhappy, and brooding most of the time. The girls were accustomed to name-calling, neglect, constant criticism, and being slapped on a regular basis in the head or face by me or Gretchen. This is also how the adults in my family treated one another, with almost constant bickering added into the insanity. It was all shamefully there. We were two unhappy people who were lost in the agony of our misery. We punished our children for the pain and emptiness we contained.

DeDe endured it by internalizing what she felt. She escaped into her world of dolls, attempting to ignore the craziness of her parents. I watched, felt, and experienced firsthand what it was like to be on the receiving end of what I generously dished out to my daughters.

In a flash, it was shown to me that it was *Deardra* who was remembering! It was *Deardra and I together* sharing these memories! Dear God, no! Please—it can't be. The cruelty of it rang with a deep bitterness. The reality crashed in, crushing me with its entire force. Deardra was my daughter DeDe, grown up! The shock drove me toward denial, so I kept repeating in my mind that DeDe was Deardra! Immediately I recognized her, or I was allowed to recognize her. Big blue eyes and brown hair. She was my sweet daughter whom I had always loved.

My emotions were a tidal wave of extremes. I was drowning in regret, guilt, shame, and the enormity of my love for her. I watched Deardra as she sat on the sunroom couch, far away in thought. I wanted to reach out and magically erase all the pain I had caused her and Annette. If only I could.

I asked Francis and Josephine, "Why is her name different?"

Josephine answered, "It wasn't yet time for you to remember that DeDe was Deardra's nickname? That memory is now available to you."

"Instantly, I recalled. "Yes. I do remember, we did call Deardra 'DeDe.'" Consumed by my overwhelming emotions, I wondered how I'd ever survive this agony.

I cried out, "Where is Annette?"

Francis answered, "Annette is doing well. Once old enough and out of your and Gretchen's control, both daughters reinvented themselves. They each engaged in therapy to understand and heal their wounds."

"Please, please stop this! I can't bear any more. I'm in hell!"

Josephine lovingly observed, "By reviewing your past actions, you are less likely to have them become your future actions. Many consider a life review hell until they realize that learning is their salvation."

Francis encouraged me. "Keep going. You are doing well. Your awareness grows with every observation. The pain will ease. All you have suffered will be worth the experience upon completion. The actions of your personality in the physical do not define your soul. All souls who come to the physical make errors and learn. Remember, you are loved and forgiven."

Another memory formed, and I again shared it as a witness and participant. This time Deardra remembered how Gretchen didn't care if the girls had food. She'd send them to school with no lunches, which reduced them to sometimes having to beg food from the other kids. The Catholic school that Gretchen insisted the girls attend didn't provide school lunches, and the nuns didn't care if some of the children had nothing to eat. It wasn't their responsibility. Deardra mostly remembered the pain of hunger and the humiliation she and Annette suffered from the other kids. The kids would whisper that she must be poor or maybe an orphan since she had no food. Deardra was sensitive and cried easily, making her more vulnerable to the kids who bullied her. With each memory, her pain echoed through my heart.

The girls not having adequate food happened after I graduated, when we moved away from my family to the foothills. Without my mother to watch over the girls, they really had no one to look after them. I was working two jobs in an effort to try and save money to get ahead. Secretly, I hadn't completely abandoned my dream of mining for gold and hitting it big.

The shared memory of my daughters going hungry brought immense pain to me and Deardra as the emotional scene continued to unfold.

In a crazy twist, I had become her dog Russell. Deardra looked my way not knowing I had been her dad, Pete. Her voice cracked as she said, "How could I have ever felt loved, cared for, protected, and safe when my parents didn't care enough about me and my sister to make sure we had food?"

My heart broke into what felt like a million pieces, and I cried like a baby.

Then she recalled how I knew they were sent to school with no lunches and were being bullied. The questions tumbled through my mind. I wondered *why* I didn't do anything to step in and take care of my daughters. But I knew the answer. It was denial that gave me the ability to ignore the obvious.

I also began to share Deardra's physical sensations. A lump formed in her throat, her stomach tightened, her eyes stung, and her tears overflowed. All of it—her feeling betrayed, unloved, neglected, and humiliated—I also felt. Then her emotions moved to anger and resentment. Again, she wondered why I, her dad, did nothing.

I was shocked to hear *Josephine* tenderly say to Deardra, "You must feel to heal, and because healing is painful, it takes bravery. Release the past and *accept* it as part of your courageous spiritual journey. Remain in faith that the challenges presented in the physical have varying roots, but all are for the highest and greatest good for the evolution of your soul."

I was surprised Josephine was also guiding Deardra, and I asked her, "So you're Deardra's Guide too?"

Josephine answered, "Yes, along with others. As I was your mother when you were Pete, I was DeDe/Deardra's grandmother. Love is an indestructible bond, so it was agreed that I would guide you both."

I attempted to lighten my sorrow for a moment. "That makes sense. Sorry. Guess I had Guide envy for a moment."

Josephine brightly responded, "Humor is important to maintain balance. I always enjoy your wit."

Then, in her mind, I heard Deardra answer Josephine. She was only partially conscious of the conversation they were having. "I'm angry, hurt, and don't understand. How could so much painful abuse and neglect be good for my soul? What I remember insults my soul."

I felt accountable for my daughter's pain, but it didn't change anything. Since Josephine was guiding us both, I asked, "I understand about reviewing my past life as Pete. But it's almost more than I can bear to experience my daughter's memories and her pain too."

Josephine stated her answer clearly. "Actions in the physical are far-reaching. For a life review to be whole in its scope, it must contain the repercussion of choices leading to actions. This includes the emotions of those on the receiving end, especially your *loved* ones."

"But you and Francis taught me we're all responsible for how we decide to respond to circumstances. Generally speaking, what if someone decides to react in a way that's the opposite of my intention?"

Josephine explained, "It is the *intention* that determines what you feel from the other person's reaction. If that person's reaction is based on his or her own soul's path, but is not relevant to you, you will not experience that person's feelings."

I sort of understood but needed more. "Can you give me an example?"

"If you give a sincere compliment and it is received as sarcasm or a question of what you really meant, you will not feel that reaction. Your life review is only relevant to your growth, not the growth of others."

"OK. That makes sense. What doesn't make sense is why, at this point, I have to go through every excruciating experience with the added anguish of Deardra's pain."

Josephine peacefully responded, "*Feeling* is a powerful teacher. And feeling the pain we caused others is part of a life review. Without this entire process, growth from each lifetime would not be integrated, stifling spiritual development. In part, this is why a life review is vital to a soul's ability to move forward."

"How could I have been so blind to my actions? Especially the ones that affected my daughters?" I shamefully asked.

Francis said, "A numb apathy shaped by your denial was what enabled you to do nothing. However, doing nothing is an action in itself, which bears its own weight of equal accountability."

Then I felt Deardra's anger grow as she recalled other memories related to Gretchen and me. One was how Gretchen never had food in the house or made dinner. The girls were limited to eating cereal, canned soup, bologna sandwiches, or nothing for dinner. I was working and didn't get home until 9 p.m. or after. They were usually in bed. I'd ask Gretchen what the girls had for dinner. She'd often say they didn't want to eat. But inside, I knew it wasn't true. For her, indulging her laziness was all that mattered, and she didn't care who she hurt with her neglect.

At the time, I also knew DeDe and Annette's emotional needs were starved. Somehow, I just couldn't seem to face reality. I felt beaten and didn't have the energy to fight with Gretchen, even for the sake of my girls.

Deardra recalled how she had always been very protective of her little sister. She felt especially bad that Annette had to endure the same painful neglect she did. Deardra's mind continued to try and solve the puzzle of why I didn't step in.

It was clear to most everyone that Gretchen "wasn't right." Yet no one stepped in to encourage her to get help. When I suggested she should get some counseling, she venomously lashed out by saying that it was me who was crazy and she was the only sane one. Back then, narcissism wasn't considered a personality disorder. It turned out that it was very destructive in our lives, especially since it was coupled with depression and paranoia.

Deardra knew I was aware of how sick Gretchen was. She continued to question how I could stand by and witness the daily abuse and then add to it with my own angry, dark moods.

The next answer that came to her was from me. I was astonished when I realized she was allowed to pick up certain thoughts I wished to share with her. And share I did. A waterfall of my overwhelming regret poured out. I told her with all the energy I could direct to her how sorry I was. I tried to explain to her. "I was too depressed, beaten down, and exhausted from my disastrous marriage to Gretchen to think and respond correctly. I was overwhelmed with working two jobs, with the loss of my dreams, and with having two unplanned children."

With a sigh, she shifted her position on the couch. The painful memories made her tired and depressed.

I continued to talk to her. "DeDe—I mean, Deardra—please forgive me, and please know how much I loved and still love you and Annette. I used denial as a means of survival. It wasn't your fault or Annette's fault. I used drinking beer every night to escape the constant barrage of nagging, criticism, and name-calling, and the most difficult circumstance of all was the lack of love. The abuse I received and then passed on caused a relentless, empty ache that became my constant companion. I deluded myself by thinking things would get better. I believed you and your sister would grow up and forget all the madness. That's what happens, I told myself. Most kids turn out well in spite of their childhoods. After all, I turned out OK—I wasn't a criminal. I was a good man in a lot of ways. I loved both of you girls, but I withheld the help you needed. Again, I'm so sorry, my sweet Deardra. I didn't want to fail you and Annette by being consumed with my own personal need for survival."

In her mind, she bitterly lashed out at what she imagined were her own thoughts. "I'm imagining all this as excuses I think my dad might give. But it doesn't change anything that happened."

Even though I knew she was only partially aware of our dialogue on a conscious level, I was absolutely thrilled that I was able to converse with her at all. I considered it a great gift to have the opportunity to be heard.

I continued my message. "None of these reasons change the outcome or excuse my actions, but I hope what I'm sharing will give you some answers—perhaps even some comfort by letting you know I was a flawed man who loved you and Annette with my whole heart." With all the energy I could project, I continued to tell her how sorry I was and how deeply I loved her.

Now it all made sense. This explained my sense of knowing her from the first day at the puppy farm. And it explained the deep love and regret I felt for her from the start. She was meant to come for me. That's why I felt so sure we were supposed to be together.

I felt Waldo smile in the background.

I believed Deardra was aware of our exchange, as her body, mind, and emotions seemed to relax. She stared out the window, then turned and gazed at me—her dog, Russell—and said, "All those trees are breathing, and we're breathing their breath. Isn't that incredible to think about? I love you, puppafied Russ."

She sat on the floor next to where I was lying, leaned over, kissed me on the head, and quietly whispered, "It's going to be all right. I know my dad loved me the best he could for who he was at the time and for all he had to endure."

With the sound of those words passing from her lips to my ears, I wept deep inside. I don't know how much conscious memory of our exchange she had, but in the infinite dimension of love, it was soothing to know she *heard* me and understood the depth of my sincerity.

I recalled, even as a small child, intuition had been one of her gifts. By her intuitively accepting that I did my best for who I was at the time, it was healing for both our hearts.

Instantly, I knew our sharing the same wavelength was over for the moment.

Francis quietly added, "Healing expands love, and love expands healing, which, in turn, liberates the soul."

"Thank you, Francis. Now I finally know some of the other reasons I'm here as Russell the dog." I was again exhausted. I felt raw from the emotional pain of my review and the shared memories. It was a shock to discover I had reincarnated to become my daughter's dog. Somehow, through it all, the new revelations helped me feel a bit more peaceful than before.

Fatigue overtook me, and I passed out in a fraction of a second. My last thought as I entered the dream world was that this had to be the ultimate spiritual adventure.

26

We Chose Our Parents

If we chose our parents, I must have been in a hurry.
—Deardra

The next day, when I awoke from my nap, Josephine was waiting. With her enduring, nonjudgmental love, she said, "We are very pleased with your progress. You are doing exceptionally well. Feeling, reexperiencing, and observing select memories bring you closer to understanding what your lifetime as Pete meant. Can you see more clearly what you did right and what you need to correct?"

I yawned. "Yes, reliving during the review is effective and instructive, but brutal. What excruciating pain do you and Francis have planned for me today?" I asked with a teasing tone.

"We are getting closer to how your life ended as Pete," she casually answered.

Terror instantly engulfed me. I announced, "I've had all the pain and suffering I can take for a while. I'm not ready to go through how I died as Pete. I need some recovery time. After all, how much can a soul take?"

Josephine seemed to understand. "The fear of pain is great for every soul in the physical. Please remember that one of the objectives for you is to find purpose in pain. We have almost accomplished your complete life review as Pete. This is another opportunity for you to rise above your fear and then complete your reason for being here."

I felt a bit calmer, but I wanted to know something. "Once I complete my review, do I have to immediately leave my life as Russell the dog?"

Francis answered, "In the physical, everything has a life cycle. You may stay until the end of your body's life cycle or you may leave sooner. If you wish, you may exit shortly after the completion of how you died as Pete. At that point, your life review will have been accomplished. Then the choice of how long you decide to stay is yours to make."

Unexpectedly, I felt sentimental. Even with all the painful turmoil, I had become attached to my life as Russell the dog. And now that my life was almost over, I felt it had gone too fast. I wanted to stay with Deardra, especially since I finally understood who she was. And I loved Heath and Maggie. But I also wanted to know more about Annette and where she was. I wondered if I could see her.

Francis and Josephine granted my request and allowed me to reach out and communicate with Annette. I watched her from the corner of her kitchen while she was eating dinner. I told her how sorry I was for all the abuse she had suffered, and I conveyed to her the same explanations I shared with Deardra. I ended by letting her know how deeply I loved her. But she didn't believe any of it. She was only able to think about how horribly I had treated her and how much she hated me for my generous abuse and my lack of love. I tearfully expressed to her again how sorry I was and how much I loved her. She rejected our interaction as only her imagination; then she pushed me from her mind. The pain for her that came from thinking about me was too great. I was devastated by the damage she had suffered from my actions. Before I left her presence, I again told her I loved her and asked her one more time to please forgive me.

After I left the scene, Josephine said, "You did your best to let Annette know your actions were regretfully harmful and incorrect. And it was healing that you shared with her how much you loved her and still do. Like many others, one of her challenges in this lifetime is to rise above the past. And she will accomplish that through forgiveness. At another point, when you and Annette are together in spirit, you will each revel in the progress you assisted each other in achieving while in this lifetime."

"It is comforting to know that at some point we will appreciate each other." Then I asked, "Was it Annette and Deardra's karma to have Gretchen and me for parents?"

Josephine sounded impressed. "Your questions are insightful. Yes, on the three-dimensional plane, most souls choose their parents. Before coming to the physical, each of your daughters' souls chose you and Gretchen as parents. And they chose each other as siblings. This is part of a complex mosaic that intricately interconnects all souls. However, the specifics of each soul's journey is that soul's own personal path, so there are no further details available to you right now concerning the reasons for their choice."

"OK. I understand. How about just a little hint?" I lightly asked. I felt the energy of delight from my two Spiritual Guardians.

For me, the whole picture had reached another level of clarity, but I still couldn't understand all the reasons that caused me to fall short. I asked, "Why didn't I express more kindness, love, and compassion? Those are the things a father should have for his children. I did—and still do—love my daughters, so why did I fail so miserably at expressing it?"

Francis answered, "You are almost ready to answer that question yourself. Know that you are asking the right questions, and you already hold many of the answers in your consciousness. Everything will come together in Divine timing."

"It's reassuring to know I already have some of the answers, and I can't wait until I know what they are. But I'm exhausted and need to rest before we continue."

Even with the kind, gentle words Francis and Josephine shared, my emotions raced across a spectrum of extremes. It was an unbearable type of fear that held me back from wanting to face the tragic end of my life as Pete. The fear brought with it an avalanche of emotion from every discovery revealed so far in my life review. I mainly felt a dark symphony of feelings, repeating over and over.

Without warning, all the emotions I had experienced so far hit me with the force of a hurricane. I cried out, "I can't imagine any suffering greater than this. It's impossible to contain the depth of the emotions that engulf me." *Everything* I didn't allow myself to feel as Pete was now a tidal wave that carried my consciousness to places I had denied. But no more denial. All was revealed—I was revealed. Yet I sensed a distant flicker of hope.

Josephine recognized the depth of my pain. I could hear the empathy in her tone. "As we discussed earlier, you will benefit from practicing self-compassion, which leads to self-forgiveness. Drama is enticing, but instead trust everything is for your highest and greatest good. Surrender will make the remainder of your life review flow more easily. I will remind you again—you are loved and watched over. No harm will come to you—no harm can come to you. Your life review is designed for the escalation of your soul's growth. Remember, you chose to have your life review as your daughter's dog. This enabled you to deeply feel the emotions you could not face in your life or upon your death as Pete. In the process, you are clearing the negative karma that resulted from your actions as Deardra and Annette's father."

I wept, feeling as if each tear cleansed my heart. I thanked Infinite Source that I had Francis and Josephine to guide my soul into a higher frequency of consciousness. I asked, "Have I completed this part of my review, or will there be more shared memories?"

Francis said, "By sharing and experiencing Deardra's memories of you as Pete, her father, you have expanded an intricate structure that assists you in your evolutionary journey. All souls have access to Divine guidance from those who have traveled the same frontier. Spirit Guides are aware of the rough areas, the parts that seem impossible. In the end, all will unfold as it should—equal to your learning stage— and only you can embrace it. *Accept* all that has taken place by surrendering to what is—and forgive yourself as we move forward."

"Is this my punishment—to endure even more pain by experiencing how I died as Pete? I suppose this is the personal hell of my own creation, but how much longer must I suffer?

Can I review how I died as Pete without the emotion? Then it wouldn't feel so much like a punishment."

"We have spoken of this before. There is a difference between accountability and punishment." Francis spoke without judgment.

I was struggling. "Considering everything that has happened so far, I still can't fully grasp the difference."

Francis patiently explained it again in a different way. "Accountability is the foundation for how wisdom forms. Understanding cause and effect is how consciousness grows, leading to greater awareness. You are not being punished although that is currently your perceived reality. Accountability can be painful, but reaching beyond the pain brings understanding, which leads to knowledge and then wisdom. Release yourself from the bondage of self-recrimination by re-forming and then redirecting that energy into your soul's growth."

The next visions were of some of the good things I did as Pete. They were the times I followed my heart or my inner guidance.

I watched myself at eight years old, poor with nothing of my own. I shared a piece of chocolate I had found with a sickly boy who lived in the same tenement. I carefully unwrapped the small piece of candy and shared it with him without a thought of what I'd get in return. My sharing came from the genuine compassion I felt for him. When he smiled from the sweet taste, I could clearly see his two front teeth were missing. He said the tooth fairy had left him a penny for each tooth, and he proudly showed me the coins. It filled me with warmth to see his face light up. That was one of the few times I felt good about myself.

He died that winter from what a neighbor said was a blood sickness. When I heard of his passing, I sobbed. I would miss him, even though we hadn't spent much time together due to his health. I considered him my only real friend at the time, and I treasured the moments we had shared.

Later in my life, I was a loyal friend and would go out of my way to help someone in need. Even so, most of my friendships were superficial. I watched many examples pass before me of how I liked to help people. And I even recognized a few from previous incarnations. It was extraordinary to observe how we are all one another's students and teachers.

Instantly the scene changed. I was holding Deardra shortly after she was born. My heart overflowed with love, admiration, and even awe for this tiny baby girl who was mine to love. From her, I hoped to receive the love I had craved my entire life. I kissed her tiny forehead and vowed to be the best father I could, as she deserved nothing less.

For the next few years, I was a good father when I was home. Joyfully, I relived all those sweet tender moments of the love I felt and expressed to her.

Next, I was cuddling Annette. How I loved her too. Her big brown eyes showed her bright awareness. She was so sweet and always loved to be rocked. I reveled in other good memories that unfolded with the girls at different ages. It was heartwarming to once again hear the sound of my girls calling me "Daddy."

Then I watched myself as Pete in various scenes of giving money to the homeless or assisting friends. Often, I'd share what I thought was encouraging advice with the intention of helping those lost souls through rough spots. At the time I didn't realize it, but I was the lost soul attempting to rescue myself.

Francis gently pointed out, "It has been said that we teach best what we most need to learn."

"I think there's truth to that thought, Francis," I said as I further contemplated his wisdom.

A warmth began to fill me as I relived the genuine love I had for my mother, Josephine. I also loved my father, but it was my mother I had the deepest connection with. I tried to bring some lightness to her difficult life. I admired how she laughed easily—a trait we shared. Often, we looked for or found humor when there was little to joke about. I think this kept us both sane.

Once again, I observed when we lived next door to my family. Since my mother took care of the girls, she became the maternal figure to DeDe and Annette. That was something I would always appreciate and treasure her for.

Then I watched the many times I tried to start over with Gretchen by attempting to make her feel loved and supported. I stressed to her the need for us to move in the same direction in order to build a life together, and I emphasized the importance of raising our girls as a team. I also tried to convince her to push herself to stay busy, hoping that would take her mind off her depression. My mother liked to say, "No matter what happens, you just have to keep going." There were times when Gretchen did try, but after a day or two, she would slip back into her dark world. That would be followed by her resenting me for trying to push her to do better.

It was all there. At times, I did do my best with a heartfelt conviction to bring about a better way of living for us all.

When the girls were little, and I was around, I would wrestle with them and play games. It was my intention for them to feel loved. Regrettably, the loving intentions I held for my daughters were sincere but inconsistent.

Francis gently commented, "The soul agreements we make with Infinite Source play out. Lesson plans are overlapping, and when the participating souls hold the highest frequency of love to overcome the slower frequencies of harm, there is a celebrated outcome. This action brings forth compassion, empathy, and merciful forgiveness. You are acknowledged for the improvements you attempted to make."

Josephine said, "We will leave you for a short period of time so that you may rest before we continue the last part of your life review as Pete."

I was relieved to hear I would have some time to process and recover. "I appreciate it, and I will make use of the time to reflect and accept what is inevitable."

Francis departed with a blessing: "Be *in* peace knowing the love of Infinite Source surrounds you. And so it is." With their absence, the energy immediately shifted.

For better or worse, I was alone with my thoughts, which bled with emotion. I knew that my biggest challenge was to rise above my fear and surrender to what was coming.

27

Weddings, Snowflakes, and Beaches

Love opened a door, showing us the reason we came here for.
—Heath

Deardra and Heath planned a December wedding. She liked to tell me and Maggie, "We're all going to live together in the House of Stone and Light."

When Heath proposed to her, she said yes, but then she held her breath and immediately asked him, "Where do you want to live—here in the mountains or your house in the city?" Her eyes were wide as she waited for his answer. This time we also held our breath, waiting for his reply. We didn't want to be city dogs.

He said, "Well, let's see, mountain house or city house?" He moved each hand like a scale. His big smile lit up his face, and he said, "Here in the mountains, of course." She threw her arms around him, kissed him, and said with relief, "That's the answer the pups and I were hoping for. I don't think I could live in Denver again after so many years of living here."

Everything was going well for Deardra and Heath, bringing me and Maggie a peaceful joy.

I was enjoying my needed break to process and embrace my ever-changing awareness. I was grateful Francis and Josephine were so loving and understanding.

It was difficult when I discovered Deardra was my daughter DeDe. However, it made a big difference in my ability to see a larger part of the bigger picture.

I cautiously wondered what else would be revealed. Would I be able to handle it? I was emotionally drained to the last cell of my being after the previous revelations. I was especially concerned about how I had died as Pete, particularly since Josephine and Francis had used the words "violently" or "tragically" to describe my death. And why was it blocked from my memory? Maybe I was the one blocking it?

Deardra and Heath sat on the couch in the sunroom and laughed, kissed, and talked. I sat down between them and put my paw on Deardra's leg. I wondered why she loved me. Could she ever fully forgive me? Then I remembered that I had to forgive myself first. She had found love and moved on to find happiness by not bringing her past into the present.

Heath and Deardra both gave me lots of pets, so, of course, Maggie came over to get in on the love, but I didn't mind. There's an abundance of love for all who desire it and even for those who don't.

They continued to talk, and Deardra cheerfully told Heath, "It's never too late to have a happy childhood." He laughed. "I like that. Let's make it one of our marriage mottos." She lightheartedly agreed.

They liked to say that I was puppafied and that Maggie was sweet as pie. Deardra smoothed down the unruly hair on my head and around my eyes. "I don't know how you can see sometimes, teddy bear dog."

Heath picked up a small flashlight that he kept on the end table, and he started making spots on the floor, which I immediately began pouncing on. He chuckled and said, "He seems to see the spots just fine." They both laughed while I did my precision spot-chasing moves, still somewhat inhibited by my almost-healed wounds from the She Cat. Maggie wanted to get in on the fun and ran off to get a toy. She came back with the green bone! Then she began hitting me with it as I was getting the best of the spots. Heath and Deardra laughed louder because of the surprise of Maggie even touching my green bone.

After a few minutes it was enough playing, and Maggie and I lay down. For the first time in a long time, I felt safe, happy, and grateful to be in a lighter mood. I was glad to share these moments with those I loved and who loved me in this world of the physical and beyond.

It was December when Deardra and Heath packed their suitcases to leave. We didn't like it when the suitcases came out because we knew it meant we didn't get to go. Maggie and I heard Deardra and Heath make their wedding plans to be married on a beach in Mexico at sunset. We wanted to go too, but we were left with a pet sitter who gave us lots of extra affection and treats. This made the week they were gone a little easier. When they came back from their wedding and honeymoon, they were happier than when they left. Maggie and I were happy too because our family was complete.

One snowy afternoon, I stood on the deck watching a flock of rosy finches in the trees across the lane. They chirped, asking me to leave so they could swoop in on the feeders and fill their bird bellies. I had felt more agreeable lately and decided to go inside so they could eat. This was another small example of my progress, which seemed to increase by the day.

Before going in the house, I noticed the snowflakes were large, larger than usual. I asked Josephine if it was true that no two snowflakes were alike.

She answered, "There are many snowflakes that share a likeness. However, no two are *exactly* the same—much like soul paths."

I felt faraway. "My soul path feels as unique as a snowflake."

Josephine answered, "And so it is."

28
Package Deals

*Your children are not your children. They are the sons
and daughters of Life's longing for itself. They come
through you but not from you. And though they
are with you yet they belong not to you.*
—Khalil Gibran

Deardra referred to Heath as "a package deal." She was thrilled he had been blessed with three sons. The youngest was seventeen when they met. One of the biggest heartbreaks of Deardra's life was when she discovered she wasn't able to have children. Now she had the chance to love Heath's sons. But she didn't want to be too eager with her pent-up maternal instinct, so she tried to pace her relationship with each of the boys. They were young men whom she didn't want to treat like children. Deardra strongly sensed the energy of a past-life connection with each one of the boys. Hopefully someday they would see her as their *other* mother, who also loved them.

Maggie and I made up the package deal for Heath, and he was better for it because he only had cats. We heard him tell Deardra that his cats were used to going outside. This would never work in the mountains, with all the animal beings here to eat them, so it was decided the cats would stay with one of the boys. It was fine with me if they didn't come and live with us since I didn't want any smelly cats in our house anyway. Pie didn't want the cats to come either, although she didn't really know what a house cat was. The only feline she had ever met was the She Cat, but I knew what cats were because of my short time at the farm.

But there were problems to test my rigid mind. The first time Heath's middle son, Sage, and Heath's youngest son, Alec, came to the house, I was sure they were little boys in long, tall bodies. Thinking of The Pit, I passionately barked and growled at them to let them know I was wise to any tricks. I tried my best to keep them downstairs, which didn't work. After hugging Heath and Deardra, they still went upstairs. I didn't like to be ignored, especially by intruders who came in the house when I didn't want them to.

Sage made sudden moves that spooked me, so I barked louder and more directly at him. Heath and Deardra told me to stop barking, but they didn't know about boys from The Pit.

Pie only barked twice, more out of happiness to see new people to pet her. This was how it usually ended up. I had to be the protector, with little or no appreciation from anyone.

After everyone sat down, they talked, laughed, and enjoyed themselves. I snorted, then finally decided to lie down, but I stayed within biting range in case the need arose. Pie wagged her tail sweetly, happy to be with them, but then she had never experienced The Pit.

No matter how much learning I received to achieve higher awareness, I was still a dog, imprinted by my past with highly protective instincts. And that's what I was going to continue to be, my best protective-dog self. Maybe this meant I wasn't progressing as fast as I thought.

After a few minutes, Alec extended his hand for me to sniff. Sage suddenly jumped to his feet, quickly moving toward me. A wave of fear hit me. I backed away, ferociously barking and growling at him with the intent to bite. This continued with Sage any time he made sudden moves, which was all the time. Then I noticed the amount of affection Pie was enjoying, so I decided since everyone was having a good time, maybe I could relax a bit. After all, they were Heath's sons. Our introductions started out rough, but the evening ended up tolerable. I was OK with Alec, but I was still leery of Sage and barked at him when he got up to leave. I growled at him not to come back because he seemed the most like a little boy to me, except very tall.

Later I met Heath's oldest son, Clint. Of course, I barked at him a little at first, and then after that we got on well. Clint's energy was calmer, and he didn't do anything to spook me. He moved in with us for a while before he left for the army. He liked to wrestle and play, so we were good pals. Maggie loved Clint and wanted to be wherever he was—she even insisted on sleeping with him at night. We both missed him when he moved away.

One day when Maggie and I were home alone, I smelled Sage trying to get in the front door. After he unlocked the door, he quickly came in the house. Bad move! I was sure he wasn't supposed to be inside if Heath and Deardra weren't home. My protective instincts kicked in, so I barked, snarled, and growled at him. Pie half-heartedly barked because she liked Sage. He suddenly stuck his hand out toward me, and I tried to bite it, but he pulled it back in time. After a few minutes he left. I was proud that we had done our critically important job not to allow anyone upstairs when we were the only ones home.

When Deardra and Heath came home later that evening, they told us, "It's OK for Clint, Sage, and Alec to come in the house when we're not home." But I wasn't having it! And I never trusted Sage again with his quick, sudden, jumpy moves.

Whenever Heath's sons came to visit, Deardra and Heath would be happy to see them. Maggie Pie told me, "I like the boys. Could you consider not acting like a grump to Sage?"

It's hard when no one understands you. Francis and Josephine agreed with Pie. Josephine suggested, "Perhaps you should consider what you are making up in your mind about Sage. He wasn't one of the boys who tormented you. He is kind and only needs a chance for you to see that." Even so, I never got far enough past my fear to accept Sage.

29

My Reason for Being Here Has Come

Life can refine us into better versions of ourselves.
—Deardra

My time has finally come to review how my lifetime as Pete ended. Francis and Josephine are both here. This time they're with others, who are in the background gently surrounding me. It feels like hundreds of hands gently holding me with loving support. All are brightly radiating with the Light of love.

I am terrified, but I'm also reassured with the extraordinary amount of love engulfing me. Then many sensations overtake me as the remembrance begins to unfold.

The scene begins in the last year of my life as Pete, which I mostly spent wandering. I was retired and free to do what I wanted. Gretchen and I had divorced after I could no longer contain my rage from her constant caustic nagging and abusive berating. Nothing had changed in our marriage. Due to my fear of being alone, I had continued to *allow* her to make my life an agonizing hell.

After separating from Gretchen, I rented a room from an old friend, Vic. We shared a taste for gambling—an addiction I continued to feed. After I lost over half of my retirement nest egg, I once again used denial to not feel. Perhaps if I had allowed myself to be remorseful, my behavior might have changed.

Then in April it happened. The accumulation of self-abuse over the years—of drinking beer, creating stress, eating chemically processed food, and smoking on and off—took its toll.

One day while driving nowhere in particular, I suddenly had a crushing pain in my head. It was a pain so severe that I had never experienced anything like it in my life. A headache followed with the same level of agony. Not knowing what was going on, I hit another car. Thankfully, I later heard that no one was hurt. Everyone at the scene thought I was drunk because I was stumbling around not knowing where I was. When the police came, they also thought I was drunk, then realized, by my speech, that I was having a stroke. Next the ambulance came. I had no memory of my name or who I was. I kept asking them to give me something for the pain. They couldn't understand me because I sounded like I was talking backward. Then I didn't feel anything on the left side of my body. They verified it; I had suffered a stroke.

For two days at the hospital, I was in and out of consciousness. When the nurse asked me for the number of a family member, I couldn't say because I didn't know who I was, and my words were garbled. The police told me my name by reading it from my driver's license. On the second day, two young women came to see me. They said they were my daughters, Deardra and Annette, but to me, they were strangers. A great deal of frustration and anger came to the surface because I didn't know what to do or how to act. I was lost. My mind was an empty shell in which every single thing seemed surreal and surrounded by fog.

A few days later my memory started to come back a little, but my words were still garbled. No one could understand me, and I couldn't write or read.

I was released after a week with nowhere to go. Gretchen and Annette didn't want anything to do with me, but I couldn't remember why that was. Deardra lived in a split-level house in the mountains with a roommate. There were too many stairs for me where she lived, and her roommate didn't want me to come and stay there. Plus, she couldn't take care of me because she had a demanding job in real estate that required many hours, sometimes seven days a week.

My mother, Josephine, at that point lived with my sister, who didn't want me to stay at her house either. My mother couldn't do anything since it was my sister's house and her decision. I couldn't drive and needed someone to take me to physical therapy. Vic let me come back to my room, but I felt he also didn't want me. I was a burden to everyone, including myself.

My speech barely improved, and I was paralyzed on one side of my body, making it almost impossible for me to be understood or get around. I was told the damage was permanent. I was devastated by the harsh reality that I would never be the same.

The paralysis on the left side of my body made it feel like dead weight. With the heaviness that I felt, I imagined I was like a wounded whale floating on a vast ocean. I was lost in a sea of confusion, pain, and fear, with no control over the direction I was headed.

The revelation that no one wanted me and only a few loved me was agonizing. As I remembered more of my past, I couldn't understand why no one was there for me. I had tried to be good to my family, but I also knew I had failed many times, and it was those times they remembered. I had hoped my mostly good behavior had made up for my abusive side. Again, it seemed my hopes were not in line with reality. Depression gripped my mind and emotions clouding my perceptions with pain. I just wanted my misery to be over. Death seemed merciful.

Not long after, I had to get up about every hour to urinate. This was more than I could bear. On top of everything else, I couldn't even sleep. It took three weeks to get an appointment to see a specialist. By that time, I was beyond exhausted. The lack of sleep further affected my energy, my ability to think, and my wherewithal to do the physical therapy correctly.

When I finally got to see the specialist, he said it was my prostate, and there was nothing he could do. He abruptly left the room, with me sitting on the cold metal table that matched his bedside manner. As he was leaving, I asked if he could do something. After all, it was 1992. He probably didn't understand what I was asking because he ignored me and closed the door without answering.

After six weeks, the insurance company decided to end my physical therapy. With every setback, my heart and soul sank to lower levels of despair.

Deardra called the insurance company several times. With each call her frustration and anger boiled over. She passionately talked about the unfeeling decision-makers at the top of insurance companies. She fumed about how they reaped the profits from good, honest people by existing as nothing more than middlemen. She said that they only covered what they absolutely had to. And for them, it was only about their profits. We could clearly see the sickness of greed by their cold-hearted decisions—decisions that ravaged my options to improve.

She cried when she asked me, "How can they make life-and-death decisions? They're not doctors."

On one occasion, I heard her ask a manager how he could sleep at night working for a company that profited from denying those most in need of medical help. He said he wasn't doing anything illegal and he slept just fine. Stunned by his heartless answer, she ended the conversation by calling him an ice man.

She was right. It was a huge, glaring moral and ethical conflict of interest. Somehow health care had continued to be a for-profit industry. This was a reality made possible by corporate contributions to certain politicians' reelection funds.

My house of doom was constructed a little more each day by the corporate decisions affecting my care. Deardra's anger grew into rage. She referred to the insurance company executives as "greedy parasites." She said she could see them at their shareholders meetings, patting one another on their backs for their growing profits while paying no attention to how those profits were being made—off the suffering of their fellow human beings. Noticing how discouraged I was, she added, "Don't worry, Dad. Nothing goes unseen. At some point, they will be held accountable and receive the repercussions for their actions."

I appreciated Deardra's efforts. The protective love she showed me was soothing. But in the end, it didn't change my situation.

I choked back the tears, struggling to finally get the words out, "It doesn't help us now." We both cried.

Over the next few months, Deardra called me regularly and came to see me at least once a week. We'd talk as she went over my medical bills. I was still difficult to understand, but she was patient, with a deep sadness in her eyes as she watched me struggle to speak. I told her I was sorry for not being a better dad to her and Annette. I said if I could do it over, I would. She paused, dropping her head, and then said, "I accept your apology, Dad, and it means a lot to me. I know firsthand the difficulties we all had to endure, but let's leave what has passed behind us and concentrate on a better future." I could tell it helped her to know I was so sorry. And it helped me to hear her say those words of forgiveness—at least I hoped it was forgiveness and not pity. However, inside me, my regrets had a life of their own. Denial no longer worked to silence their voices. Even with Deardra's words, the sins of the past brutally haunted me with no mercy.

I didn't think it was possible to be so miserable and still live. To survive with so much emotional, physical, and mental pain was unbearable, and I told Deardra I wanted to die. Her eyes filled with tears as she asked me not to say that. She said she thought things would end up OK, but I could read the uncertainty in her eyes.

In early October, I had a request. I asked Deardra if she would ask Gretchen and Annette if the four of us could have Thanksgiving dinner together. She said she would do her best to make that happen. Then two weeks later she tearfully broke the bad news. Gretchen and Annette had said that they wouldn't agree to the four of us having Thanksgiving or any other meal together. The devastation broke my dam of tears. I sobbed, unable to respond for several minutes. For me, this was the final blow. I understood I hadn't been the best man over the years. I was deeply damaged, flawed in many ways, but I had always been generous with money and ready to help if things were bad. When I asked Deardra why, the tears flowed down her face. She shook her head and said that she was sorry, but it was the way they felt. She was unable to change their minds.

I tried to convince myself that I deserved it, but the punishment seemed much harsher than my crimes. Then I reflected on how harshness was one of the traits that I had generously dished out. There were many times I had been severe, even physically abusive, to Gretchen and my girls. Maybe this was poetic justice—my karma. But the thought didn't help to ease my agony.

At the time, my most pressing need was to seek out anyone—besides Deardra and my mother—who loved me or thought well of me. This would be a way to substantiate that my sins were forgivable, and I wasn't a bad man, just deeply damaged. I was contemplating my exit and wanted to know that there were others who thought I had some redeeming qualities. I thought this might bring me a bit of peace.

Toward the latter part of October, after receiving more wounds to my heart, I started to have the symptoms of another stroke. The right side of my body began tingling, followed by numbness. I could barely get around with the paralysis on my left side. If I had another stroke, that would be it for me. I couldn't allow myself to become fully paralyzed and become even more of a burden. I knew what I had to do—I had to end my life before I became incapacitated. The thought of ending my suffering gave me comfort—it was a way to end the torturous hell my life had become.

Raised Catholic, I didn't believe in suicide. I was taught that those who did such a thing went to hell—but I was already there. In my present circumstances it felt more and more like the right thing to do. My top priority was to make sure I didn't become a bigger burden. It was the only thing I could still control. I had lived my life; now it was near the end. Planning my exit, I purchased a gun.

When I told my sister I was going to end my life, she requested I not do it on her birthday. The ugly reality crashed in further. No one cared if I lived or died. Deardra and my mother were the only ones who truly loved and cared about me. But my mother was old and couldn't help me. Deardra was divorced, attempting to rebuild her life, and didn't need me weighing her down. Time would heal the wound of my self-inflicted death. Or so I hoped. I could not allow myself to become completely paralyzed; then I'd have no way out.

I prayed and prayed, constantly asking for grace, for a miracle—but nothing changed in the slightest. Bitterness and sorrow became my constant companions. I turned my back on God. I believed He didn't care about me either, and that massively increased my emptiness.

When the day came for me to end my life, I went to the house Gretchen and I had lived in for many years. It was the most familiar place for me to be. I left the garage door open, with the radio blaring so that when Gretchen came home from work, she'd know something was wrong and not go inside. The last thing I tasted were my tears as I put the gun to my head. I heard a deafening sound and fell into a dark, empty space where a bright Light immediately appeared. My soul reached for it. My life as Pete quickly flashed before my eyes.

The love emanating from the Light engulfed my soul. My detailed life review as Pete began. I felt the pain of the additional sorrow I had caused by ending my life. Immediately I refused to have my life review go any further. Each time it began again, I would stop it, refusing to let it start again. I was advised of how unusual my choice was and of the repercussions that would follow. But I didn't care—I couldn't bear it. Finally I was put into a state of limbo. I stayed in nothingness until I was ready to face what I would not. Many loving Guides worked with me, teaching me about release, compassion, forgiveness, love in all its forms, and acceptance. Slowly, with their loving Guidance, I agreed to review my life as Pete under certain circumstances.

Francis and Josephine were silent as I processed the weight of what I re-lived again in my life review.

After I recalled my life ending as Pete, I was in a state of unparalleled *relief*. I had finally accomplished my soul's mission to move forward. Instantly I understood the recurring patterns repeated over my many incarnations. As Edmond and Pete, I had chosen to end my life each time. And I had been shown other lifetimes when I was self-destructive, choosing to commit a slow suicide.

I felt unconditional love from Josephine, Francis, and the other souls who were present. Collectively, they continued to energetically hold me in the dimension just barely beyond the physical. There was no judgment, only immense unending love.

Josephine tenderly spoke first: "One of the many blessings of incarnating in the physical is the powerful instruction the soul receives through the full spectrum of feeling emotions. That is coupled with the opportunity to fully experience how your developed strengths can overcome weaknesses. You have excelled in your courage to continue your spiritual evolution. Congratulations, my sweet one!"

I could fully see a greater view of a bigger picture, one where I had complete compassion for myself. I wondered and asked, "In my next life, am I likely to continue with the same dominant traits, destined to make the same choices?"

Francis said, "Joyfully we all congratulate you! You have come far and achieved much." Then he gently answered my question: "That is your choice. Let us observe the entire picture."

Instantly, I was shown the other probable futures of Pete and Edmond—if they had not ended their own lives in each of those incarnations.

First, I observed myself as Pete, in an alternative future, where I was unable to end my life. The scene unfolded with my living beyond my choice to die.

I did have another stroke two weeks later, and my worst fear of becoming fully paralyzed came to be. I watched Deardra admit me to a nursing home. I was crushed by the circumstances of what my life had become. The despair of hopelessness was one of the unbearable emotions I was overcome with.

While asleep, in the nursing home, thirty-seven days later, my life ended, and I peacefully left my body. But in those thirty-seven days, miracles had occurred in my life.

Family and a few friends I thought didn't care about me came to share their hearts. What was told to me in those last precious few days filled me with the warmth of reassurance. My sister came to see me with an apology. A great deal was tearfully healed between us on that day. My heart leaped when I got to see my mother, Josephine, again. We cried and laughed together one last time. Gretchen and Annette also brought me the gift of their presence. Our visit was tearful, filled with the regrets of love we held back. I clearly understood that the love we withhold hurts us the most because of the regret of not expressing that love.

I could clearly see that if had I chosen to stay, it would have been possible for them to forgive me and themselves. We all played our parts in the years of unhappiness when we lived in pain. Because of our egos, we again and again needlessly wounded one another, then later acted as if nothing of consequence had happened. But the damage infected each of our personal realities. We were all complicit in the misery we created. All those moments added up to years—years during which we continued to actively express harm rather than love.

As I watched the probable future of a scenario in which I didn't end my life, there was no judgment from Francis and Josephine. And surprisingly, I had no judgment about not remaining in my life as Pete. I fully understood that each choice reveals the lessons we have yet to learn. This perspective is a powerful way to transform pain into purpose.

Then I observed how my life would have been as Edmond had I decided to stay. After Sofie and Beth died, alcohol would have consumed me for the next seventeen months as I made an effort to kill my emotional pain. It was a way to insulate myself from the heartbreak, self-hatred, and guilt of choosing the pursuit of gold over my Sofie and Beth. Eventually, I would have decided not to live in the bottom of a whiskey bottle. I would have forced myself to focus on mining enough gold to leave Idaho Springs and become a lawyer, as Sofie had wanted.

About three years later I would have met an intelligent, attractive blonde woman from the Midwest. We would have married and lived in Denver. The kind, sharp-witted woman would have brought me six children. I would have had a full life. Over the years, on occasion, the guilty pain of losing Sofie and Beth would have festered, leading me to drink. In my early sixties, I would have realized that alcohol didn't help the pain of my loss, but instead only made me more depressed, with the added misery of a horrible headache. So I would have quit drinking, no longer permitting a bottle to be in control of my life.

I could see that Sofie came back to me as Gretchen. Sophie was extremely angry and disgusted with me from having to watch our beautiful Beth die before her. So my sweet Sofie had died hating me. This was something I knew as Edmond, and I couldn't bear it. Sofie's hatred for me was part of the reason I chose to give up by ending my life that night in the graveyard.

Now I understood why Gretchen was distant when we first met, then became hateful when she was forced to marry me. Her soul's test was to rise above the angry resentment she held for me by replacing it with forgiveness. Had I not ended my life as Pete, she may have made the choice to finally accomplish that.

My lifetime as Edmond would have ended at age sixty-seven, when I would have died from a fever. I observed my large family around my deathbed saying their goodbyes. Had I not ended my life as Edmond, I would have overcome the addictions of gold fever, alcohol, and gambling. This would have freed me to seek higher levels of my soul's evolution. Even so, I was still at peace, accepting that we only call to us the lessons we need based on the actions of our choices.

Once again, Francis and Josephine praised me on my successful review of my lifetime as Pete. I could have never accomplished it without their guidance filled with love, wisdom, and support. And again, I gave them my heartfelt gratitude.

I reflected on what a hard journey it had been, filled with more heartbreaking anguish than I thought was possible to experience. But experience, I did. My soul leaped forward into a state of peaceful, indescribable love.

I bowed to all the souls present with a deep admiring love. I thanked them for the purification resulting from the full spectrum of emotions I had finally faced. And I thanked them for the gift of transformation—from acceptance into peaceful understanding.

I could feel Francis and Josephine's love expand, surrounding me in their Light of love. Francis pointed out, "If you wish, there is more to experience as Russell the dog before you rejoin us in the realm of spirit. Or you may leave now."

Without pause, I answered, "Thank you. I'll see it through until the end of my body's life cycle. I've decided that I really like my life as Russell the dog." After I made my choice, the next few years flew by quickly on the wings of time.

30

Completion Brings Beginnings

I am complete, bathed in the highest frequencies of love.
—Russell

My dog body is now ten years old. The pain from the cancer in my bladder is severe. Though I'm at peace, I'm fully aware that this lifetime has been one of my most enlightening, with considerable movement forward. I have expanded my soul's growth by accomplishing my purpose for being here. Still, I don't want to leave yet. Deardra's warm, affectionate love compels me to stay with her and Heath for as long as possible.

As I look back on my life as Russell the dog, I'm extremely grateful to all who played a key part in my journey. We are all instrumental in one another's growth. I started by blessing and thanking my sweet mother, Tess, who brought me into the physical. Then the angel ladies who lovingly rescued us from the cruelty of The Pit. And Deardra, who adopted me, then patiently loved me with all her heart. And I thanked Waldo, my beloved brother and kindred spirit, who taught me what was truly important. And Josephine, my mother when I was Pete, who became one of my most loving Guides. And, of course, I thanked Francis, my patient and persistent wisdom Guide. And it just went on and on. Perfectly and completely, our souls learn and learn, forever advancing and expanding in the power of love. With endless gratitude, I love you all.

The intricate fabric of my life design is astounding. Everything fits. My daughter Deardra still loves me, forgiving me for my flaws. Then there's Heath—well, I love Heath for many reasons. When we first met, I was aware of knowing him from before. Later, Josephine showed me the two primary reasons why I recognized him. The first was we shared a previous brief incarnation. It was a happy time for us both. The second was based on a premonition, an awareness that he was the one Deardra had waited for.

The love Heath and Deardra shared was exquisite, spanning time and space. Francis showed me they had experienced two previous incarnations together. One of their most expansive happy lifetimes they shared was in the late 1400s. They were married and lived in Paris. Heath's three sons today were their children in that lifetime.

The other lifetime took place in the mid-1940s, when they loved each other, but both died in their early twenties as casualties of World War II. Then, in this present incarnation, both were born in the 1950s. Each of their souls designed a present lifetime covering several lessons, and the reward was Heath and Deardra finally got to be together again.

Gretchen had visited Deardra a few times here in the House of Stone and Light. When she came, I barely recognized her.

The ache of sorrow was all I felt as I sat next to her. I tried to let her know on a deeper level that I forgave her, hoping she had also forgiven me. Sadly, she still lives in a dark shell, not having extended her free will to rise above it. Of course, in the end, that's only my observation. Ultimately, it is between her soul and Infinite Source.

Because Gretchen had not changed for the better, Deardra had decided to release herself from any further harm. She forgave her mother, but no longer wanted Gretchen's abusiveness as part of her life. Deardra learned to reach beyond the fallacy that blood relations might be a justifiable reason for a person to continue being abused. Instead she has embraced the strength of self-respect, empowering her to form healthy boundaries. This was one of her lessons. By not speaking to Gretchen for years, she found peace. This has proven to be a wise decision for both Deardra and Heath.

Josephine gave me a gentle reminder that my time to leave this body was quickly approaching. However, there was no need to remind me. I sensed the presence of my energy fading from the physical world.

Francis asked me, "Do you recall the times you were offered to leave your body?"

"Yes. It would be hard to forget," I said with a lightness of heart.

"Each time was a test, inspired by your past choices to end your life as Edmond and Pete."

"Since I stayed each time the choice was presented, have I passed the test?"

Francis replied, "Actions are revealing. And yes, you have succeeded. Though you should be aware that this test may be presented to you again in other lifetimes."

With sincere gratitude, I said, "I know I will do well if you and Josephine are there to watch over me and Guide me."

Francis thanked me for the compliment. "In spite of the high level of difficulty you presented to us, it would be my honor to guide you again. However, we never know what we may craft next with the Infinite. Whatever it is, I will see you in the etheric field, my dear, kindred soul."

I then experienced a quick recap of the full review of my entire lifetime as Pete. Again, I felt every moment not only from my perspective as Pete, but also from the other affected embodied souls' points of view. However, this time I didn't feel the emotions in the same way or with the same intensity as I did before. It was more of an objective observer's view of what I had done correctly or could have done better. I'm able to fully embrace the meaning of the idea that what we do to others we do to ourselves. It is the energetic essence of cause and effect rooted in the choice between harm or help. Nothing goes unseen. I hope to take this awareness into my next incarnation to create a kinder, less fear-based identity.

Maggie and I have always loved the sunroom the best, so we lie side-by-side, gazing across the hills and listening to the trees breathing. Maggie whimpers and says, "I'll miss you, puppafied Russ, and I'll be lonely without you." I let her know that I'll miss her too until we meet again.

When I see the late afternoon sun shimmering off the pine needles and aspen leaves, it reminds me of the multitude of souls that Josephine said are waiting to come into the physical. They linger, as light beams, in a dimension of etheric space. They observe, sometimes assisting us in the physical, while they wait for their next learning incarnation. It's beautiful to see how the soul sparkles with love.

I'm weaker with each passing moment. Heath, Deardra, and Maggie must feel it too, as they are heaping more affection on me. Pie tenderly licks my face. I can feel her missing me already.

As I reflect, I fully appreciate how each incarnation compels us to play our parts in the brilliant drama of being in the physical on planet Earth. All parts are significant. Each part played is to ultimately manifest love, grace, and integrity, bringing forward our highest frequency to rejoin with Infinite Source.

My soul is rising from my body, then descending down again. There is an expanding when out of my body, then contracting when reentering.

Waldo, Charlie, Nicholas the Newf, Henry the cat, and many others, in different forms, are waiting for me in the Light. My breathing is labored. Heath and Deardra panic.

Deardra is crying as she begs me, "Please don't go, Puppa. I love you so much. You have brought us so much joy and laughter that I can't imagine being without you." On a deeper level, she knows her grieving extends beyond this lifetime, to when she was my daughter.

My heart has stopped beating. The Light is extremely bright, drawing me closer—I reach for it. Then I rise for the last time from the red teddy bear dog body that once housed my soul. Oh, the lightness of being without a body is blissful. The Light engulfs me, but I'm still aware of Deardra and Heath's desperation. Then I hear Heath gasp, "He's gone." But I'm not gone; a part of me is still with them. Our love has formed an everlasting connection. I say to them, "We take all the love with us. I live in your hearts. I'm only a thought away."

Waldo lovingly embraces me in our spirit form. I realize I have known Henry and The Newf from other incarnations. Josephine, my mother and Guide, holds me with overwhelming love as we too have experienced many incarnations together. A multitude of souls are present to welcome me. All are illuminated with the celebration of being reunited in love. Surprisingly, I embrace some whom I had considered enemies when in a physical body. But the platform for drama is no longer needed, nor the attachment to the performances we've played to be one another's students and teachers.

My soul has achieved the perfection of transformation through the agony and elation of learning from my life review. I continue to receive many congratulations from my soul group for a lifetime well lived. I too am satisfied with my progress.

In the distance, I can hear Deardra and Heath cry. On a soul level, their tears are tears of joy, rejoicing for me that I am home. It's a home they will someday also return to. And I will be here to greet them with all the love my soul can express.

Together, a message of inspiration is sent from the other side. It is sent on the Light of love to Deardra, Heath, Maggie Pie, and anyone who wishes to receive it. The message from all the Spirit Guides is this: "We are watching over you. We will Guide you and see you through. We are right here next to you."

Deardra and Heath hear the message with their hearts, holding each other, aware we will all be together again.

Another beginning can unfold for my soul since I have left my body as Russell the dog. I take with me all the love I gave and received. I'm secure in the knowledge that all things are possible.

Heath snapped this picture of me, not aware at the time that he was capturing a future moment of me in the world of spirit.

Here I am watching over you.

Epilogue

For me it was a blink in time although three years have passed since I left the physical as Russell the dog. Waldo and Henry the cat are on to other spiritual adventures. I've spent much time with Deardra, mostly in the sleep state, when she dreams about me as her dad, Pete, or as her dog Russell. We often talk on an astral wavelength of many things spanning numerous dimensions.

One morning Deardra marveled at the beauty of the sunrise, when large snowflakes began to gracefully float in the air. The sunbeams shimmered on the ice crystals of the flakes. She felt inspired as she sat in the sunroom, typing in bold letters at the top of a blank page: *The Spiritual Adventures of Russell the Dog: A Blend of Truth, Fiction, and Inspiration from the Other Side.* And so another new spiritual adventure unfolds.

Acknowledgments

Of course I have to start with Russell, my sweet teddy bear dog. His unusual behaviors, challenging personality, and loving heart will always be with us. He brought laughter into our lives daily. We will always miss his mischievous spirit.

My husband, Mark Watson, is an inspiration and the love of my life. Without him, my heart probably would not have opened to the many possibilities of what life has to offer. Mark's sons—Clayton, Seth, and Andrew—have blessed us with the light of their bright souls. I love them as my own. Andrew's wife, Nabila, and their son, Lucas, and Seth's partner, Kate, have all continuously brought so much joy to our family.

I wish to acknowledge my paternal grandparents, who inspired me with their personal stories of survival and taught me by example how kindness and triumph of spirit is what counts in the end. I thank them for their consistent, stable, nourishing love.

Thanks go to my friends who continued to give me encouragement by patiently listening to this story and reading what I wrote. Special thanks go to Julie Roth and Jim Schwartz, Elizabeth Gonzales-Renals and Jake Renals, Madeline Ray, Mary O'Rourke, Elizabeth Stensing, and all our other friends who make up our family of choice We love you all.

Thanks also go to my editors, Julie Cameron and Tom Locke. My cover and interior designer, Nick Zelinger. And Jerry Fabyanic, for his generous and patient mentoring.

I'm also grateful for Maggie and Cooper, our dogs who have given us love and have reminded us every day of the magic these souls in dog bodies bring to us.

And I greatly appreciate my Spirit Guides—for the patience, love, wisdom, and direction they have always given me, even when I didn't listen.

And here's a wish: may you know your Spirit Guides, who love and assist you on your unique spiritual adventure.

About the Author

Trisha Watson, holds a deep reverence for nature and compassion for those in need, especially animals. Of course that encompasses pets too, and thus all her dogs and cats over the years have been rescues or strays. One of her passions is to save animals through adoption, so a portion of the proceeds from the sale of each book will be donated to an animal rescue charity.

Twenty years of self-employment helped her develop a can-do attitude, so writing her first book, while intimidating, was something she felt driven to do. When asked about the process of writing a book, she said, "It wasn't my intention to write a book, but this story wouldn't leave me alone. Much of it flowed easily. Some of it I don't remember writing, which at first was spooky but later made complete sense as the story revealed itself. My hope with this book is to, in some way, touch all who read it."

At sixteen, Trisha began her spiritual journey. At twenty-six, she had an out-of-body, near-death-experience, almost dying of pneumonia. She said, "This was the most transformational experience of my life." Over the years she has delved into many facets of life with an open mind and a dash of healthy skepticism. Always looking forward, she seeks to encounter, learn, and share with others. Her philosophy says it best, "We are all each other's students and teachers."

Trisha was born in Rhode Island. A few years later her family moved to the "Mile High City," Denver, Colorado, where she grew up. As an adult she was drawn to live in the mountains, eventually settling in Evergreen, a small mountain town outside of Denver. It is there she's built a life with her husband Mark and their two dogs, Maggie and Cooper.

Trisha is available for interviews and speaking engagements. To schedule a time with Trisha email her at: *TheSpiritualAdventures@gmail.com* or visit her website: *TheSpiritualAdventures.com* where you can sign up for Russell's free guide and link to her Facebook and Twitter accounts.

Book Club

Have questions for the author?

You can invite Trisha to connect with your book club either by Skype or in person.

To schedule an appearance with Trisha, please contact her at: TheSpiritualAdventures@gmail.com.

To see the color version of the last picture in the book: Russell In the World of Spirit.
Go to www.TheSpiritualAdventures.com
and click on Pictures link.

You are not a drop in the ocean.
You are an entire ocean in a drop
—Rumi

CPSIA information can be obtained
at www.ICGtesting.com
Printed in the USA
FSHW020006060620
70733FS